MensPulpMags.com # new texture

The Men's Adventure Library Journal: Maneaters is a New Texture publication. ISBN 978-1-943444-25-0 This book is also available as an abbreviated softcover. Designed by Wyatt Doyle. Archival materials reproduced via arrangement with The Robert Deis Archive. The editors can be contacted at WeaselsRippedMyBook@gmail.com © 2021 Subtropic Productions, LLC. All rights reserved. NewTexture.com MensPulpMags.com

With gratitude to **Jessica Myers, Jeff Krulik,
Team Künstler, Jacqueline Pollen,** *and* **The Asylum**

Foreword

Steve Cheskin, creator of Shark Week

It was 1987. Discovery Channel was in about a third of the number of homes it's in now, and trying to get noticed in the cable universe. We were brainstorming at a meeting I'd been invited to join at the last minute. *How do we get noticed? How do we get people to notice Discovery?* I was not high up in the company, but I had a say in what programs we were developing and buying. I knew our program inventory, and I knew we had a lot of shark programs, and I knew sharks did really well for us. So I said, "What about doing 'shark week'?"

And John Hendricks, founder and president of Discovery, said, "That's it."

That first year, we knew it was something, because we got press. And press is what you want, when people don't really know your network. Viewers responded to the idea and it took off, but it was gradual. At one point a few years later, I got a new boss and he said, *I don't know about Shark Week, maybe we should just end it.* But Shark Week had momentum; it just kept going and going. At one point, it was twice a year!

I ended up having a great career. I was the number two person at Discovery Channel, I was EVP of Programming and Interim General Manager at TLC, General Manager of Travel Channel, and head of programming at multiple networks. Now I'm Senior Vice President of Programming at Reelz. We've done a couple of shark programs. We timed the first one to appear right before Shark Week, just when people were getting all worked up for sharks. It did a big number. Now we're doing a second one. Nat Geo Channel, they do it, too. And Nat Geo Wild, they do *two weeks* of sharks leading up to Shark Week! Trying to ride on that tail, riding on the huge success of Shark Week.

Although there never was any kind of financial reward for coming up with the idea of Shark Week, it sure is cool to be the creator of an idea that became a part of pop culture. I'll be watching something, and somebody mentions Shark Week, and I'll think, *Holy cow! I came up with that idea!* It's amazing to me that the idea still resonates all these years later.

At the time, I was driven by ratings: *What's going to get us noticed? What's going to do a rating for us?* If I'd thought elephants would've got the rating of sharks…

But there's something about sharks. There's the natural fear of them that many people have, and there's a mystery about them—the stories in this book recognize and exploit both. And the different kinds of sharks! I learned myself there were so many different kinds of sharks, and that most aren't dangerous to humans. I've visited many aquariums, across the country. And you see the same reaction at all the shark exhibits: People sit there, and they're just mesmerized. Mesmerized! Watching those sharks swimming around and around. ▼

Preface

BY ROBERT DEIS

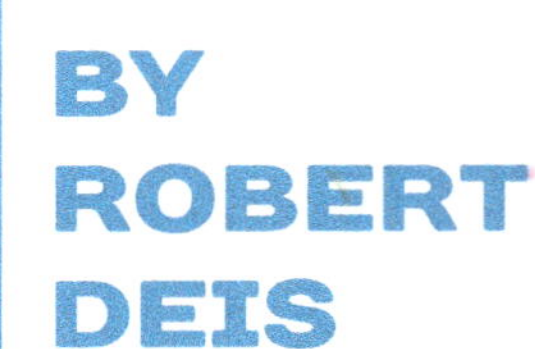

There are many misperceptions about both sharks and vintage men's adventure magazines. And, as you'll see in this book, some of the misperceptions about the former were echoed and amplified by stories in the latter.

Sharks have traditionally been viewed as monstrous, bloodthirsty killers of humans. Most people are unaware of the differences between the more than 500 species of sharks and the important and beneficial roles they play in ocean ecosystems. Many have a fear of sharks that's totally out of proportion with the relative rarity of attacks on humans by the small number of species considered "maneaters."

Similarly, vintage men's adventure magazines (aka MAMs) are subject to many ill-informed misperceptions and exaggerations. Ironically, their stories helped reinforce misperceptions and exaggerations about sharks. In fact, they paved the way for *Jaws*.

During the 1950s, '60s and early '70s, more than 160 magazine titles that fit into the MAM genre were published by 30 or so different publishers. Some lasted decades; some only a few issues. Some were one-offs. In total, I estimate over 6,000 individual issues of various MAMs were published.

Most share certain qualities, such as using wild, arresting painted covers, an element they inherited from the earlier pulp fiction magazines they are partly descended from. Like the pulps, MAMs are full of action/adventure, war, Western, exotic adventure, and crime stories. These stories are often gritty, exciting, shocking and bloody. Most of these yarns feature manly men and sexy women. However, the approach, focus, and quality of the magazines (and the stories and artwork in them) varied. It's true that MAMs are outdated with respect to modern political correctness. But that's true of most media from the 1950s, '60s and '70s. MAM fiction is certainly violent, outrageous and over-the-top, but not all that extreme when compared to what's typical in modern movies, TV shows, and books..

MAMs may not have been entirely respectable in polite company, but they were popular entertainment and read widely. The least politically correct MAMs, the lower-tier "sweat mags," notorious for their seamier fiction and cover art, had limited circulations. The more popular and somewhat more respectable mid-tier MAMs had hundreds of thousands of readers; these were mags like *For Men Only*, *Male*, *Men*, and *Stag*, published by Martin Goodman's Magazine Management Company (which also gave birth to Marvel Comics). Top-tier MAMs like *True*, *Argosy*, and *Saga* enjoyed peak circulations of 1 million or more.

MAN'S CONQUEST August 1955   Artist uncredited

MEN April 1966

A high percentage of MAMs published "Book Bonus" versions of novels by leading crime, mystery, and action/adventure writers of the day, such as Mickey Spillane, Ed McBain, Brett Halliday (creator of Mike Shayne), Richard Matheson, Quentin Reynolds, Lawrence Block, John D, MacDonald, Alistair MacLean and many others. A fair number of writers who would later become famous started out as writers and editors for MAMs, such as Bruce Jay Friedman, Mario Puzo, Walter Wager, and Martin Cruz Smith. Most of the cover artwork and interior illustrations were done by talented illustration artists who also did cover art for paperbacks. Some later became famous for their fine art paintings, like Mort Künstler, James Bama, Robert McGinnis, Ron Lesser, and Frank McCarthy.

Man vs. animal stories are common in MAMs. Most are fiction. Some are actual first-person accounts. Others are a third type of story, perfected by the mid-tier MAMs. They are yarns portrayed as true but actually either barely based on facts or pure fiction, dressed up with photos and subheads designed to make them seem like true stories.

Some classic examples appear in our anthology *I Watched Them Eat Me Alive* (a title taken from a story about killer crabs included in the collection). My own all-time favorite is "Weasels Ripped My Flesh," which first appeared in the September 1956 issue of *Man's Life*. That story helped spark my fascination with MAMs, and we borrowed its title and included it in our first anthology of MAM stories.

When it comes to stories set on the ocean, sharks are by far the most common killer creatures in MAM stories. These stories predated and, in many ways, presaged *Jaws* and the slew of other killer shark novels and movies *Jaws* inspired—as well as the unfortunate anti-shark hysteria its popularity ignited.

Indeed, the popularity and ubiquity of MAMs in their time suggest the killer shark stories they featured, usually accompanied by artwork or photos of sharks with huge, toothy, gaping mouths, were surely something Peter Benchley and Steven Spielberg had been exposed to. Such images are forerunners of the iconic *Jaws* movie poster by Roger Kastel—an artist who also painted cover and interior artwork for MAMs.

ONE INTERESTING forerunner of *Jaws* was written by Mario Puzo, before he became famous as the author of *The Godfather*, Puzo began his professional career as a writer and associate editor for the MAMs published by Magazine Management Company. Under the pseudonym Mario Cleri, which he commonly used for his MAM stories, Puzo wrote a semi-factual story titled "The Six Million Killer Sharks That Terrorize Our Shores." That article, published in the April 1966 issue of *Men*, has an opening that will seem prescient to everyone who has seen *Jaws*:

> *As carefree summer vacationers frolic on beaches all over America, horrible death waits a few yards off-shore in the maws of giant sharks who've developed an insatiable taste for human flesh. But despite a rocketing toll of maimed, crippled, scarred and dead casualties, resort towns everywhere have dropped a blackout curtain on this hideous new menace—preferring to expose millions to death rather than let the frightening truth scare off tourist dollars.*

Puzo's shark story is a non-fiction piece—sort of. It does recount some actual historic shark attacks, but it's full of exaggerations and some outright fiction, as "true stories" in MAM stories often were. And the sharks featured in the two main photographs are whale sharks, a docile species that is a plankton eater, not a meat eater—let alone a maneater. Of course, the exaggerations and inaccuracies about sharks in MAM stories were not unique. They reflected common misperceptions and myths, some of which have only recently begun to be busted by scientists.

WE'VE included some of our favorite MAM shark stories in this book, along with the original artwork and photos that went with them. We think they're ripping good, escapist yarns that few readers today have had the opportunity to enjoy. And they're accompanied by some amazingly cool illustration art that has gone largely unseen since the magazines' original publication.

We know that, like *Jaws*, most are scientifically flawed. So we've also included notes and commentary by shark experts that describe what the stories got wrong and help clarify the real facts about sharks.

The MAM genre is extinct. The populations of many shark species are now in danger of extinction due to unfounded fears, misguided attempts at eradication, overfishing and climate change. We hope this book sheds some light on both MAMs and sharks and, ultimately, helps both to live on. ▼

DEATH HAS SHARP TEETH

BY WYATT DOYLE

The men in men's adventure magazines (MAMs) never went quietly. They squared off against death in exotic places, in unconventional circumstances. After all, editors were tailoring their content to a post-WWII male readership who'd been dispatched to all corners of the world during wartime to experience all the horrors, fascinations, and unexpected delights their minds could process—and more than a few they couldn't. The scope of raw experience the average fighting man absorbed during his service could be nothing short of staggering, and when those who came home tried to settle into their old lives (or carve out new ones), their interests and diversions had taken on a different complexion, and the content of the magazines they read for pleasure reflected this.

Today, more passive varieties of entertainment dominate the cultural landscape and command the majority of consumer interest, attention, and leisure dollars. But that landscape was very different in the mid-20th century, when reading fiction was as prevalent and compelling a diversion for consumers as video games or binge-viewing today. Despite television's growing popularity and the then-sturdy appeal of movies and radio, magazines publishing short fiction and unusual true-life accounts were incredibly popular—business was booming, in fact, and reading was an egalitarian pursuit that cut across social and economic lines. It was a time when most Americans enjoyed reading, and the ever-expanding publishing industry went all-out to keep pace with demand. Publishers turned out periodicals in tried-and-true genres while also inventing brand new ones, blending elements old and new in hopes the fresh combinations would strike a popular chord and hit paydirt. Whatever worked was promptly copied, industry-wide. Anything that didn't was abandoned, sometimes after only a single issue.

The MAM formula was one of the most successful blends, ultimately leading to over 160 titles issued by multiple publishers over three decades. Targeting a working-class male readership, they merged elements of vintage pulp fiction, "bachelor" and pin-up mags, outdoor and travel periodicals, true crime and detective magazines, and celebrity scandal rags. They were a little of everything then considered masculine and manly, and it was emphasized in their branding: *Male. Men. Action For Men. Adventure. Challenge. For Men Only.* The assertive, unapologetic masculinity of such titles seemed to confer a degree of manliness on their readers, as though congratulating purchasers for being man enough to seek them out in the first place.

Reassurance was most definitely part of the equation, and most definitely

ADVENTURE December 1953   Art by Rico Tomaso

part of the appeal. Editorial voices adopted the familiar, straight-dope tone of a pal in the know, and despite an emphasis on unconventional and controversial subject matter, editorial viewpoints were not provocative, and promoted attitudes readers were comfortable with. Though outrageousness and outright fabrication defined much of their content, ambitions for MAMs were straightforward, even old fashioned: To supply the American working man with a bit of titillation and escape, and hope they came back the next month for more of the same.

Intensity was a key element of MAM fiction. Stories grabbed readers by the lapels and shook. In MAM fiction, life was often cheap, and it moved fast. There were no recurring characters, and in many titles, even obvious works of fiction might be presented as true accounts, no matter how over-the-top the narrative, no matter how preposterous the scenario. Neither science, logic, nor the limits of reality were permitted to get in the way of a good story or slow the action. But despite storytelling sometimes heightened to the point of absurdity, there were no knowing winks to the reader, no authorial tongues in cheeks. Ironic detachment was not part of the vocabulary. MAM fiction wasn't formulated to impress the reader with its literary finesse, it was meant to knock him on his ass.

Indisputably, MAMs were wild, but wild within the confines of their era and marketplace. Publishers were well aware and observant of social mores, and understood where to draw the line. MAMs didn't exist to shake things up, and posed no threat to anything, except at times good taste. If MAMs didn't have all that more upmarket men's mags offered, those other mags couldn't deliver what MAMs did: Pure, escapist entertainment without apology—whatever that might mean, whatever form that may take. (And it would take some far-out forms.)

In MAMs, the surest path to excitement was making it *big*—not only bigger than the competition, bigger than *life*. While conventional hunting mags of the time published stories of stalking big game with occasional tales of animal attacks, MAMs upped the ante, regularly throwing their protagonists into gory hand-to-claw battles with just about anything that walked, crawled, flew, or swam. And while Hemingway's Old Man allegorically wrestled his marlin in the respectable, mainstream pages of *Life* magazine, MAMs set whole crews of desperate survivors adrift at sea, dozens of frenzied sharks snapping at their ramshackle rafts. From the earliest days of the format, MAM editors recognized the visceral and commercial appeal of turning it up to eleven.

SHARKS were an ideal adversary for MAM fiction, an arena constantly in search of new villains to pose threats to the health and safety of their stories' fictional average Americans. Sure, MAMs had humans squaring off against every wild animal imaginable in their pages. Animal attack yarns were a cornerstone of MAM fiction and cover art. But even among the onslaught of tigers, alligators, and bloodthirsty rodents, sharks were something special. As several MAM stories and articles acknowledge, shark science was then in its infancy, and even what were then accepted notions about their habits and behavior were regularly debated, disproved, or reconsidered. And facts that seemed up for grabs in the first place were easy for writers to ignore in service of a better story.

Such widespread ignorance only made sharks more appealing—and versatile—as MAM villains. Writers could draw on centuries of specious ocean lore and fish stories about sharks that encrusted public perceptions like barnacles, reinforced by a global lack of insight into and understanding of the various shark species and their contributions. Longstanding phobias and hostility were handily exploited in the service of wilder and more resonant storytelling. Sharks could be whatever the story needed them to be. They were anthropomorphized, assigned all manner of human traits. They could be sadistic, or vengeance-minded. They could develop a taste for human flesh, or even cultivate a preference for the flavor of one gender over another. They could guard Nazi gold. They could be evil.

Who did MAM authors pit against such evil? Who were the protagonists who squared off against these apparently soulless monsters of the deep? Usually they were average, blue-collar guys—stand-ins and idealized avatars for the mags' average, blue-collar readers. In the stories included here, they're plumbers, oil riggers, marine biologists. Demolition and salvage guys. Airmen. Cargo pilots. Often they're veterans. Not James Bond, Joe Sixpack. Unlikely leading men are an essential component of MAM fiction in general, and in animal attack stories particularly. Often they're guys doing a job (or trying to unwind from one) who get caught in situations they never anticipated or bargained for. Guys who find themselves—usually through no fault of their own—deeply out of their depth. (In the stories here, literally.) They can be tough and resourceful, but they're not supermen. The worry that's often in their narration and their uncertainty about how their stories may play out make their plights more vivid, and their

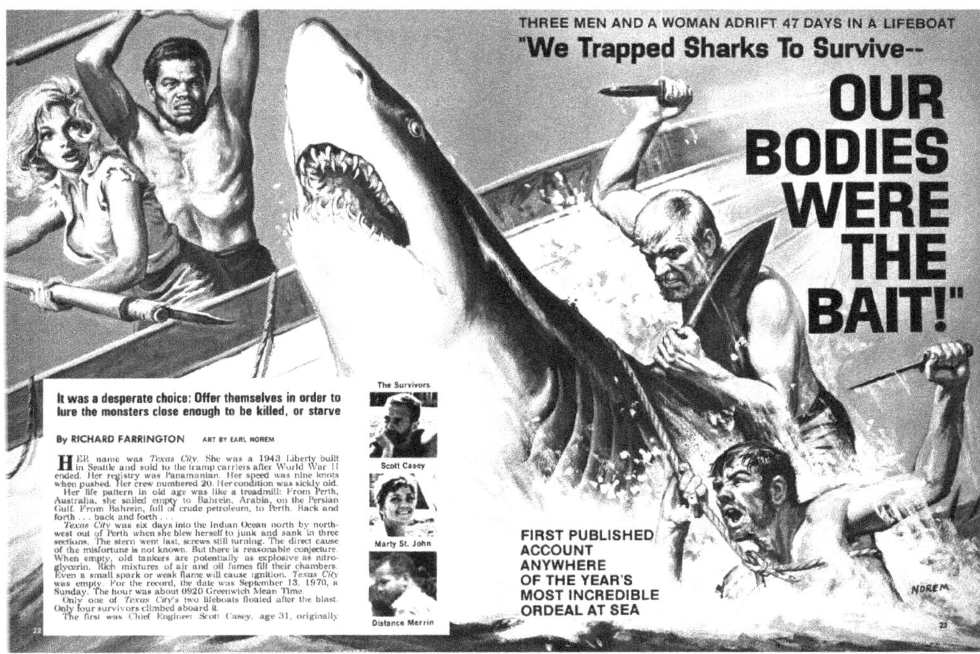

uncertainty is justified. Unqualified victories in MAM fiction are rare, and despite uninformed perceptions, there is little conventional chest-thumping machismo in the actual stories or artwork. Read the stories; you won't find many indestructible action heroes there. Take a closer look at some of those magazine covers; most of those guys look scared as hell. Because at its heart, much of MAM fiction is not about trouncing enemies or triumphing over adversarial conditions. It's about surviving them. And ultimately, invariably, acknowledging the scars, physical and psychological, that remain. In this, MAMs could be unexpectedly therapeutic.

The violence and extremity that helped define the format spoke very directly to a readership who'd endured comparable life-threatening dangers and their own heightened experiences during wartime, and continued to wrestle with them after. Could they personally relate to battling a shark from a sinking lifeboat? Maybe not. But did they understand what it was to feel powerless? Did they know what it was like to wonder if they'd survive an injury? Could they identify with watching a pal not survive theirs? Did they understand trauma? As an audience comprised largely of American war veterans, the answers were yes, definitely.

Bad luck is the axis animal attack stories turn on. They make the case that at any moment, life could trip into chaos, introducing trouble that you didn't ask for and can't avoid. And MAMs' take on sharks took them out of the animal kingdom to make them literal forces of nature; cold, mysterious, and profoundly unsympathetic. You can't reason with sharks, and you can't out-pace or out-maneuver them—at least not for long. Stories describe their hides as like iron, so rough to the touch that just brushing against them left men bleeding. Even guns prove mostly ineffective. For the most part, they're unbeatable. The only real hope is to endure, and somehow escape—ideally with as many of your appendages as you entered the water with.

MAM fiction trades heavily in metaphor, and this was a potent one. Making his way in 20th century America could chew a man up, leave him maimed and bleeding…and MAMs had the perfect villains to express that. Agents of dark, unstoppable fate. Violent, elemental, beyond our understanding. *Maneaters.*

THE PRICE of such effective villainy comes at sharks' expense, and MAMs played a role in their demonization, perpetuating attractive but dangerous canards and embracing some deeply troubling attitudes that were in the water, so to speak, at the time. (Some still are.) Even stories created with no agenda other than brief diversion inevitably incorporate prevailing attitudes of their era, some past their sell-by date. Separate from the stories' worth as pulp entertainment, their misapprehensions drive home how little we knew, and how far we've come.

Sadly, it's not far enough. Despite well over a half-century of scientific research and education since many of these stories first saw print, sharks, vital to the health and survival of our oceans, continue to be irrationally feared, loathed, and constantly killed—irresponsibly, pointlessly—as a direct, tragic result of not decades but centuries of misinformation, misinterpretation, and ignorance.

Compelling fictions have staying power. ▼

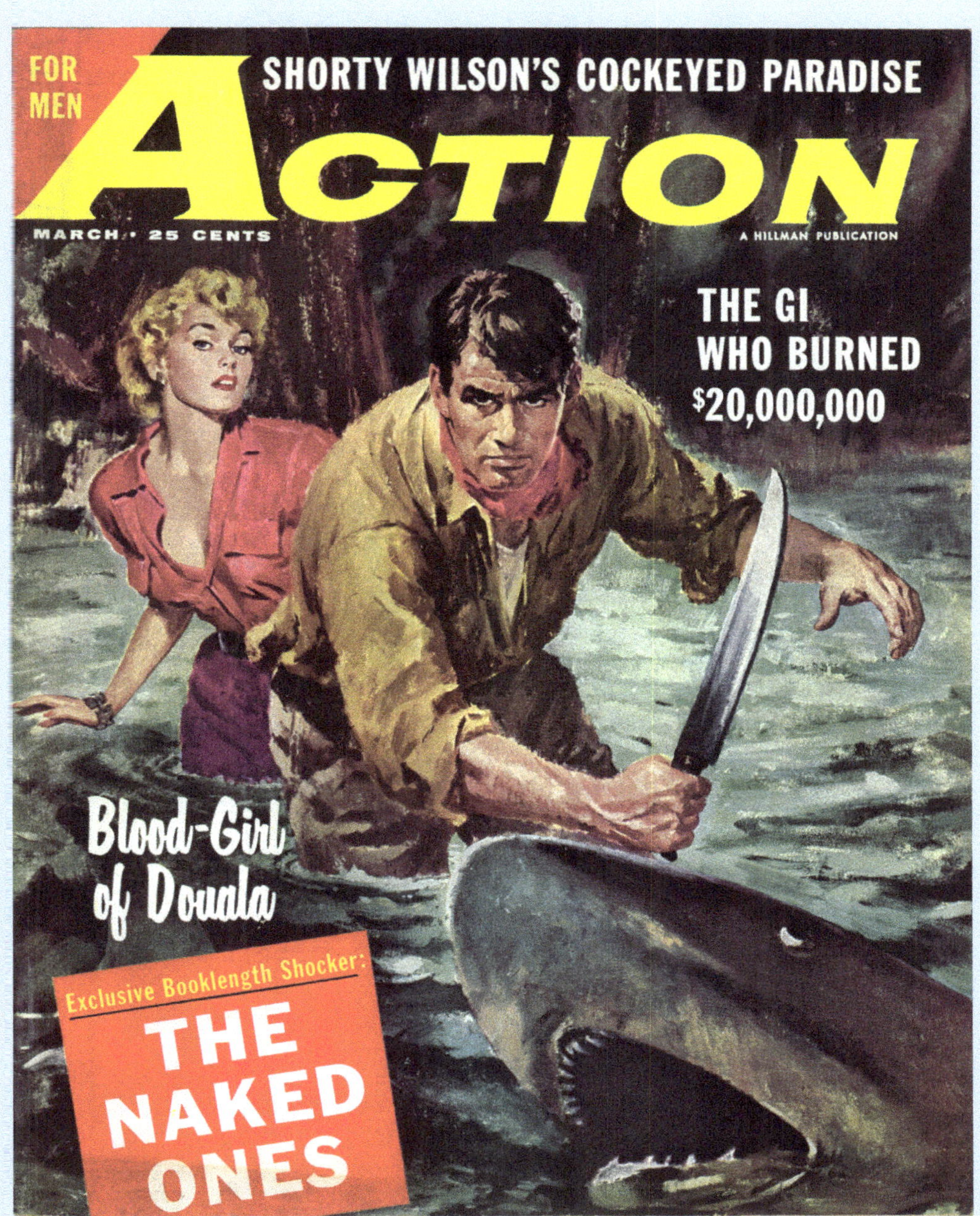

ACTION March 1958 Artist uncredited

STAG February 1952 Art by Harry Schaare

"The Mail-Carrying Shark"

STORY BY RAY NELSON

COVER ART BY RAY JOHNSON

THE MAIL-CARRYING SHARK

A fish story, but every word of it true, about a nice big one that surprised a skipper

IT WAS 2:00 A.M. in the glassed-in lounge of the Grand Hotel at Yarmouth, Nova Scotia, and one by one the press and radio boys who had converged on the spot to cover the International Tuna Cup Matches yawned and shuffled off to bed.

Finally only Boudreau and I were left. This particular Boudreau, that is—for in Yarmouth a man's name tends to be Boudreau, if it isn't Comeau, and the bustling port would be a pretty desolate waste if the Boudreaus and the Comeaus happened to pull up stakes.

This Boudreau tamped a fresh pipeful down with a horny thumb, and regarded the ceiling thoughtfully as he lighted up. Then, exhaling a blue cloud, he said, "You've seen big sharks, more than likely. What I mean are the really big babies."

"I have," I answered. "Lots of them. Why?"

"Ever hear about the mail-carrying shark?"

I did a double-take on that one, and my companion chuckled. Then he told me the following story:

The old windjammer, *Socony*, Percy Crosby captain, rolled lazily along in mid-Pacific, case oil in her hold, a fairish breeze ruffling her sails. She was about two weeks out of Los Angeles, Shanghai-bound, and her timbers creaked and groaned with the weariness of age, answering the muttering, gurgling water that slapped at her bow.

Crosby, finishing his morning coffee in his cabin, lit a cigarette and looked out the porthole at the placid Pacific. It had been a good voyage, even a pleasant one, he mused, except for one thing—a huge shark that had followed doggedly in the wake of the *Socony* for the last five days.

Tamping out his cigarette, Crosby went on deck to have a look. Sure enough, the shark was still there, less than a hundred feet astern. Half a dozen sailors were leaning over the rail, regarding it glumly, mindful of the seaman's superstition that if a shark follows a ship one of the crew will die during the voyage.

The captain watched the scene for a moment, then

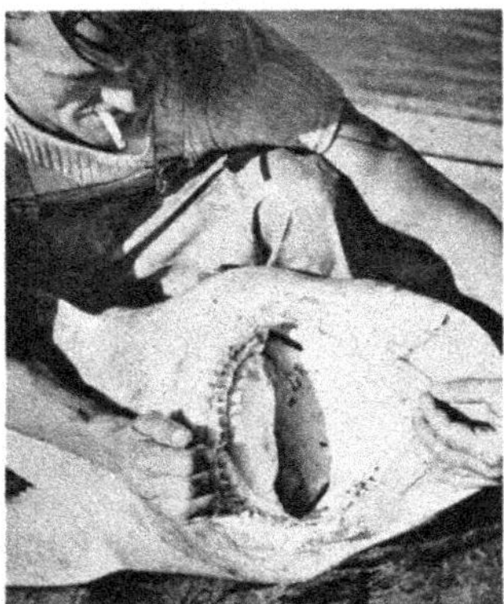

THE BUSINESS END of a shark is a fearsome thing. A hungry one will eat anything in sight.

called for action. A heavy hook, baited with chunks of salt pork, went over the stern with a splash —and in a matter of minutes there was a frantic thrashing as the big fish hit.

A block and tackle was brought into play, and soon the glistening body of the shark was lying on the deck of the ship. The sailors gave it plenty of berth, all 18 wicked-looking feet of it.

They finally decided to open it up, however, on the premise that no shark is deader than a disembowled one.

Suddenly, one of the men straightened from his task with a surprised exclamation, walked over to the captain and silently handed him four bundles of letters, neatly tied and in good condition. And every letter was addressed to Percy Crosby, captain of the *Socony!*

Boudreau paused to light up, which gave me a chance to break in with, "Who on earth dreamed that one up?"

"Nobody," he answered. "I got the story from Crosby, who lives here in Yarmouth. You want the rest of it?"

The explanation was almost disappointingly simple.

It seems that, accompanying Captain Crosby on this trip, were his wife and two small sons, Keith and Percy, Jr., aged five and seven. The boys had decided to vary shipboard routine by playing a form of post office. Rounding up the letters in the cabin, they tied them into four bundles and tossed them out the porthole. The bundles had floated astern, where the shark—not averse to taking a crack at anything even faintly resembling food—gulped them down. Which accounts for the return of the captain's mail, delivered by the only postal shark on record.

I didn't see Boudreau again until the next afternoon, aboard a tuna boat some 20 miles out of Wedgeport, where half a dozen of us had decided to try our luck with the giant blue-fins we'd been writing and talking about all week. We'd just boated a 500-pounder when Boudreau tapped me on the shoulder.

"When you get around to it," he said, with a grin, "you might see if there's any mail for me." **END**

Ray Nelson, who conducts a monthly feature page for REAL, is the well-known sportsman and narrator-producer of the "Rod and Gun Club of the Air," heard over the Mutual Broadcasting System every Thursday at 9:05-9:30 P.M., EDT.

It was 2:00 AM in the glassed-in lounge of the Grand Hotel at Yarmouth, Nova Scotia, and one by one the press and radio boys who had converged on the spot to cover the International Tuna Cup Matches yawned and shuffled off to bed.

Finally only Boudreau and I were left. This particular Boudreau, that is—for in Yarmouth a man's name tends to be Boudreau, if it isn't Comeau, and the bustling port would be a pretty desolate waste if the Boudreaus and the Comeaus happened to pull up stakes.

This Boudreau tamped a fresh pipeful down with a horny thumb, and regarded the ceiling thoughtfully as he lighted up. Then, exhaling a blue cloud, he said, "You've seen big sharks, more than likely. What I mean are the really big babies."

"I have," I answered. "Lots of them. Why?"

"Ever hear about the mail-carrying shark?"

I did a double-take on that one, and my companion chuckled. Then he told me the following story:

The old windjammer, *Socony*, Percy Crosby captain, rolled lazily along in mid-Pacific, case oil in her hold, a fairish breeze ruffling her sails. She was about two weeks out of Los Angeles, Shanghai-bound, and her timbers creaked and groaned with the weariness of age, answering the muttering, gurgling water that slapped at her bow.

Crosby, finishing his morning coffee in his cabin, lit a cigarette and looked out the porthole at the placid Pacific. It had been a good voyage, even a pleasant one, he mused, except for one thing—a huge shark that had followed doggedly in the wake of the *Socony* for the last five days.

Tamping out his cigarette, Crosby went on deck to have a look. Sure enough, the shark was still there, less than a hundred feet astern. Half a dozen sailors were leaning over the rail, regarding it glumly, mindful of the seaman's superstition that if a shark follows a ship one of the crew will die during the voyage.

The captain watched the scene for a moment, then called for action. A heavy hook, baited with chunks of salt pork, went over the stern with a splash—and in a matter of minutes there was a frantic thrashing as the big fish hit.

A block and tackle was brought into play, and soon the glistening body of the shark was lying on the deck of the ship. The sailors gave it plenty of berth, all 18 wicked-looking feet of it.

They finally decided to open it up, however, on the premise that no shark is deader than a disemboweled one.

Suddenly, one of the men straightened from his task with a surprised exclamation, walked over to the captain and silently handed him four bundles of letters, neatly tied and in good condition. And every letter was addressed to Percy Crosby, captain of the *Socony!*

Boudreau paused to light up, which gave me a chance to break in with, "Who on earth dreamed that one up?"

"Nobody," he answered. "I got the story from Crosby, who lives here in Yarmouth. You want the rest of it?"

The explanation was almost disappointingly simple.

It seems that, accompanying Captain Crosby on this trip, were his wife and two small sons, Keith and Percy, Jr., aged five and seven. The boys had decided to vary shipboard routine by playing a form of post office. Rounding up the letters in the cabin, they tied them into four bundles and tossed them out the porthole. The bundles had floated astern, where the shark—not averse to taking a crack at anything even faintly resembling food—gulped them down. Which accounts for the return of the captain's mail, delivered by the only postal shark on record.

I didn't see Boudreau again until the next afternoon, aboard a tuna boat some 20 miles out of Wedgeport, where half a dozen of us had decided to try our luck with the giant blue-fins we'd been writing and talking about all week. We'd just boated a 500-pounder when Boudreau tapped me on the shoulder.

"When you get around to it," he said, with a grin, "you might see if there's any mail for me." ▼

ACTION FOR MEN January 1972 Art by Bruce Minney *(colorized cover detail)*

18

"I Fought the Suez Sea Beast"

STORY BY MICHAEL DUBALL   COVER ART BY MORT KÜNSTLER

by Michael Duball

I FOUGHT THE
SUEZ SEA-BEAST

"I recognized the creature, then, as a huge moray eel, the ocean's

deadliest monster — and I was trapped in an underwater cage!"

It was on the 26th of November, late afternoon. The sudden and violent outburst of action over the Suez Canal area had ceased. English aircraft had droned off to their Cyprus bases and French and British troops bowed to the United Nations security forces. In retribution against western opposition, the Egyptians had scuttled vessels in the entrance to the canal to seal off passage into the Red Sea, and as an engineer formerly with the Bezane Company in Cairo, I was called to assist in the demolition and salvage.

I was on the stern of the *Mistral,* a Belgian vessel, with Gamal Fuad, a young Egyptian engineer educated at Columbia University in the States, when one of our demolition men bobbed up to the surface about twenty yards from the marking buoy. We both caught sight of him at the same time. He hung heavy on the water, his head jerking up and down, not like someone acting out of a tremendous fear or compulsion, but more like a man waking himself from a nodding sleep.

We shouted to him but there was no response. A dark, eddying pool stirred up about him and I grabbed at a life-jacket and started lowering myself down over the small kedge anchor. Simultaneously, Fuad dashed for the cabin and burst out of it with a Manlicher rifle clutched in his hands.

The water, characteristic of the Red Sea, was sluggish, tepid and because of the fuel contamination and high mortality of sea life, stinking and nauseous. I came at the man from the side, facing his back and shoulder. I grabbed at him under the armpits. He was Rayber, a New Zealander and a big man, over 220 pounds. But his body was strangely buoyant and unbalanced. He went over on his side against me, and his eyes rolled in a filmy daze, his blue eyes tremoring like an epileptic.

I heard the crack of the high-powered rifle first. I turned to follow the line of its discharge and I saw the triangular fin slicing the water like a keen blade.

"Shark, Rayber—shark!" I shouted trying to frighten him into consciousness. I tugged at him violently and as he toppled forward, I saw the jagged stump of his left leg at the thigh, the raw tendons and severed tissues running blood.

I moved around Rayber, getting in front of him, pulling one of his arms over my shoulder to keep him from going under. At the same time I kept my face to the shark (distinguishable as a tiger shark, by the width of the fin). Then I began kicking up a froth.

The shaking up was bad, perhaps even fatal to a man in Rayber's condition but I had no alternative. His lacerated limb was pumping blood, staining the water within eight or ten feet, a pinkish, milky hue. And if the shark ventured close enough to make contact with it, it would be incensed enough to tear us into pieces.

Fuad discharged several shots before he was joined by other armed crewmen and the water spanked up under the impact of the bullets.

The fin shuddered, disappeared and reappeared again, moving swiftly now, without any pattern, like a wounded animal gone beserk. I glanced back for an instant and caught sight of a dinghy being lowered over the side. It was a mistake to look back; I lost sight of the shark. I began shouting to the men in the dinghy, "I can't see it! Where is it? Where is it?"

I made several turns in the *(Continued on page 76)*

(Continued on page 76)

ILLUSTRATED BY EMMET KAY

"I twisted and turned desperately to avoid the creature. I felt panic, wondering if I would ever leave that cage."

ART BY MORT KÜNSTLER

It was on the 26th of November, late afternoon. The sudden and violent outburst of action over the Suez Canal area had ceased. English aircraft had droned off to their Cyprus bases and French and British troops bowed to the United Nations security forces. In retribution against western opposition, the Egyptians had scuttled vessels in the entrance to the canal to seal off passage into the Red Sea, and as an engineer formerly with the Bezane Company in Cairo, I was called to assist in the demolition and salvage.

I was on the stern of the *Mistral*, a Belgian vessel, with Gamal Fuad, a young Egyptian engineer educated at Columbia University in the States, when one of our demolition men bobbed up to the surface about twenty yards from the marking buoy. We both caught sight of him at the same time. He hung heavy on the water, his head jerking up and down, not like someone acting out of a tremendous fear or compulsion, but more like a man waking himself from a nodding sleep.

We shouted to him but there was no response. A dark, eddying pool stirred up about him and I grabbed at a lifejacket and started lowering myself down over the small kedge anchor. Simultaneously, Fuad dashed for the cabin and burst out of it with a Mannlicher rifle clutched in his hands.

The water, characteristic of the Red Sea, was sluggish, tepid and because of the fuel contamination and high mortality of sea life, stinking and nauseous. I came at the man from the side, facing his back and shoulder. I grabbed at him under the armpits. He was Rayber, a New Zealander and a big man, over 220 pounds. But his body was strangely buoyant and unbalanced. He went over on his side against me, and his eyes rolled in a filmy daze, his blue eyes tremoring like an epileptic.

I heard the crack of the high-powered rifle first. I turned to follow the line of its discharge and I saw the triangular fin slicing the water like a keen blade.

"Shark, Rayber—shark!" I shouted trying to frighten him into consciousness. I tugged at him violently and as he toppled forward, I saw the jagged stump of his left leg at the thigh, the raw tendons and severed tissues running blood.

I moved around Rayber, getting in front of him, pulling one of his arms over my shoulder to keep him from going under. At the same time I kept my face to the shark (distinguishable as a tiger shark, by the width of the fin). Then I began kicking up a froth.

The shaking up was bad, perhaps even fatal to a man in Rayber's condition, but I had no alternative. His lacerated limb was pumping blood, staining the water within eight or ten feet a pinkish, milky hue. And if the shark ventured close enough to make contact with it, it would be incensed enough to tear us into pieces.

Fuad discharged several shots before he was joined by other armed crewmen and the water spanked up under the impact of the bullets.

The fin shuddered, disappeared and reappeared again, moving swiftly now, without any. pattern, like a wounded animal gone berserk. I glanced back for an instant and caught sight of a dinghy being lowered over the side. It was a mistake to look back; I lost sight of the shark. I began shouting to the men in the dinghy, "I can't see it! Where is it? Where is it?"

I made several turns in the water with Rayber in my arms and suddenly he came around.

The dinghy was less than twenty yards left of us and I began shoving Rayber toward it.

"We've got him!" Melsher called to me from the dinghy. He was a small man, wiry and with a single eye, and despite his English nationality, a great favorite with the Egyptians. As he reached over the side to grab at Rayber, I saw the last thrashing throes of the great shark. It was out of sight, before I was dragged aboard.

Rayber opened his eyes but never regained complete lucidity.

He died within two hours. He was the third man attacked by a shark within two weeks of the initial salvage operation.

Bodies and supplies from the vessels sunk during the brief and fierce hostilities had littered the water with provender for the roving scavengers, until virtual schools of them ventured up to the entrance of the canal.

The hazard to the men during the salvage inspection, the preparatory workmap period, turned out to be our gravest problem. And our first approach to its solution was the construction of two four by five wire "stileen" cages suspended from the ocean-going salvage tug. Here, equipped with an especially-fitted Bolex camera and vulcanized sacks of the powdered shark repellant used with effectiveness in the South Pacific during World War II, Fuad and I were lowered into the depths. Steel cables held us in position above, from the Belgian vessel. Ours was a two-fold function. Firstly to photograph the damaged and scuttled ships for study as to the best method for demolition and clearance. Secondly, to seek out the shark and to flood the area around our demolition men with a stream of repellant.

Almost three weeks later, the work was proceeding without any hitches, except for the one instance of a shark which had drifted aboard the scuttled Egyptian vessel *El Meber*. Lubbock, a powerful young Jamaican acetylene torcher, had seared through a water-tight bulkhead and run head-long into the tiger.

"It come right at me belly and I shove me hand out afore I know what's at me," the man told us when we applied a tourniquet to his hand where it had been severed at the wrist. Lubbock, a dark, handsome mulatto, a devastating Casanova with the women, displayed steely nerves. His only comment: "One hand can only love one woman at a time!"

But within days of this incident, the work around the *El Meber* proved almost fatal a second time. I was port side of the vessel, recording on film the angle of the

El Meber, and the depth to which it was submerged in the sinking sands. I had the camera up to my line of vision, as a result of which I did not see the creature until its long, slithering form had cleared the steel cage.

It went beyond me and over my head and I whirled and flung my back against the front of the cage. I recognized it then as a massive moray eel, of the voracious species inhabiting the warm waters of the Red Sea. Black, snub-nosed, thick across the top as a shillelagh, its maw packed with deadly cutting teeth.

It moved with the jagged and slithering quickness of a water-serpent, its movements difficult to discern in the glinting undersea reflections. I went for the sack of shark repellant, lifting it and shaking out a dark cloud of its murky contents. It was my intention to drive out the creature with the noxious chemical…a serious mistake.

Once aroused, the moray eel, like many forms of sea life, expands, and the whip like form charging against the cage was now inflated to the thickness of a heavy cable—and could not clear the steel openings. It thudded head-on, in quick, successive thrusts and then it went wild.

I swung the emptied sack up before me, snagging the moray. But the powerful jaws gnashed through instantly and I felt a tearing pain high on my thigh. I slugged at it with the camera. The resistance of the water deflected the forward force of the instrument and the moray went up—striking me flush in the face. The impact was like the powerful jolt of a hammer. I went back against the cage, conscious of the loose flesh-flap of a lacerated cheek.

I got back on my feet. I felt trapped, half torn to pieces. The grainy repellant, still clogging the water, singed into the raw flesh on my face. I lost all caution, fearing that I would never leave that cage. Instead of bashing the camera, I shoved it; creating less resistance and I trapped the moray against the steel mesh. I leaned into it with all my weight. It tore from between the camera and the cage, leaving stripped edges of flesh on steel. It slithered on a side, flipped over and twitched in one position. I chopped down on top of it forcing it down.

Water caught at the grimy innards of the desperately wriggling, moray and it smeared over the camera, and onto my hands. I continued crushing it, afraid to release it. Then my knees went out under me…

I WAS revived back on aboard the Belgian vessel and the Egyptian doctor in attendance repaired my face with twenty-four stitches. The repair of the thigh wound was not as easily remedied. A chunk of flesh half the size of my fist was torn out, exposing delicate nerve fibers which required skin transplants in the American Hospital in Beirut, Lebanon.

Lubbock, the amiable Jamaican with the one-track mind, had the last (and for him, characteristic) words on this episode: "You lucky moray bite flat chunk. He bite chunk higher up, you have real big troubles." ▼

BRUCE AVERA HUNTER, MARINE CONSERVATION & NATURALIST PHOTOGRAPHER: It is true that tiger sharks are among the most dangerous sharks (along with great whites and bull sharks), and they would certainly be attracted to so many dead sea creatures floating about, leading to a feeding frenzy—a dangerous scenario for any creature in the water. Tiger sharks are known as "garbage eaters" because not only are they predators, but as scavengers, they will eat almost anything, including man-made indigestible objects. However, many dive alongside tiger sharks with no problem—albeit without the presence of rotting carcasses in the water.

The story's presentation of the moray eel is rather hilariously unbelievable. Moray eels are nocturnal, and prefer the cover of darkness and crevices. They have very poor eyesight, and therefore are rather timid; they mostly scavenge for food. It is highly unusual for a moray eel to attack or eat anything larger than a baseball. On rare occasions humans do get bitten by morays, but usually as a result of an attempt to feed them.

I have been fortunate to dive and photograph some of the most beautiful, weird, and wonderful creatures on Earth. I am keenly aware that approaching any wild animal too closely can present a risk of danger, and I never forget it.

In the Coral Sea of Papua New Guinea, crossing a channel in open water, I spotted a four-meter hammerhead shark ahead of me. I swam to catch up to capture a 3/4 angle shot with my camera. Each time I gained ground and moved up alongside him, he'd whip his tail sharply and surge ahead another five meters. This happened three or four times until I was finally winded. He could tolerate my presence, but only so much. I was surprised that this creature twice my size was so uncomfortable with my proximity.

In the Sea of Cortés off the Baja Peninsula, I was tasked with photographing a nine-meter female whale shark. I was dropped into her path on the surface of the water about fifteen meters away. I was free diving without the drag of a tank, and before I reached her she began to dive, then suddenly reversed her dive, arching upwards. She had spotted me, and aimed directly towards me. I was nervous but exhilarated as her white spots and gaping mouth zoomed up to me. But as she approached, she slowed her pace to a gentle drift. She could have swallowed me whole if she wanted, but I wasn't on her meal plan, and she had more fun posing and letting me scratch her belly.

Some animals have a reciprocal passive curiosity, and others have almost no interest at all. Reading their behavior, knowing their patterns, respecting their space, and remaining constantly vigilant are my essential tools to coexisting safely with wild animals.

STAG February 1954 Art by Gail Phillips

"Kiss Me, Killer Shark!"

STORY BY LARRY C. GRAYBILL & JAMES B. HENDERSON

COVER ART BY JOHN GARGIUILLI

On September 18th, 1953, at 4 P.M., an Air Force B-29 weather reconnaissance plane was 250 miles east of Savannah, Georgia, and headed for its home base in Bermuda, when it exploded over the Atlantic Ocean. The following is an eyewitness account of one of the most incredible stories of man's survival at sea.

PART I

Staff Sergeant Larry C. Graybill:

OUR SHIP was up about 10,000 feet and cruising at about 250 miles per hour. There were about 16 of us—all of the 53rd Stratosphere Reconnaissance Squadron—the crew of 11 and five ground crew maintenance men. The week before, we had been evacuated from Kindley Field in Bermuda when a severe hurricane threatened to smash headlong into the islands. By Friday, September 18th, the danger was over and we were returning.

It was a day to be up there. Brilliant sun. Not a cloud. I could see a lot of ocean from where I was positioned in the right "blister," the plexiglass bubble built into either side of B-29s. As Right Scanner it was part of my job to keep an eye on Number 3 and 4 engines—out of the pilot's line of vision. It was quiet except for the even hum of the engines. And you got so that from inside the pressurized cabin you never even noticed it.

Suddenly there was a deafening roar—like another plane swooping down on us. I looked out quick. My eye caught the blur of motion up front and then—boom! An explosion rocked the plane.

I started hollering through the intercom to our pilot, Captain Broughton: "Number 3 engine on fire—no, it's 4, sir—it's burning!"

Thick black smoke was pouring out of Number 3 and Number 4 was ringed with flame. "Number 3 blew clear of its mount and crashed into 4."

"How fast is she burning?" Captain Broughton barked through the intercom.

"Looks bad," I said—and I kept talking fast, describing the progress of the flames. "She's burning back to the wing." I turned around and hollered to the guys, "Everybody get your chute, Mae West and dinghy!"

The bail-out alarm was ringing, shrill and continuous. The flames were crawling up the wing fast. If it ever got to the wing gas tanks we'd be blown to bits.

A sudden flash of flame blinded me for an instant. Then I made out the wing burning from top to bottom. It got so hot in the "blister" I had to get out. My lids felt dry and

swollen and blinking irritated my eyeballs.

There was another flashback, worse than the first. It was a solid wall of flame. Everybody was scrambling out. I watched the last couple of men bail out through the rear door.

I got to my feet and made a dash for the rear door. A loud report like a giant firecracker went off in my ear. It ripped a gaping hole clear through the fuselage. Next thing I knew I was pinned to the floor.

Flames were shooting through the compartment. I thought I was going to be burned alive.

The ship was in a spin. I tried to crawl for the hole in the fuselage.

I couldn't move—it was like being glued to the floorboards. I could feel the exposed parts of my body burning, my face, my hands . . .

"Hit the water," I cried out—"If it would only hit the water!"

There was another blast and it blotted out everything. I found myself hurtling through the air. I saw chutes above me. It dawned on me that I was falling with my back to the water. I strained to turn myself around. I jerked the rip cord. The chute billowed and jolted me to my heels as it pocketed air. I looked down. I was almost on top of the water.

I set myself for the impact. I knew what I was doing now. A ditching and survivor course the Air Force put us through, every year, prepared us for such emergencies.

As I struck, I pulled myself free of the chute and inflated my Mae West jacket. The chill of that water was like an ice pack. I tried to inflate the dinghy—the one-man raft that was folded and hooked to the chute pack—and my Mae West. I pulled the cord on the bottle of gas but the dinghy wouldn't inflate. I figured I had somehow damaged the valve release when I was flung

out of the plane.

Then I saw one of the six-man rafts from the aircraft. It was half submerged. Three such rafts are stored on the plane, two on either side of the fuselage on the wing, and the other between the two "blisters" on the rear section of the fuselage. I started swimming for the raft. I'm a fairly strong swimmer. I did a lot of spear fishing in Bermuda in my off time. But my Mae West held me back somewhat and my right arm was hurt. I thought I had twisted it or struck it against something when blown from the plane. The heavy running swells made the going tougher.

When I was within 20 yards of the raft I saw someone close to it. I hollered out and he waved back. It was my closest buddy, Airman Second Class James B. Henderson.

"Jim — what's happened to my face?" I asked anxiously. It felt swollen to twice its normal size.

"Nothing," Jim said. But I could tell from the way he said it that he was lying.

The raft turned out to be badly ripped up. In another minute it sank. But a sudden swell carried Jim upward and forward and he pointed excitedly over my shoulder.

"Larry—another big one!"

It was another six-man raft.

We swam the several hundred yards toward it and it was sheer anguish trying to snag it. The raft shifted elusively back and forth like a wet rubber ball. When we got our hands on it we groaned our disappointment. It was almost in as bad a condition as the other raft. Only one end was above the water. The gas bottle was discharged and the hand pump smashed. We clung to the raft for maybe an hour, waiting, looking around, trying to spot some of the others. No sign.

The waves kept smacking us in the face. Sometimes they'd break over us, but most of the time we got

KILLER SHARK!

By S/Sgt. Larry C. Graybill
and A/2C James B. Henderson

ART BY JOHN GARGIUILLI

On September 18th, 1953, at 4 PM, an Air Force B-29 weather reconnaissance plane was 250 miles east of Savannah, Georgia, and headed for its home base in Bermuda when it exploded over the Atlantic Ocean. The following is an eyewitness account of one of the most incredible stories of man's survival at sea.

Part I
Staff Sergeant Larry C. Graybill:

Our ship was up about 10,000 feet and cruising at about 250 miles per hour. There were about 16 of us—all of the 53rd Stratosphere Reconnaissance Squadron—the crew of 11 and five ground crew maintenance men. The week before, we had been evacuated from Kindley Field in Bermuda when a severe hurricane threatened to smash headlong into the islands. By Friday, September 18th, the danger was over and we were returning:

It was a day to be up there. Brilliant sun. Not a cloud. I could see a lot of ocean from where I was positioned in the right "blister," the plexiglass bubble built into either side of B-29s. As Right Scanner it was part of my job to keep an eye on Number 3 and 4 engines out of the pilot's line of vision. It was quiet except for the even hum of the engines. And you got so that from inside the pressurized cabin you never even noticed it.

Suddenly there was a deafening roar—like another plane swooping down on us. I looked out quick. My eye caught the blur of motion up front and then— boom! An explosion rocked the plane.

I started hollering through the intercom to our pilot, Captain Broughton: "Number 3 engine on fire—no, it's 4, sir—it's burning!"

Thick black smoke was pouring out of Number 3 and Number 4 was ringed with flame. "Number 3 blew clear of its mount and crashed into 4."

"How fast is she burning?" Captain Broughton barked through the intercom.

"Looks bad," I said—and I kept talking fast, describing the progress of the flames. "She's burning back to the wing." I turned around and hollered to the guys, "Everybody get your chute, Mae West and dinghy!"

The bail-out alarm was ringing, shrill and continuous. The flames were crawling up the wing fast. If it ever got to the wing gas tanks we'd be blown to bits.

A sudden flash of flame blinded me for an instant. Then I made out the wing burning from top to bottom. It got so hot in the "blister" I had to get out. My lids felt dry and swollen and blinking irritated my eyeballs.

There was another flashback, worse than the first. It was a solid wall of flame. Everybody was scrambling out. I watched the last couple of men bail out through the rear door.

I got to my feet and made a dash for the rear door. A loud report like a giant firecracker went off in my ear. It ripped a gaping hole clear through the fuselage. Next thing I knew I was pinned to the floor.

Flames were shooting through the compartment. I thought I was going to be burned alive.

The ship was in a spin. I tried to crawl for the hole in the fuselage.

I couldn't move—it was like being glued to the floorboards. I could feel the exposed parts of my body burning, my face, my hands...

"Hit the water," I cried out — "If it would only hit the water!"

There was another blast and it blotted out everything. I found myself hurtling through the air. I saw chutes above me. It dawned on me that I was falling with my back to the water. I strained to turn myself around. I jerked the rip cord. The chute billowed and jolted me to my heels as it pocketed air. I looked down. I was almost on top of the water.

I set myself for the impact. I knew what I was doing now. A ditching and survivor course the Air Force put us through, every year, prepared us for such emergencies.

As I struck, I pulled myself free of the chute and inflated my Mae West jacket. The chill of that water was like an ice pack. I tried to inflate the dinghy— the one-man raft that was folded and hooked to the chute pack—and my Mae West. I pulled the cord on the bottle of gas but the dinghy wouldn't inflate. I figured I had somehow damaged the valve release when I was flung out of the plane.

Then I saw one of the six-man rafts from the aircraft. It was half submerged. Three such rafts are stored on the plane, two on either side of the fuselage on the wing, and the other between the two "blisters" on the rear section of the fuselage. I started swimming for the raft. I'm a fairly strong swimmer. I did a lot of spear fishing in Bermuda in my off time. But my Mae West held me back somewhat and my right arm was hurt. I thought I had twisted it or struck it against something when blown from the plane. The heavy running swells made the going tougher.

When I was within 20 yards of the raft I saw someone close to it. I hollered out and he waved back. It was my closest buddy, Airman Second Class James B. Henderson.

"Jim—what's happened to my face?" I asked anxiously. It felt swollen to twice its normal size.

"Nothing," Jim said. But I could tell from the way he said it that he was lying.

The raft turned out to be badly ripped up. In another minute it sank. But a sudden swell carried Jim upward and forward and he pointed excitedly over my shoulder.

"Larry—another big one!"

It was another six-man raft.

We swam the several hundred yards toward it and it was sheer anguish trying to snag it. The raft shifted elusively back and forth like a wet rubber ball. When we got our hands on it we groaned our disappointment. It was almost in as bad a condition as the other raft. Only one end was above the water. The gas bottle was discharged and the hand pump smashed. We clung to the raft for maybe an hour, waiting, looking around, trying to spot some of the others. No sign.

The waves kept smacking us in the face. Sometimes they'd break over us, but most of the time we got a mouthful of salt water.

"This raft isn't going to last long," Jim said. I knew he was right. It was submerging gradually.

I felt flushed. Above my eyes, in the area of the sinuses, sharp pains throbbed. I tried not to think of my face and what had happened to it. Then something rushed past me. I could feel the motion of the current and then it was at my leg. I reached down and I felt my hand in a mouth. I let out a yell and the fish came right out of the water on its white underbelly.

"A shark, Jim," I screamed. "A shark!"

I began punching and moving like a maniac. I was scared sick. I guess it was about five feet long but it looked three times that to me. Jim caught it a good, square kick in the belly. And we both kicked and splashed at it until it went away.

I clung to the raft, what there was of it still above water, trying to catch my breath. "The shark repellent—" I said to Jim, half choking out the words. He reached down into the safety pocket of his Mae West and removed the squeeze sack that contained the gritty powder. The repellent was supposed to be effective up to two-and-a-half hours, but we were spreading it so violently and the water was so rough it kept washing away.

We'd clung to the raft about an hour, maybe two. Then I felt it slip away from under my armpit. "It's going down, Jim," I said.

He grabbed the nylon rope out of the raft. "We'd better tie ourselves together," he said.

I nodded. It was getting dark and the swells were getting steeper. It was no time to become separated. We strung the rope through the rings on our Mae Wests. A couple of minutes later, the raft sunk out of sight. Then a movement close to my body under water made me pull away. My little finger caught the razor edge of a tooth.

"It's back!" I hollered to Jim.

"Hit him in the snout!" Jim yelled.

I punched at it, missed it, then caught it flush. Jim got a solid smash into its snout. We both kept kicking like crazy all the time. It went away.

"I read somewhere about smashing them in the snout," Jim said.

It seemed to work.

The flesh on my finger was slashed to the bone and it bled a lot. I was afraid for the blood to drop into the water and attract the sharks. So for a couple of hours I swam with my arm above the water, letting the blood run into my sleeve until it dried. The waves were maybe 10 feet high by now and we had to swim with our backs to the sea to keep from drowning, but still they came over our heads. And it was cold—we were shivering and fighting to keep our arms, necks and legs from cramping.

My right hand hurt. It wasn't only the little finger. I saw that the flesh from the knuckles had been completely ripped away by the shark. My face felt like a masked covering and the pain in my head was making me delirious. I heard myself speaking and half the time I didn't know what I was saying. But Jim and I kept talking to each other, trying to keep from falling asleep and going under. There was a full moon illuminating the water but it was still so dark we could barely make each other out at four feet apart. When we brushed against each other we panicked, thinking we'd made contact with a shark.

I heard Jim yell and smash furiously at the water. I began doing the same thing until he stopped. Then I heard him moan.

I came close to him. "Did it get you bad, Jim?"

He shook his head. "It wasn't a shark," he said. "It was a Portuguese man-of-war."

This large, bladder-like, gelatinous fish can inflict severe stings. Jim held up his arm. It was badly swollen. Five minutes later he started beating up the water again and the fish got at him. I was worried. Jim seemed dazed for about a half hour after that. It was only when I yelled "Sharks!", and went half crazy in the water at the pressure exerted against my leg, that he snapped out of it.

We had developed a one-two punch by now. It must have been good, because when the sharks closed in, they came up at us, instead of coming along the surface where we could hit at them.

But I was getting so weak it was an effort to raise my arms. I was so miserable that I sometimes wanted to die. But each time I got a gullet full of sea water it made dying seem more like an agony than staying alive. Then I got a terrible pain in my stomach. I doubled over. It was so bad I can't describe it, worse than the burns or the shark bites. I started screaming. Jim came over to me.

PART II
AIRMAN SECOND CLASS JAMES B. HENDERSON:

LARRY was bad off, but I was afraid if I showed too much concern I'd alarm him. It was getting tougher for him to hold his face and head out of the water, and he kept swallowing salt water.

"Can I help you, Larry?" I asked him.

"No," he said, "nobody can help me. I wish you had a knife so you could kill me."

He kept on screaming as we swam for an hour or more in the black of night. At one point he said, "Tell Jeanette I died thinking of her, if I don't make it and you do."

"Don't talk like that," I said. "They'll have half the Air Force looking for us by morning."

My body was quivering from the chill. I clamped my jaws together as tight as I could but I couldn't stop the chattering of my teeth. And since I had been stung by the Portuguese man-of-war, a dull, pounding headache persisted. I wondered whether the stings had resulted in some kind of infection.

As I watched Larry screaming and writhing with stomach cramps I felt it was a hopeless, losing battle. Then I saw it—a light moving across the sky.

"Larry—a search plane!" I cried out.

We shouted, flailed our arms, used our signal whistles—although we could barely blow them between cracked lips. But the plane's spotlight swept the water —and went by.

We saw a couple of more planes swinging in wide arcs. They didn't even come close. We saw two or three boats, or what we thought were boats, and we made a futile effort to blow our whistles. They were too far off to hear us, and it was too dark to see us. Then we were alone again, except for the sharks.

Then dawn started creeping up. Exhaustion, salt water sickness and heavy seas had taken a terrific toll of us. The salt encrusted my eyelids, smarted on my eyeballs and itched in the inside corners of my eyes until I wanted to rip them out of their sockets. But we both kept squinting, straining to see.

We spotted them about the same time—search planes! They'd sweep down in circles but they didn't come near enough to us.

Both of us were about ready to give up. I thought about Heaven and what it was like…and Hell. I began to wonder why I was so afraid to die. Nothing, it seemed to me could've been worse than being out there in that water—watching the planes fly out of sight.

Occasionally I would feel or imagine I felt the movement of a shark near me and I would kick out and splash. But mostly we just drifted, swept along, lifted and dropped by the swells, buffeted by waves. Then, after what I guess was about three hours…

"Larry—Larry, I see a ship!" I said. It was about two miles off.

"We'll never make it," Larry said. His voice was so cracked I could hardly make out what he said. We swam toward the ship, fighting, pushing ourselves every foot of the way. If there had been any last resource of energy—and I couldn't believe there had been—we used it then.

Then we saw that the ship was moving in a straight line away from us. We said nothing, we just about gave up. We just bobbed up and down trying to keep our faces out of water. That was all.

That's when a number of planes, different types, began making circles. There must have been four or five of them. Once one of them came in so low that for a fleeting instant I saw a face peering out of a blister window. But the plane was going so fast, the observer never saw me.

Suddenly one of the planes spotted us.

Later I found out that when they started circling us they kept finding and losing us as we rode the crest of a swell. The plane started dropping six-man life rafts. Frantically we tried to get to them. But the closest moved too fast for us. Another dropped and then another. We couldn't get them.

"I—I'm all done," Larry said weakly, "I can't swim—"

I knew it was so. "Hang on," I told him. "Just stay afloat until I get a life raft to you."

I unsnagged us and started swimming. Not very fast at first. Then something came over me like one of God's miracles—a new-found strength. I could almost picture somebody in that raft telling me to come on. I could hear my own voice saying, "I'm trying!"

I started sinking and the water rose over my head. When I came up I saw the sharks. I splashed hard with my hand and started flailing away with fast, overhand, splashing strokes but I couldn't get to the raft. The plane made a pass. I begged out loud for another raft. In fact I screamed, "Please, God, send another raft!"

The plane dropped another two rafts, together, directly ahead of me. Then suddenly everything got hot, my face, hands, legs, everything. Something nipped at my hand. Shark. I took a punch at it. Then I saw three or four more sharks following me. I started kicking and splashing.

But there was one shark in particular, about two feet long, I won't forget. It came up alongside of me and nudged me in the side. I jumped and pushed it away.

I grabbed at a raft. I got it!

I put both hands over the side. The rafts were lashed together. Two brand-new, beautiful rafts. I fell in and passed out face down. I was out for seconds only. Something brought me around. I pulled the snaps loose on the oar kit. I could hardly move my hand and I had trouble getting the small metal oar out. I could grip the oar but I couldn't paddle with it. The water made my hands flabby, puffed up.

I tried to holler for Larry, who was out of sight. But I couldn't, my throat cracked. I couldn't hear him and I couldn't see him. I drove a shark away from the raft and I dove into the water. I moved out a little way, taking the rafts with me, over the swells.

Then I saw a raft with men in it, right near the spot where I thought I left Larry. I learned later these were men from a Navy amphibian. They had spotted sharks and decided to investigate. But in landing on a choppy sea they'd broken a pontoon. I struggled back into the raft and passed out. This time, I guess, for about 15 minutes.

When I came to, I was looking broadside at the luxury liner *SS Nassau*. A lifeboat pulled up alongside me and I looked up into the face of a strapping big Italian. It was the nicest face I think I ever saw in my life. He jumped down into the raft and lifted me into the lifeboat. I asked for something to drink and a crew member handed me a bottle of cognac. I took a swig. My mouth was raw and my throat parched. The stuff almost burned my insides out!

I sank back to rest. The lifeboat headed for the Navy amphibian and its crew in the life raft. I was feeling sure that I'd find Larry with them. But when we pulled alongside them he wasn't there. I started to go over the side of the lifeboat to look for him. A crew member grabbed me and pulled me down. I was too weak to fight.

"What about my buddy?" I asked.

I was told he was already aboard the *Nassau*. They took me aboard the *Nassau*, thinking they had already saved Larry. But Larry was fished up about 20 minutes after I was brought aboard. Two young women passengers had spotted him three-quarters of a mile off. The ship had almost run him down in picking him up—but he was safe.

On board the *Nassau* we were brought up to date on the fate of the other men of our squadron. Six of us were picked up by the *Nassau*. Three other men were rescued by the *Seatrain Georgia*, a railroad car transport vessel.

Nine men saved out of the 16 who were in that B-29.

Larry and I had been in the water 22 hours. I'll always think of it as a far bigger piece of my lifetime. ▼

BITING BACK   commentary

This story is true, and is mentioned in the non-fiction book, *Shadows in the Sea: the Sharks, Skates and Rays* (Chilton, 1962) by Harold W. McCormick and Tom Allen with Captain William E. Young:

> *A man adrift at sea, far from land, never knows, however, when or whether a shark will be drawn to him. Two Air Force men parachuted into the Atlantic about 200 miles east of Savannah, Georgia, one night in 1953. The men. Sergeant Larry C. Graybill and Airman Second Class James B. Henderson, kept afloat by their lifejackets, lashed themselves together back to back. They floated for 22 hours until they were rescued. And for most of those hours, they fought off sharks.*
>
> *"I remembered something I had read—if you hit them on the snout, they take off. It worked," Henderson said.*
>
> *Graybill was not so lucky. "Something rushed by me," he recounted. "I felt one hand in a mouth, so I took a poke at him to get loose."*
>
> *Graybill's hands were both cut and scraped by the sharks. Henderson's forearms were raw with Portuguese men-of-war stings. Their blood in the water should have doomed them to the jaws of gore-crazed sharks. But no such mob-feeding frenzy occurred. Once more, sharks showed how unpredictable they could be.*

"The Killer Sharks Caught Us"

STORY BY CLIFTON MILLER

COVER ART BY CASEY JONES

Death is eighteen feet long and has a maw as big as a barrel. It comes at you like a racer on a speedway, staring at you with ugly little eyes, and then the maw opens and you see the flash of sawteeth that can rip you in half.

Those teeth are usually the last thing you see before your world turns into agony and eternal darkness. I saw them, and they held me spellbound so I could hardly move. I was full of horror because I had just seen Tony Boquist die; and there's nothing like catching a sneak preview of your own death.

The big killer shark took a quick swipe at Tony; he didn't even seem to stop. The white-blue monster passed in a flash, and my friend's body split like an overripe tomato. Just like that.

His body opened at the hip and his entrails spilled out, squirming like green worms in the shark's wake. Blood pumped from the ragged gash in Tony's side. The ocean water turned a frothy pink.

Tony's arms went up, and he hung like a weird puppet in the bloody bubbles gurgling from his open belly, and then the shark made a quick turn and was back, and his teeth ripped Tony from the other side.

One leg came off and slowly sank away; the other dangled by fibres. He looked like an odd jelly fish with the dangling leg and the squirming bowels, all wrapped in a red cloud. There were no screams, no sounds; the ocean is a silent world, and death under water is a pantomime.

But it was all over in a hurry. Because on his next pass the shark stayed, and the slaughter scene turned into a whirlpool of fish flesh and blood. Frayed chunks of Tony's body dropped away and floated, sinking slowly, and at last when the killing was done, the heavy oxygen tanks still hooked to Tony's mask dragged down his goggled head and what was left of his body.

That was the end for him, but not for me. I had seen him die, and there was nothing I could do about it, and seeing him torn into butcher chunks I'd know it would be my turn next.

I knew that my only chance—if any—lay in playing

THE KILLER SHARKS CAUGHT US...

by Clifton Miller

possum. The least movement would betray my presence. I hung in the wet nothingness of the Pacific, clammy and chilled despite the warmth of the water, and I wished I didn't have to breath. I clutched my knife and waited. Would the killer shark see me? Or would he swim off? He churned around now, snatching little pieces of Tony's body that sank slower than the others had. He sucked them into the gash of his evil mouth, and kept swimming in circles.

I didn't have much oxygen left. If the shark didn't take off soon I'd have to cash in my chips anyway. Because when you're 150 feet down it takes you a while to come up. You've got to stop every so often and hang in the water for a few minutes so your system adjusts to the pressure. If you don't stop, if you pop to the surface like a cork, you end up with the bends; and there's little choice between bends and a shark's ugly teeth. In either case, you've missed a better death.

The shark swam in circles, and my oxygen bubbled away. Sharks have damn sensitive noses, and my bubbles smelled of man. The minutes ticked away. The shark sensed he wasn't alone, but he hadn't seen me yet. I waited. I tried to pray.

And then a cold horror turned my insides into an icy lump. In the greenish never-never world of the ocean depth, I saw a second telltale shape. Another shark!

The second killer must have smelled the blood from far away; he must have felt the vibrations of the slaughter. Scientists say there are sounds under the water, sounds of frequencies you cannot hear but sharks can, and these sounds only mean one thing to the butchers of the deep: a killing and a free meal.

The two sharks cruised around me, uncertain with greed and excited by the lingering smell of Tony's blood. I could almost feel them sniffing for me, sensing the presence of another warm-blooded being, a tasty tidbit for lunchtime. The torpedo-shaped butchers swam with a slinky deadly grace that knotted my pounding heart with panic. I wanted to scream. Inside my mask I bit my lips until I could taste blood.

The second shark wheeled six feet from me, flipped himself upwards and passed over my head.

I peered up.

The shark had stopped. Hovering like a submarine he was sniffing at my bubbles. He opened his maw and inhaled my air. He scented *man* and tasted the man smell and the faint flavor of the blood from my lips. His long tail fin whipped the water in excited agitation. He moved his flat head up and down, trying to find out where the taste came from.

I looked at the great shark's white belly.

Slowly I raised my knife hand.

No, it didn't reach. At least one foot of water separated the gleaming knife tip from the monster's underside. There was no chance.

What if I lunged upward to sink my blade into the shark's soft gut? I couldn't think clearly, but I decided against it. (Continued on Page 48)

39

Death is eighteen feet long and has a maw as big as a barrel. It comes at you like a racer on a speedway, staring at you with ugly little eyes, and then the maw opens and you see the flash of sawteeth that can rip you in half.

Those teeth are usually the last thing you see before your world turns into agony and eternal darkness. I saw them, and they held me spellbound so I could hardly move. I was full of horror because I had just seen Tony Boquist die; and there's nothing like catching a sneak preview of your own death.

The big killer shark took a quick swipe at Tony; he didn't even seem to stop. The white-blue monster passed in a flash, and my friend's body split like an overripe tomato. Just like that.

His body opened at the hip and his entrails spilled out, squirming like green worms in the shark's wake. Blood pumped from the ragged gash in Tony's side. The ocean water turned a frothy pink.

Tony's arms went up, and he hung like a weird puppet in the bloody bubbles gurgling from his open belly, and then the shark made a quick turn and was back, and his teeth ripped Tony from the other side.

One leg came off and slowly sank away; the other dangled by fibers. He looked like an odd jellyfish with the dangling leg and the squirming bowels, all wrapped in a red cloud. There were no screams, no sounds; the ocean is a silent world, and death underwater is a pantomime.

But it was all over in a hurry. Because on his next pass the shark stayed, and the slaughter scene turned into a whirlpool of fish flesh and blood. Frayed chunks of Tony's body dropped away and floated, sinking slowly, and at last when the killing was done, the heavy oxygen tanks still hooked to Tony's mask dragged down his goggled head and what was left of his body.

That was the end for him, but not for me. I had seen him die, and there was nothing I could do about it, and seeing him torn into butcher chunks I'd known it would be my turn next.

I knew that my only chance—if any—lay in playing possum. The least movement would betray my presence. I hung in the wet nothingness of the Pacific, clammy and chilled despite the warmth of the water, and I wished I didn't have to breathe. I clutched my knife and waited. Would the killer shark see me? Or would he swim off? He churned around now, snatching little pieces of Tony's body that sank slower than the others had. He sucked them into the gash of his evil mouth, and kept swimming in circles.

I didn't have much oxygen left. If the shark didn't take off soon I'd have to cash in my chips anyway. Because when you're 150 feet down it takes you a while to come up. You've got to stop every so often and hang in the water for a few minutes so your system adjusts to the pressure. If you don't stop, if you pop to the surface like a cork, you end up with the bends; and there's little choice between bends and a shark's ugly teeth. In either case, you've missed a better death.

THE SHARK swam in circles, and my oxygen bubbled away. Sharks have damn sensitive noses, and my bubbles smelled of man. The minutes ticked away. The shark sensed he wasn't alone, but he hadn't seen me yet. I waited. I tried to pray.

And then a cold horror turned my insides into an icy lump. In the greenish never-never world of the ocean depth, I saw a second telltale shape. Another shark!

The second killer must have smelled the blood from far away; he must have felt the vibrations of the slaughter. Scientists say there are sounds under the water, sounds of frequencies you cannot hear but sharks can, and these sounds only mean one thing to the butchers of the deep: a killing and a free meal.

The two sharks cruised around me, uncertain with greed and excited by the lingering smell of Tony's blood. I could almost feel them sniffing for me, sensing the presence of another warm-blooded being, a tasty tidbit for lunchtime. The torpedo-shaped butchers swam with a slinky deadly grace that knotted my pounding heart with panic. I wanted to scream. Inside my mask I bit my lips until I could taste blood.

The second shark wheeled six feet from me, flipped himself upwards and passed over my head.

I peered up.

The shark had stopped. Hovering like a submarine he was sniffing at my bubbles. He opened his maw and inhaled my air. He scented man and tasted the man smell and the faint flavor of the blood from my lips. His long tail fin whipped the water in excited agitation. He moved his flat head up and down, trying to find out where the taste came from.

I looked at the great shark's white belly.

Slowly I raised my knife hand.

No, it didn't reach. At least one foot of water separated the gleaming knife tip from the monster's underside. There was no chance.

What if I lunged upward to sink my blade into the shark's soft gut? I couldn't think clearly, but I decided against it.

Sharks are faster than men underwater. He'd be gone at the first movement, and then he'd be back in a deadly flash. Better to sweat it out. Softly and slowly I lowered my hand.

I cursed myself for having come on this trip. I cursed myself for having learned to love the deep, for having learned to live in it; because now, and perhaps quite properly, I would have to learn to die in it. I'd already had part of my bitter lesson from Tony, my best friend.

ONCE, a long time ago, I'd had a conversation about sharks with a fish specialist at the Hopkins Marine Station in Pacific Grove. Sharks are something every skin diver thinks about even when he doesn't admit it.

"There's only one way," the guy had told me, "to avoid sharks."

"What's that?" I asked him.

"Stay out of the water," he said.

And that's stinking advice for somebody like me who works his fanny off all week, 50 weeks a year, just so that on weekends and vacations he can slip his feet into flippers and buckle on an aqualung.

"Why do you suppose," the fish man had said at the marine station, "so many skin divers get it when they're out spearfishing?"

I didn't know. There are lots of things a guy like me doesn't know.

"That's because of the death sound," the scientist told me. "A fish makes a sound when it dies. That sound travels 1400 feet a second underwater. You can't hear it, but other fish can. So every time you spear a fish it's like sending out a telegram to all the fish in the neighborhood. They head for the source of the sound with the accuracy of a guided missile."

Good deal. So Tony and I had been spearfishing off a rock between La Jolla and San Diego, same place we usually go on weekends after sweating all week at the aircraft plant, and this time there were sharks around and they got our telegram. We'd each speared a couple of big rock bass and cabezons, and Tony had just fired his gun—and missed his target—when the first shark showed up. It was to have been our last and parting shot on that trip because we were running out of air and wanted to take our time going back up.

The whole massacre went like lightning. The shark made his pass at old Tony before he even knew what was coming off, and I guess that was just as well because it made his death more merciful.

The shark nozzled my air bubbles and gulped them, and the other shark was still swimming around the spot where Tony had died. I thought of trying to dive slowly, down maybe another 50 feet, then swimming away and coming up someplace else and taking my chance with the bends, but just then the sniffing shark made up his mind.

QUICKLY I turned to face the shark. It was wheeling in the water for a fatal pass. Again I could see his serrated jaws as he opened his maw for the attack. I expelled air and dropped. I wanted to get below his belly.

But I hadn't made my decision soon enough. My face was on a level with his eyes. His nose flashed toward me, twisting, and I held my knife in front of my face to stick it in his jaws as a last gesture.

Fear saved me that time. For I must have shifted instinctively to avoid the attack. The shark's hide scraped over my shoulder, and his blunt snout banged against my oxygen canisters.

The impact toppled me over so I lay in the water on my side, facing away from the shark, not seeing either of them now, and not knowing when I'd feel sharp teeth ripping into my body.

My mouthpiece loosened, and I felt water pressing between my lips. God! I screamed to myself, not that! I managed to keep hold of the water that had gotten in, and I tried not to choke. It burned in my lungs and my stomach.

The shark was in a rage now, having missed his victim a second time; wildly he hammered through the water, mouthing for me, fixing me with his staring pin eyes.

He came straight for my chest; his nose whipped toward me. I tried to twist out of the way. I couldn't do it. His sharp teeth ground into my shoulder; I felt them ram into my bone. The impact was a blaze of fire. Instinctively I tried to ward off the shock, and as the shark whanged off part of my shoulder, my knife sank deep into the belly he had turned to me.

In up to the hilt, the knife sliced lengthways through his body; then it struck something hard in his gut as the monster flashed past me, and it dropped out of my hand. I was weaponless. I gave up.

Fighting my pain I looked over my darkly bleeding shoulder whose flesh rung in ragged shreds, and I saw the shark beating through the water, himself now in agony and trailing a stream of blood. My knife must have punctured his air bladder, as I think about it now, because he didn't seem to be able to control his swimming. He veered wildly, out of control, bleeding harder all the time, with bits and pieces of his insides creeping out of the knife gash .

Then a shadow flashed through the water: the other shark, the first one. I was too weak to do anything but look on in desperation.

But the monster did not go for me. He attacked his butcher brother, curving off as he hit the trail of his blood, and I saw him rip into the wounded shark's side, and the two killers curled up in a wild whirlpool in a fight to the death.

I rose up like a rocket. I flippered frantically and popped to the surface.

I still limp from the bends. It's almost a year now, and I'm only just starting to live again. ▾

BITING BACK — commentary

JESSICA MYERS, MARINE SCIENTIST: I'm a scuba diver; I've been diving for six years. So I felt a connection with the narrator, and I was able to put myself in his fins. I've been down there, and I understand the uneasiness of certain situations.

One of the first things that's mentioned is how fish make "silent sounds" they can hear and you can't. And that is something that occurs. It's not menacing; it's just fish talk, in different frequencies than we're able to hear. They're all tuned into that channel and we're not, like birds chirp and communicate with each other. But what the sharks in this story would have actually picked up on would be the electrical and the physical vibrations of the fish dying—after being struck by a spear, fish will send out a fear response or a stress response. And *that's* going to alert the sharks, though not through their ears, necessarily. So they're not talking on that silent level that the first part of the story talks about; they're using something called the *lateral line*.

All fish have this. It's a series of sensory organs that run along their bodies that picks up on vibrations and movements in the water, and it can help direct them where to go. So that wasn't *too* off-base. It was played up for dramatic effect, but there is that communication in the ocean.

A minor detail, but worth correcting: The narrator mentions slicing the shark open, and suggests it couldn't swim because he thought he cut its swim bladder. But sharks don't have swim bladders. Instead, they have a really large liver. Oil and water don't mix; oil floats to the top. A sharks' liver is very oily, and that's what causes them to stay neutrally buoyant in the water, instead of having an air bladder or swim bladder like a fish does. So there's no way he popped anything, because it's not there.

A meeting of scuba divers and sharks is a rare thing. If you're diving and see a shark, it's an honor, it's a blessing. Because sharks don't like the bubbles and they don't like the noise and they don't know this thing that's in front of them that's close to their size. You've got this big tank, you're really loud, you're clunky. They're just very confused by you! The idea of sharks recognizing man's scent by his bubbles is misleading. Sharks don't know what those bubbles are; most things in the water don't create bubbles like that.

But the narrator conveniently added that they were spear fishing. That made a lot more sense, because now you have blood, you have that panicked motion of the fish and the prey. So the sharks are of course going to pursue that opportunity, because a lot of them are active hunters, and also scavengers. They pick off the weak and the sick fish. If something's moving in a fashion that suggests it's injured? That's something that's weaker, and can be preyed upon.

Sharks maintain an essential role in the food chain. Many shark species act as keystone species, regulating and supporting their ecosystems by eating sick and injured fish, so the fittest survive and go on to reproduce. If sharks are eating off animals that are more prone to sickness, the healthier fish are going to live on and reproduce, we get healthier and healthier oceans. Sharks are not just eating any and all fish that they find, and they're not the maneaters they've been painted as. They are strategic hunters, and they pick off the weakest, the sickest. They are helping regulate the oceans. They help keep systems in balance.

Removing apex predators from an environment, on the other hand, can cause what's called a trophic cascade. The popularity of *Jaws* led to a big shark cull, because the mood was, *"We've got to find the sharks, we've got to get them out, they're bad."* One person would be attacked by a shark, and people would kill 30 of them in that area. Sharks reproduce very slowly. So removing even 30—which doesn't seem like a lot—can be profoundly damaging to the ecosystem. With fewer predators, their usual prey increase in population. Because there are more of them, they will eat more, using up *their* resource of prey. And with no more food to eat, *they* will start dying off—because they weren't being regulated by their top predator.

"Shark Bait"

STORY BY ANDERS McCLAIN   COVER ART BY VIC PREZIO

The reef, waist deep in water,
was no protection. The sea wolf
charged, his jaws spread
wide with evil, greedy triumph.

SHARK BAIT

by ANDERS McCLAIN

Illustrated by SID SHORES

IT HAPPENED SO FAST, we hardly had time to make preparations! One minute we were cruising serenely over the Pacific Ocean, and the next, the old DC-4 was fluttering like a wounded bird — three of her four props were dead, idly windmilling in the breeze.

We never did have time to find out what the trouble was. At the time, the drive for survival was a lot more important than puttering around, trying to make like a detective. My own guess is that it was a gas lock. But it's a little late now for speculation.

There were six of us aboard. Myself, the pilot; Bob

Hightower, co-pilot; Gin, our young Chinese-American relief pilot; Dick Olsen, engineer; Dom Ventresca, cargo chief; and Jenny MacDougall, paying passenger. Our run, Hawaii to Wake, was strictly routine. We'd flown it a hundred times before, in both directions, without incident enough to snap an insomniac out of a light catnap.

"*Mayday — Mayday!*" I screamed into the radio like a madman—the plane began to bounce like a busted bazooka. "We are preparing to ditch. Repeat, we are preparing to ditch! Position approximately 19 degrees 43 minutes north; 179 degrees 27 minutes west. *Mayday! Mayday!* We are preparing to ditch!"

I didn't wait for a reply—I couldn't, because suddenly the power went dead. Lights, instruments, engines, radio—everything was out. We were falling, settling into a long, fast glide; down, down, toward the black, empty water.

We hit the choppy sea with a jarring smash that was like running into a brick wall. I rammed forward into the instrument panel with a sickening jar that sent lights flashing through my brain.

Behind me in the cabin, I could hear the roar of the cargo as it tore loose and started to crack against the sides of the plane. There were screams, wild anguished screams of pain.

The plane started to sink almost immediately, just as I threw myself against the door leading to the cabin. I saw Jenny's face—dead white. She was writhing in hysterics, screaming and sobbing in terror and pain. There were jagged scratches on her face from flying debris.

"The other man—Dom!" she cried weakly. "Help him . . . a case fell on him. Maybe he's dead!"

Even as she spoke, the ship began to settle. I grabbed the girl's wrist and literally dragged her toward the upper escape hatch. Water was lapping about our knees and was rising fast. We didn't have a second to spare!

I heard her scream again as she slid across a jagged edge of metal. But there wasn't any time to worry about that—we made it into the water just in time. The plane gave a final sick lurch, blew up a greasy bubble, and sank beneath the ocean surface. For one frantic moment, the suction pulled at our bodies, trying to drag us below with the dead plane. We went under for a moment. . . .

THEN WE WERE bobbing in the water like a pair of corks. I looked around, trying to see if I could spot anyone else.

There were some weak splashings to my left. I swam over to investigate —it was Hightower.

"You all right?" I yelled at the top of my voice.

"Well, I'm still in one piece," he shouted back. "Olsen's around someplace. But I haven't seen Gin, Ventresca or the girl!"

"I got the girl—she's OK. Dom's dead; he went down with the plane. You stay here. I'll swim back and get the girl. If you see Gin, get him over here too!"

It took me about five minutes to negotiate the swim. It's amazing how difficult it is to keep a sense of direction and distance in any empty ocean. By the time I got back, Olsen had joined us. There was no sign of the relief pilot, and in the darkness, it was impossible to make an extensive search. All we could do was hope that somehow he was still afloat.

Bob and Olsen had life-jackets, but neither Jenny nor I had had time to grab anything. We hadn't been in the water more than an hour, but I was already beginning to feel numb and exhausted. I grabbed one of the boys with preservers, but realized that the very weight of my water-soaked clothes was dragging us both down.

If anyone was the hero, it was Olsen. He gave Jenny his life-jacket --he practically forced it on her. Her hysteria had passed, and she tried to refuse. But Dick wasn't having any—he was too much of a man. While Bob and I held her, he slipped the jacket around her shoulders.

As soon as I had regained some strength from this bit of exertion, I slipped out of my water-logged flight suit. Dick did the same. Then, each of us hanging to one of the more fortunate pair, we floated on the water.

Luckily — and it was the only "lucky" thing that happened — the water was comparatively warm, around seventy degrees. But there was certainly nothing else to be thankful for. The life raft was a good four or five miles away — straight down, inside the plane. The nearest land, Johnson Island, was some 450 miles to the southeast; Wake, our destination, was better than 1000 miles away. In between, there was empty, barren ocean — nothing else. *Except the sharks . . .*

Up to that point, we hadn't noticed them. I suppose our continual splashing had kept them away. But now, as the kicking and spluttering stopped, we could practically feel them rippling through the water toward us. The first time I heard the sound, I could have sworn it was a skate blade hissing over ice. But even in the starlit dimness, I could see the pointed fins sliding toward us. My blood froze. . . .

We started slapping away at the water again, trying to keep them off. Jenny was screaming at the top of her lungs. I envied her—I wouldn't have minded giving out with a few myself. (Continued on page 56)

It happened so fast, we hardly had time to make preparations! One minute we were cruising serenely over the Pacific Ocean, and the next, the old DC-4 was fluttering like a wounded bird—three of her four props were dead, idly windmilling in the breeze.

We never did have time to find out what the trouble was. At the time, the drive for survival was a lot more important than puttering around, trying to make like a detective. My own guess is that it was a gas lock. But it's a little late now for speculation.

There were six of us aboard. Myself, the pilot; Bob Hightower, co-pilot; Gin, our young Chinese-American relief pilot; Dick Olsen, engineer; Dom Ventresca, cargo chief; and Jenny MacDougall, paying passenger. Our run, Hawaii to Wake, was strictly routine. We'd flown it a hundred times before, in both directions, without incident enough to snap an insomniac out of a light catnap.

"Mayday—Mayday!" I screamed into the radio like a madman—the plane began to bounce like a busted bazooka. "We are preparing to ditch. Repeat, we are preparing to ditch! Position approximately 19 degrees 43 minutes north; 179 degrees 27 minutes west. *Mayday! Mayday!* We are preparing to ditch!"

I didn't wait for a reply—I couldn't, because suddenly the power went dead. Lights, instruments, engines, radio—everything was out. We were falling, settling into a long, fast glide; down, down, toward the black, empty water.

We hit the choppy sea with a jarring smash that was like running into a brick wall. I rammed forward into the instrument panel with a sickening jar that sent lights flashing through my brain.

Behind me in the cabin, I could hear the roar of the cargo as it tore loose and started to crack against the sides of the plane. There were screams, wild anguished screams of pain.

The plane started to sink almost immediately, just as I threw myself against the door leading to the cabin. I saw Jenny's face—dead white. She was writhing in hysterics, screaming and sobbing in terror and pain. There were jagged scratches on her face from flying debris.

"The other man—Dom!" she cried weakly. "Help him…a case fell on him. Maybe he's dead!"

Even as she spoke, the ship began to settle. I grabbed the girl's wrist and literally dragged her toward the upper escape hatch. Water was lapping about our knees and was rising fast. We didn't have a second to spare!

I heard her scream again as she slid across a jagged edge of metal. But there wasn't any time to worry about that—we made it into the water just in time. The plane gave a final sick lurch, blew up a greasy bubble, and sank beneath the ocean surface. For one frantic moment, the suction pulled at our bodies, trying to drag us below with the dead plane. We went under for a moment…

THEN we were bobbing in the water like a pair of corks. I looked around, trying to see if I could spot anyone else.

There were some weak splashings to my left. I swam over to investigate—it was Hightower.

"You all right?" I yelled at the top of my voice.

"Well, I'm still in one piece," he shouted back. "Olsen's around someplace. But I haven't seen Gin, Ventresca or the girl!"

"I got the girl—she's OK. Dom's dead; he went down with the plane. You stay here. I'll swim back and get the girl. If you see Gin, get him over here too!"

It took me about five minutes to negotiate the swim. It's amazing how difficult it is to keep a sense of direction and distance in any empty ocean. By the time I got back, Olsen had joined us. There was no sign of the relief pilot, and in the darkness, it was impossible to make an extensive search. All we could do was hope that somehow he was still afloat.

Bob and Olsen had life-jackets, but neither Jenny nor I had had time to grab anything. We hadn't been in the water more than an hour, but I was already beginning to feel numb and exhausted. I grabbed one of the boys with preservers, but realized that the very weight of my watersoaked clothes was dragging us both down.

If anyone was the hero, it was Olsen. He gave Jenny his life-jacket—he practically forced it on her. Her hysteria had passed, and she tried to refuse. But Dick wasn't having any—he was too much of a man. While Bob and I held her, he slipped the jacket around her shoulders.

As soon as I had regained some strength from this bit of exertion, I slipped out of my waterlogged flight suit. Dick did the same. Then, each of us hanging to one of the more fortunate pair, we floated on the water.

Luckily—and it was the only "lucky" thing that happened—the water was comparatively warm, around seventy degrees. But there was certainly nothing else to be thankful for. The life raft was a good four or five miles away—straight down, inside the plane. The nearest land, Johnson Island, was some 450 miles to the southeast; Wake, our destination, was better than 1000 miles away. In between, there was empty, barren ocean—nothing else. Except the sharks…

Up to that point, we hadn't noticed them. I suppose our continual splashing had kept them away. But now, as the kicking and spluttering stopped, we could practically feel them rippling through the water toward us. The first time I heard the sound, I could have sworn it was a skate blade hissing over ice. But even in. the starlit dimness, I could see the pointed fins sliding toward us. My blood froze…

We started slapping away at the water again, trying to keep them off. Jenny was screaming at the top of her lungs. I envied her—I wouldn't have minded giving out with a few myself.

I have no idea why the sharks didn't attack us that night. According to every rule book, the monsters don't scare that easily. And as any lifeguard who works in shark-infested waters will tell you, thrashing about will probably bring on an attack.

But whatever the reason, they didn't charge in. They kept circling about us, never very far away, guarding us almost as a sheepdog herds in a group of lambs.

It was a frantic, murderously tense night. We rested in shifts, continually keeping up a barrage of splashing and howling. At times it almost seemed preferable to just give up and sink beneath the surface. What was the use? Our survival odds were less than one in a hundred million!

Suddenly, a bright flash of color literally shot up across the eastern horizon. It was the nearest thing *to the day of salvation I've ever experienced*—dawn, then morning! Sunlight filled us with hope and life.

BUT THE morning brought more than merely a sensation of hope. There was something else. As a swell caught me and floated me upward a few feet, I distinctly saw some white water about four or five hundred yards to the north.

"Bob! Dick!" I shrieked at the top of my lungs, "look over there!" I pointed. "There's some surf. Maybe it's a reef of some sort. It might give us something to hold on to!"

I watched the girl's eyes, at first so sleepy and so full of resignation, suddenly open wide. "Please God," she murmured, "make it true!"

"I see it! I see it!" Hightower was laughing like a maniac. "There's *got* to be something near that surf!"

We started swimming, slowly. It was hardly a championship performance. We were all so tired and dragged out from the hours in the water, that it was all we could do to move our arms and legs. If it hadn't been for the two life-jackets, we'd never have made it.

The school of sharks didn't cotton to the idea of us leaving them. We hadn't moved ten yards before they began to circle in closer. They seemed to move so slowly, so lazily, that we weren't even conscious of the change at first. But then without warning, one of them suddenly straightened out and charged!

I was hanging on to Jenny's jacket. Before I could even tum, the sea killer was hurtling toward me like an express train! His jaws were slightly parted—his long rows of gruesome teeth looked as deadly as a flying buzz saw.

I knew I couldn't turn fast enough. There was only one way to avoid him—*straight down*. I turned my head into the water and dived as hard and fast as I could. I felt the current of water eddy through my hair as he passed over me, hardly inches away. And then I was shooting toward the surface again as the shark turned and came back for another try.

As I broke water, I heard a blood-chilling scream that sent fear racing through my veins. Olsen, his mouth contorted, his arms flailing against the water, was shrieking, "My leg! Oh my God! They ate my leg. I can't swim! Help me, somebody! Please, please, please…" Then his voice gurgled into his throat in a horrible, unintelligible sound.

The water all around was rapidly staining crimson. The sharks, dozens of them, driven crazy by the sight and smell of blood, were swarming towards him. The water was being beaten to a scarlet froth by the thrashings of tails and fins and bodies, fighting for a chunk of human flesh!

The sharks ignored us while they feasted on Olsen. The gurgling screams stopped after a few minutes, and we didn't have to look to know that he was dead. We didn't want to watch while sharks gnawed off globs of meat from his carcass, to see them swimming off with bits of arms and legs, or even to think of one sea monster swimming away, holding Olsen's horror-contorted head between its grinning jaws. The sensation of what it feels like to be eaten alive was too real and close as it was.

But the short distraction saved the rest of us. It gave us a chance to put open water between ourselves and the ravenous sharks. We had found new, panic-driven strength from the horror. We swam like demons—by a miracle, *we made it.*

There *was* a reef there. It wasn't much—a small, sharp outcrop of coral reached to within about two feet of the surface. We found that by exercising our senses of balance to the limit, we could plant our feet on something solid and stand up with the water lapping around our knees.

We were ghostly wrecks. Our skins were wrinkled and sore from the long immersion in the ocean. There were salt-encrusted cracks on every inch of our bodies.

IF I WAS naked, the other two were hardly dressed much more. Bob's flying suit was in tatters. Jenny's dress, torn during the crackup and our escape from the sinking plane, had literally gone to shreds in the water. Even after her long swim, she looked beautiful. Her young firm breasts were uncovered—her long lithe legs were bare to her thighs… Desire flushed through me, and for a flashing instant I was amazed at my reaction in such a situation.

But any thoughts I might have had disappeared immediately. The sharks had found us again and were swarming toward us! They had tasted blood once—they wouldn't stop now until they had drunk a lot more.

Somehow, the very sensation of standing upright gave us new confidence. We didn't feel quite so helpless with a bit of our own element—land—working for us. We stood there and faced them, ready to fight…

Under the water, I felt a piece of the coral work loose. I stumbled! But then, as I reached down to steady myself, I had an idea. Grabbing under the surface, I took hold of the jagged piece of rock. It was a weapon, and a good one. Its sharp, knifelike edges were fully capable of cutting through even a shark's tough hide.

I stood poised, waiting for the first hungry killer to come within range. Then, when it was only about a foot away, I struck! Smashing the sharpest edge down across its face, I raked out one of its eyes and slit along right to the edge of its jaw.

The sea turned red again. But this time the shark's blood was flowing.

To the rest of the school, that newest scarlet stain was another signal to go kill-crazy. They turned on their wounded companion. Right before our eyes, only five or ten yards away, they began tearing him apart.

Then we heard it; the low, distant drone of a search plane. We stood paralyzed, hardly daring to believe that the sound existed.

"Bob," I shouted, "your life jacket! It's yellow. Take it off and wave it! I'll watch the sharks. Make them see us!"

Bob was out of his preserver in two seconds flat. Then Jenny ripped a piece of her dress and was waving it, right beside him, both of them roaring at the top of their lungs. As if the pilot could possibly hear their shouts!

The drone of the plane got louder and clearer. We could see it now, weaving back and forth across the sky—searching, looking, inspecting every square inch of the ocean.

But I didn't have time to watch. The sharks, having finished off their wounded member, were coming back. They were swarming in now, from three sides!

I slashed at the water again with my coral weapon. I felt it rasp across one back. Then I was conscious of a deep stabbing pain in my leg…

Instinctively, I cracked out once more with my stone. I was lucky—I caught the beast that was cutting at my leg and he backed away. But I was bleeding badly and could hardly stand. If the water hadn't given me a bit of buoyancy, I'd have tumbled right over.

Still, as the sharks moved off to gather for another lunge, I stole a glance skyward.

The plane had seen us! It was waggling its wings and dipping low to buzz over us in a sign of recognition.

As the plane roared over, hardly twenty feet above the surface of the sea, the sharks scattered. The noise and vibration of the huge bird was too much for them. In less than a minute they were gone—the sea was as calm and empty as if they had never been there.

The plane made a second run. This time it dropped a life raft, landing it on the ocean hardly fifty feet from our reef. Bob swam out and got it. A quarter of an hour later we were sitting in it, dry for the first time in more than fifteen hours. There were emergency rations in the raft—*and fresh drinking water…*

That's about the story. Other planes gathered over us like a swarm of flies, circling, mothering us for the few remaining hours until a ship could make its way to our location. When we saw the smooth, sleek lines of a US Navy destroyer climb over the horizon, we cheered as if we were watching the winning run in the World Series.

They carried us aboard like helpless babies. We were so weak that we couldn't make it under our own steam.

I'm back flying the Pacific runs again, and Bob is still my co-pilot. Frankly, I wouldn't have anyone else.

Jenny? She's working as a civilian employee on Wake, where she was heading in the first place. But we're far better acquainted now. After all, we have a lot in common. We'd been swimming together!

Let me assure you, now that circumstances are normal again, I find her tempting figure a lot less resistible. But then, that's only human. Isn't it? ▼

MARK ROYER, PHD: The shark behavior in this story is actually accurate for the most part. That might be because this story reads similar to the accounts of several US Navy sailors and pilots who experienced shark attacks after bailing out of sunken ships and downed aircraft in the open ocean during the WWII Pacific Campaign. Oceanic whitetip sharks *(Carcharhinus longimanus)* are the likely species that were responsible for the aggressive interactions and deaths of pilots and sailors in the open ocean. Bloody injuries incurred from ship or aircraft wreckage along with the prolonged periods of thrashing at the surface can indeed attract oceanic whitetips.

Oceanic whitetip sharks are widely distributed across tropical and warm-temperate oceans and typically occupy the upper surface layers over deep pelagic habitats. This species will roam long distances and go for extended periods (days to weeks) between feeding events, as food is often scarce in the wide expanse of the open ocean. This requires this species to be "inquisitive" and "bold" whenever they come across anything that can potentially be food. Similarly in this story, they will generally swim around lazily and keep their distance when they initially approach the object of interest and eventually commit to aggressive contact for feeding, though they would never actually 'herd' their prey as the main character has suggested.

At the time that this story was published (late 1950s), oceanic whitetip sharks were one of the most abundant marine apex predators in tropical and warm-temperate oceans around the world. Their inquisitive nature and preference for swimming near the surface makes this species highly susceptible to small and large-scale open ocean purse seiners, long-liners, and gill nets. Decades of bycatch (incidental catching) in commercial fishing fleets and direct targeted-fishing for their fins due to the increased demand for shark fin soup have caused populations of this species to decline by 80-98%. Their global status is now listed as "critically endangered" by the International Union Conservation of Nature (IUCN) Red List. Scientists are conducting research on their behavior and biology to contribute to the conservation of this species through science-informed management measures. This species has also become the focus of several open ocean ecotours around the world that attract divers who wish to see these iconic sharks in person.

TRUE MEN STORIES April 1957 Art by Wil Hulsey

TRUE BOOK BONUS

On the first day out, Tiira smashed his paddle against the snout of the killer-shark as the Swede held on.

Art by Bob Stanley

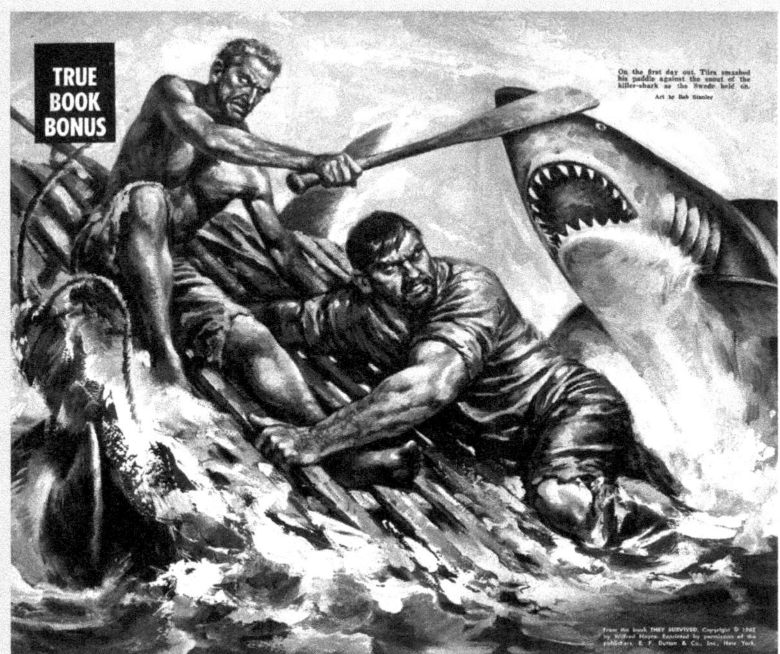

ONLY ONE MAN SURVIVED

THE TERRIBLE 32-DAY OPEN-RAFT NIGHTMARE

To escape the Foreign Legion, two men jumped into a blazing hell where thirst, hunger and sun turned them to shark-bait skeletons too weak to resist.

By WILFRED NOYCE

The two men, one big and powerful, the other short and slightly built, paced back and forth nervously on the troopship *Skaubryn*. Suddenly, a flashlight beam cut through the darkness, played a few seconds on a small rubber raft bobbing on the black waves below. Even before the beam went out, the two men had climbed the ship's rail and jumped out into the night.

The raft was close by and they struggled towards it, then climbed in. Once inside they found it smaller than they thought, only a four-foot square of metal tubing. The flooring, now inches under the sea, was a network of canvas strips, each about five inches wide, with gaps between. Around the metal rim were draped a number of rope grips, to which drowning men could cling. The paddles were

PLEASE TURN PAGE

19

From the book THEY SURVIVED. Copyright © 1962 by Wilfred Noyce. Reprinted by permission of the publishers, E. P. Dutton & Co., Inc., New York.

Action For Men August 1963 Art by Robert Stanley

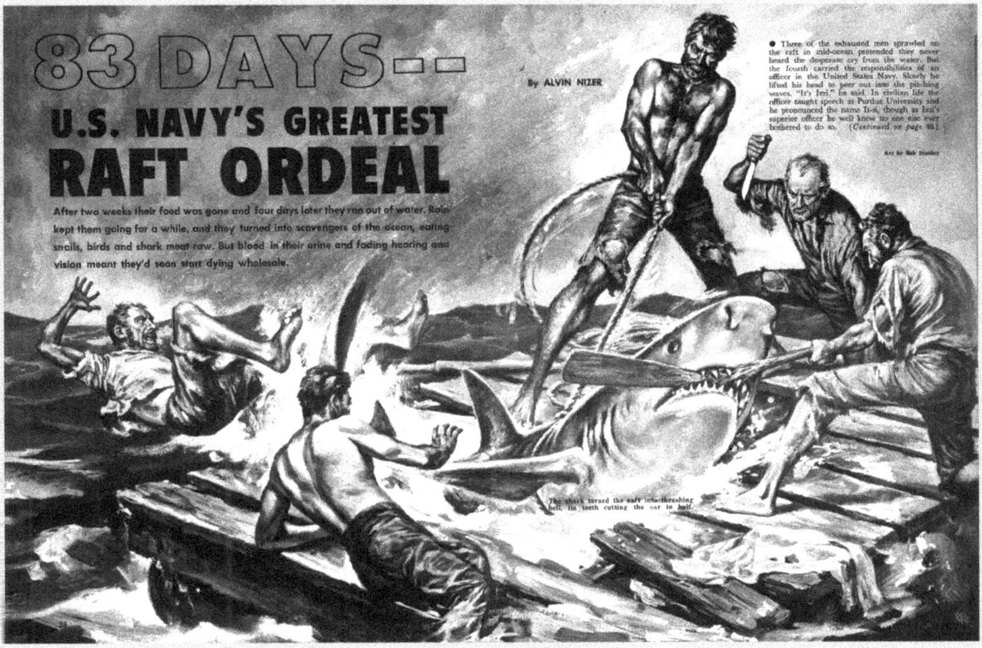

83 DAYS--

U.S. NAVY'S GREATEST RAFT ORDEAL

By ALVIN NIZER

After two weeks their food was gone and four days later they ran out of water. Rain kept them going for a while, and they turned into scavengers of the ocean, eating snails, birds and shark meat raw. But blood in their urine and fading hearing and vision meant they'd soon start dying wholesale.

● Three of the exhausted men sprawled on the raft in mid-ocean pretended they never heard the desperate cry from the water. But the fourth carried the responsibilities of an officer in the United States Navy. Slowly he lifted his head to peer out into the pitching waves. "It's Izzi," he said. In civilian life the officer taught speech at Purdue University and he pronounced the name It-si, though as Izzi's superior officer he well knew no one else ever bothered to do so. (*Continued on page 40*)

Art by Bob Stanley

The shark turned the raft into thrashing hell, its teeth cutting the oar in half.

Action For Men March 1964 Art by Robert Stanley

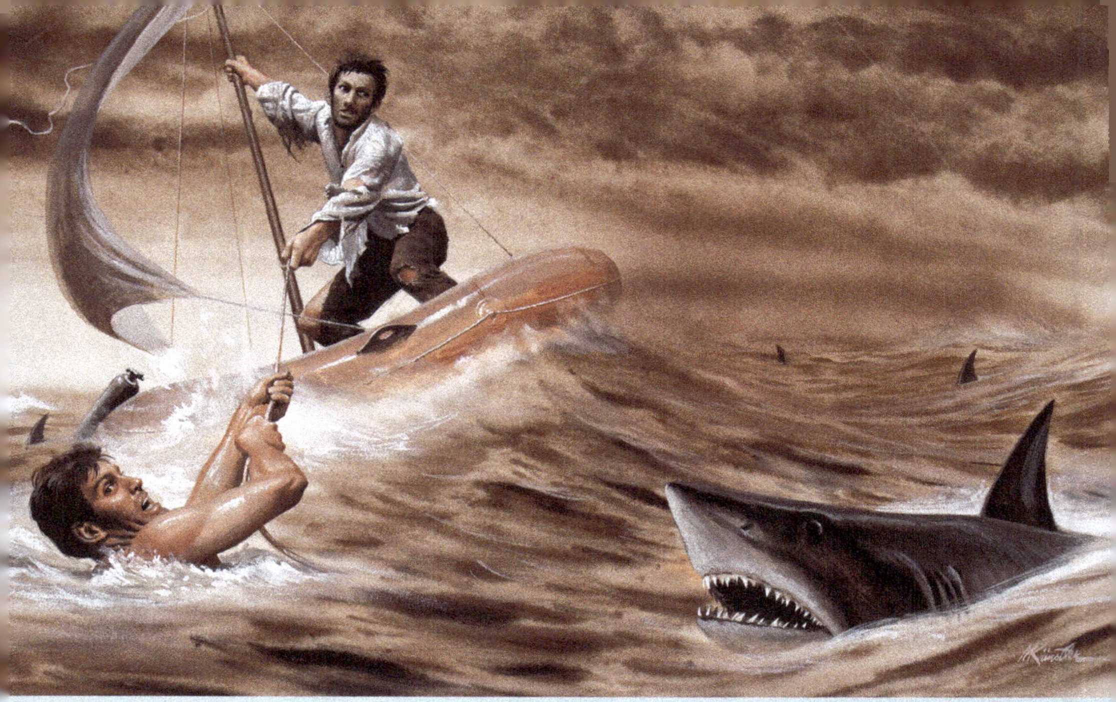

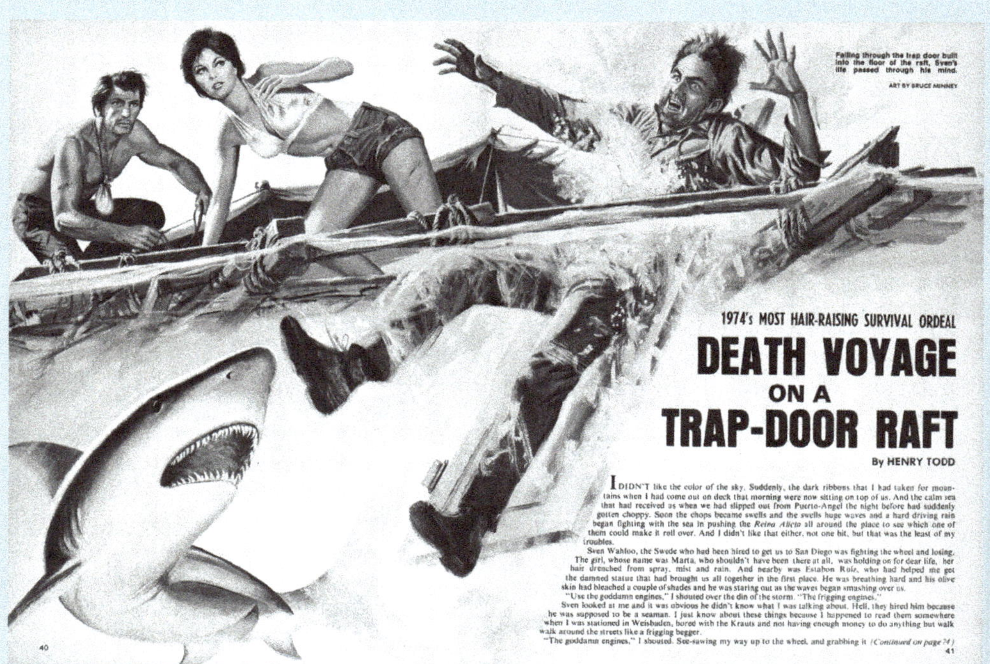

Original interior artwork by Mort Künstler from **MALE** April 1968

Falling through the trap door built into the floor of the raft, Sven's life passed through his mind.

ART BY BRUCE MINNEY

1974's MOST HAIR-RAISING SURVIVAL ORDEAL

DEATH VOYAGE ON A TRAP-DOOR RAFT

By HENRY TODD

I DIDN'T like the color of the sky. Suddenly, the dark ribbons that I had taken for mountains when I had come out on deck that morning were now sitting on top of us. And the calm sea that had received us when we had slipped out from Puerto-Angel the night before had suddenly gotten choppy. Soon the chops became swells and the swells huge waves and a hard driving rain began fighting with the sea in pushing the *Reina Alicia* all around the place to see which one of them could make it roll over. And I didn't like that either, not one bit, but that was the least of my troubles.

Sven Wahloo, the Swede who had been hired to get us to San Diego was fighting the wheel and losing. The girl, whose name was Marta, who shouldn't have been there at all, was holding on for dear life, her hair drenched from spray, mist and rain. And nearby was Estabon Roiz, who had helped me get the damned statue that had brought us all together in the first place. He was breathing hard and his olive skin had bleached a couple of shades and he was staring out as the waves began smashing over us.

"Use the goddamn engines," I shouted over the din of the storm. "The frigging engines."

Sven looked at me and it was obvious he didn't know what I was talking about. Hell, they hired him because he was supposed to be a seaman. I just know about these things because I happened to read them somewhere when I was stationed in Weisbaden, bored with the Krauts and not having enough money to do anything but walk walk around the streets like a frigging begger.

"The goddamn engines," I shouted. See-sawing my way up to the wheel, and grabbing it (Continued on page 74)

40 41

TRUE ACTION August 1975 Art by Bruce Minney

MEN December 1956 Art by Stanley Borack

Overleaf: Original Stanley Borack cover art for MALE March 1955

FROM THE PAGES OF MAN'S ADVENTURE, OCTOBER 1959

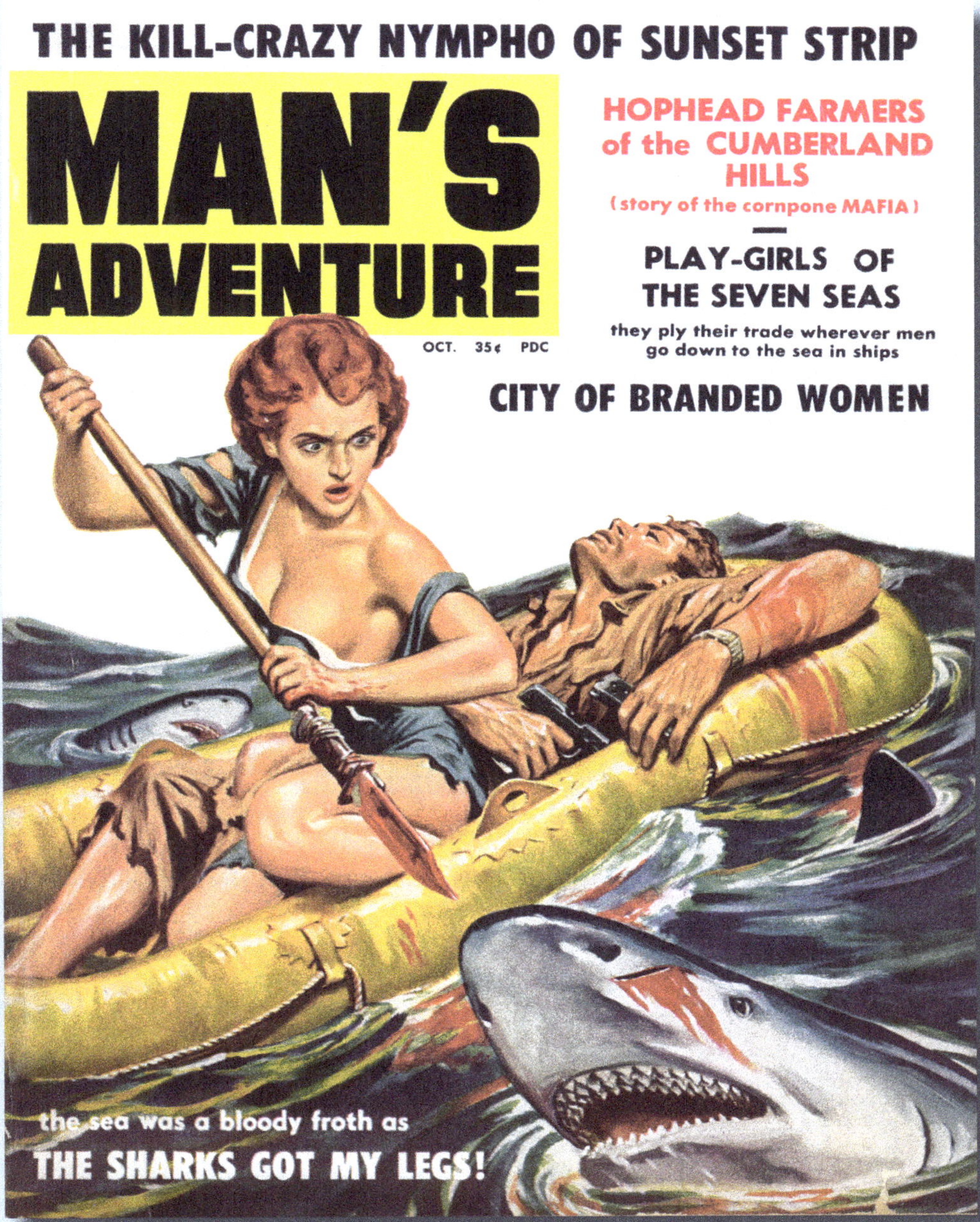

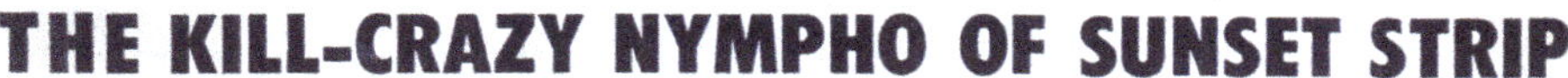

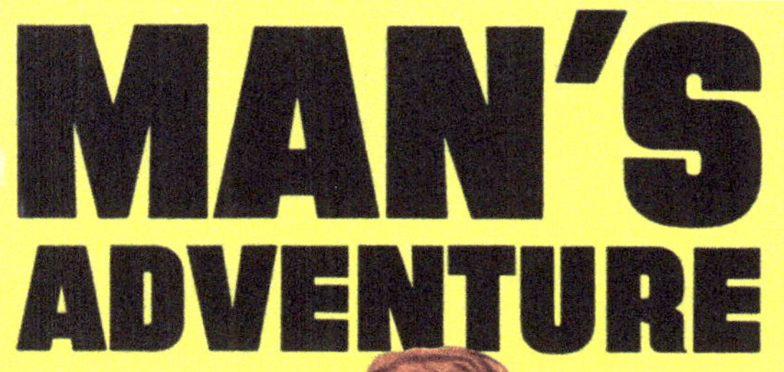

"The Sharks Got My Legs"

STORY BY TOM DARCY

COVER ART BY CLARENCE DOORE

The Sharks Got My Legs

by TOM DARCY

ALL NIGHT LONG the edge of the rubber raft had kept coming up and smacking me in the back of the neck. Sleep was nearly impossible. If I hadn't been so exhausted I wouldn't have slept at all. I looked over at Irene Earn and she smiled wearily at me. She hadn't gotten any more sleep than I—and possibly less.

The sun just looming over the limitless horizon promised we were in for another day's baking. And the sharks were still keeping up their

Driven insane by the smell of my blood, the killer sharks were attacking from all sides.

The Sharks Got My Legs (continued)

never ending patrol, their monotonous circling. Like vultures, they seemed to know we were about to die. And they were waiting.

I rested there, conserving strength, two feet up on the raft edge, watching their sharp, cruelly hooked fins cut water. They were man eaters all, the great white sharks of Australia, and they were getting hungrier.

One torpedo shape—a giant, thirty-five feet long —came in on a flashing run. By the raft he slowed his impetuous rush in a swirl of foam. His sharp snouted head rose out of the sea lazily, like a water logged barrel. The cavernous jaws snapped open, displaying rows and rows of triangular shaped, bone shattering teeth. I tried to move, but I was too sick, too tired, too near death to do anything. The jaws closed with a quick muscular snap, and a good part of my legs dropped away with the shark.

I shrieked as a million volts of agony electrocuted my brain. Irene screamed as a cascade of blood fountained out of the stumps, splashing over the raft and into the water. I bellowed as white hot pain converted my entire body into a mass of writhing torture. My back arched as the shock tautened muscles spasmed, my ruined legs curled as even my battered insides tried to recoil from the racking torment. Scream after scream ripped from my throat, echoing far over the quiet sea. The raw gaping wound still pulsed blood into the water. And the sharks went wild as they smelt it. Turning the sea white with lashing tails, they made a fierce, insane rush for the raft.

Piloting between New Guinea and Australia, you fly over a lot of water, but somehow or other, you never think you'll actually dunk in it. That always happens to the other chap—not to you. Of course, when I first learned to handle aircraft with the RAAF, I took a course in ocean survival. Or at least they threw the information at me but I never stood at the bat very long. Like the rest of my buddies, I thought it was merely one of those nuisance courses and dozed through most of it.

After Korea, I was mustered out, and started scratching my head about what to do. Most of the soft jobs with the commercial air lines had been snapped up by the lads from War II. I couldn't wait around for them to grow old and retire. The old savings account was kaput and I was down to nothing minus when I read a notice in the Brisbane *Times*.

The Sullivan Gold Exploitation Company wanted a pilot to service their (Continued on page 66)

8

ARTIST(S) UNCREDITED

All night long the edge of the rubber raft had kept coming up and smacking me in the back of the neck. Sleep was nearly impossible. If I hadn't been so exhausted I wouldn't have slept at all. I looked over at Irene Earn and she smiled wearily at me. She hadn't gotten any more sleep than I—and possibly less.

The sun just looming over the limitless horizon promised we were in for another day's baking. And the sharks were still keeping up their never ending patrol, their monotonous circling. Like vultures, they seemed to know we were about to die. And they were waiting.

I rested there, conserving strength, two feet up on the raft edge, watching their sharp, cruelly hooked fins cut water. They were man eaters all, the great white sharks of Australia, and they were getting hungrier.

One torpedo shape—a giant, thirty-five feet long—came in on a flashing run. By the raft he slowed his impetuous rush in a swirl of foam. His sharp snouted head rose out of the sea lazily, like a waterlogged barrel. The cavernous jaws snapped open, displaying rows and rows of triangular shaped, bone shattering teeth. I tried to move, but I was too sick, too tired, too near death to do anything. The jaws closed with a quick muscular snap, and a good part of my legs dropped away with the shark.

I shrieked as a million volts of agony electrocuted my brain. Irene screamed as a cascade of blood fountained out of the stumps, splashing over the raft and into the water. I bellowed as white hot pain converted my entire body into a mass of writhing torture. My back arched as the shock-tautened muscles spasmed, my ruined legs curled as even my battered insides tried to recoil from the racking torment. Scream after scream ripped from my throat, echoing far over the quiet sea. The raw gaping wound still pulsed blood into the water. And the sharks went wild as they smelt it. Turning the sea white with lashing tails, they made a fierce, insane rush for the raft.

PILOTING between New Guinea and Australia, you fly over a lot of water, but somehow or other, you never think you'll actually dunk in it. That always happens to the other chap—not to you. Of course, when I first learned to handle aircraft with the RAAF, I took a course in ocean survival. Or at least they threw the information at me, but I never stood at the bat very long. Like the rest of my buddies, I thought it was merely one of those nuisance courses and dozed through most of it.

After Korea, I was mustered out, and started scratching my head about what to do. Most of the soft jobs with the commercial airlines had been snapped up by the lads from World War II. I couldn't wait around for them to grow old and retire. The old savings account was kaput and I was down to nothing minus when I read a notice in the Brisbane *Times*.

The Sullivan Gold Exploitation Company wanted a pilot to service their mines in the Mandated area of New Guinea. Before the war, a few Aussies had waltzed into the Otto mountains and found heavy deposits of gold. Now the problem was getting in and out. It was a real never-never land.

The aborigines were no longer dangerous, although they had been at first. The abos came squibbing out of the bush and stoushed the first miners in the head. They even used stone axes.

Now that was all changed. Nowadays, some of the best coffee in the world is grown by these wild gentlemen. Only to grow coffee right on the equator, it has to be mountain country. The Otto mountains soar up to thirteen thousand feet over the wildest country in the world. It was quite a trick threading a few of those passes with a DC-3. Most plane jockeys bowed out of that show, but I didn't have much choice. I took the job and held it for three years right up to 1956.

The gold mine was actually the whole side of Wumuwumu Mountain. It was a huge operation. They were literally tearing the mountain apart, dumping it into the valley, and washing out the gold. There was a regular company town to house all the laborers. My job was to keep it supplied.

On the ground, I sometimes dated Irene Earn, the company nurse. I say "sometimes," because not only was she the prettiest sheila I ever laid eyes on, but she was the only eligible female in that section of New Guinea. There was a waiting list just to bid her the time of day. The hospital, not the pub or paymaster's office, was the most popular building in town.

I had the inside track because I had access to the outside world. Occasionally, we dated at Port Moresby in that square box they call a hotel. A few times I flew her to Brisbane when she felt she needed a shopping spree. But Irene would have looked good in a burlap bag—brunette, five four, all swelling curves and soft planes.

It was Monday, July 16, 1956. I was due for a run to Australia and Irene was scheduled to go with me. The prospect of being alone for some ten hours with Irene didn't make me feel too grim. For quite awhile I had been trying to induce her into other situations besides the one she presently held with the company, and had been notoriously unsuccessful. Not that Irene was a puritan, but she was looking for something more permanent.

For the first few hours I was kept too busy flying over the Otto and Owen Stanley mountain ranges to have much conversation with Irene. When we finally left them behind I breathed a sigh of relief, and began to think about Irene. But first, I checked in with Port Moresby radio for local weather conditions. The news was all black.

"There's a storm to the south and west of you," the operator said. "Growing in intensity—moving east by north."

"Can I skirt around it?" I asked.

"I think so. Swing out over the Coral Sea. You can turn in again around Cairns, or fly the circular route to Brisbane. Perhaps that would be safer."

I checked out. Irene had heard the whole conversation, but she didn't look alarmed. Her voice was still even.

"Anything serious?"

"No," I lied. "Just have to pop around some mucky weather. Might be nasty in spots, though, so you'd best strap yourself to a chair."

Soon I hit the heavy weather. And as I fought the bouncing wheel, black thunderheads started blotting out the horizon ahead of me, and everywhere between me and touch down in Australia. I couldn't go east; it was just more ocean. I couldn't go back; I had reached the point of no return. So I tried for altitude.

That didn't help. It was one of those circular storms that reached much higher than a DC-3 can go. I had both engines wide open and sometimes, I'm sure, we stood still. Again, we would suddenly be shot forward as from a cannon. There wasn't any calm air at all. We'd drop two thousand feet in a second, stop with a crash, metal groaning and complaining, your spine tip climbing for your jaw bone. Then we'd be caught and flipped three thousand feet straight up. Then it would be that sudden sickening fall again. I had absolutely no control of the ship.

Suddenly we were out of the wild blackness and the storm was behind us. I turned due west for any part of Australia and didn't particularly care which part. All I wanted was solid land under me. Then the radio bugged out and I had to fly by dead reckoning.

I threw a quick glance at Irene. There was a big swelling on her forehead where she had bashed into the cabin wall. But she winked to show me she was all right, and laughed, "That was quite a show, wasn't it?"

"It's all over now," I consoled her.

And just then, to prove me a liar, the port engine started spitting.

I TRIED switching petrol tanks, but it didn't work. It was something more serious than a lack of fuel. The overworked engine kept coughing and coughing, started smoking—and died in a blaze of flame. I smothered it with carbon dioxide, feathered the prop, and prayed the other engine would take up the burden.

It kept us in the air but that was all. We kept losing altitude. I hoped we'd sight the Australian mainland, or an island, or even the Great Barrier Reef, before we'd have to ditch. We didn't.

As the ocean came closer and closer to us, Irene calmly went about preparing a survival kit. She indicated the rubber raft and nodded. I told her to strap in for ditching.

The water was still fifty feet below. I was bringing the nose up, trying to get the tail slightly down, when the starboard engine died. I flapped the rudders quickly, stalled out, lost flying speed, and we fell like a stone.

Hitting water at one hundred miles an hour has the same effect as hitting concrete. There was a metallic crash and the belly skin of the ship split wide open. Water flooded in. Irene was up like a shot, kicked out the door, grabbed survival equipment, and was swimming away.

I jerked the rubber raft free. There was a sudden lurch and the ocean was all around the plane, swallowing it. I lunged for the fountain that was the door and strained against the tremendous water pressure. Somehow, I fought my way clear. The last thing I saw as I swam through the green sea, kicking for the surface, was the DC-3 swirling downwards, leaving a string of air bubbles.

We got settled on the raft and I took stock of our equipment. There was the survival kit with fishing tackle, a jerry can full of water, my American Army .45 automatic—a souvenir of Korea—and a heavy knife. I looked glumly at the few things that had to keep us alive for…how long?

Irene made a better show. "It's short rations for us," she said. "I've been promising myself a diet."

"We'll be all right," I said. "We can catch fish and squeeze water out of their flesh. And, besides they'll supplement our diet. It's just a matter of waiting until search craft find us."

THREE days later, I didn't take such a cheery view. We were catching fish right enough, but the sun was blasting the life from our bodies.

I had tried rigging a sun screen with a collapsible paddle and my shirt, but it didn't help much. The reflections bouncing off the water still broiled us. Then there was the constant salt spray that split your lips and desiccated your tongue.

Irene had found a stick floating by, and attached the knife to it as a lance. It was handy in gaffing the fish I had hooked.

The sun was playing hell with Irene. She had started out with a sensible bush shirt but the salt was rotting the seams and button thread. Her beautiful white skin was gradually being exposed to the burning rays as more and more of it showed through the rents and gaps. At first, as the buttons dropped away, she had tried tucking the whole affair tight into her skirt. Then she gave it up. She retained the shirt not for modesty, but as a sun shield.

You've read about men and women in open boats. Well, it's true. As the puffy breezes blew the ragged shirt away from her, I'd grow terribly thirsty—and not for water. But I never said a word or made an approach to her. I thought she had enough troubles. There is no privacy or modesty on a raft.

Towards sundown, she looked at me and asked, "Tom, tell me frankly, what are our chances?"

"Good," I lied to her. "It's just a matter of waiting. That's all we have to do: be patient, keep ourselves in good condition, and wait."

"I asked you to tell me the truth, not a fairy story. Do you even know where we are?"

I shrugged. "No, I don't. Somewhere in the Coral Sea, I suppose. But they must be searching for us at this very moment. After that storm, when we didn't reach Brisbane they'll know what happened."

"Only they haven't found us, have they?"

"They will," I reassured her. I was a lot less confident than I sounded. The Coral Sea is an immense ocean of nothing, and we were less than a fly speck from the air.

That evening, I poured her out a half cup of water. She came over and knelt in front of me, looking directly in my eyes. Even as she drank, she stared at me. When she finished, she still looked intently. The night breeze was just springing up, fluttering her shirt. She let it flutter. And she saw how I looked.

"Tom," she whispered, "we're all alone out here—just the two of us. We might never get back. We might never know each other. Let's not be silly."

She came closer. I took her softness in my arms.

I WAS CLEANING fish the next morning when Irene said, "Tom, we've got company."

I looked up and saw massive black fins slicing through the water. It was to be expected. The fish guts had brought them.

The shark is a wandering appetite. It has to eat constantly to live, and it's an indiscriminate eater. It's also a cold, cruel, savage killer. It will eat its young. It will eat anything.

The most savage of all the sharks is the great white shark of Australia. They say it's the worst in the world, and any Australian will agree.

Now we had these beauties for traveling companions. Irene picked up her lance and stabbed at one which came too close. The knife sank into the monsters snout and blood spurted out, dyeing the sea a bright red.

"Don't do that," I shouted. "The smell of their own blood will drive them crazy. They'd be crawling in here after us.

"You have a gun," she pointed out.

"A bullet won't stop a shark. Maybe an explosive harpoon, but that's about all. If a school of fish comes along, they'll leave soon enough."

The presence of the dreaded killers meant an end to our fishing and our water supply. You don't find fish where there are sharks.

For days they followed us. When some went away to feed, others would take their place. And day by day, the juices were being baked out of our bodies. The sharks waited for us to die. And just their presence meant our death.

The lack of food didn't bother us too much. It was the lack of water—lovely, cool, trickling water—that nearly drove us insane. I could feel the tongue swelling in my mouth, my lips turning to sandpaper. No matter how we cut our water quota, it seemed to go rapidly. And as the drops dwindled, so did our lives.

And ceaselessly, the killers circled. Their glaring eyes would shine out of the sea, watch us, never leaving us. It was hard holding on to sanity with death just inches away. As the raging torment of thirst increased, I wondered if it wouldn't be easier to use the .45 on Irene, then myself.

Then, suddenly, my legs were ripped from my body.

Irene screamed when she saw the shark roll over, its grey underside appear, its bayonet studded mouth open and clamp shut. She screamed when she saw what had happened to me. But she reacted.

Almost immediately, her nurse's training came through, and sent her flying at my mangled legs ripping at her skirt. She pinned the quivering limbs down, twisted lengths of material around them tightening, tightening relentlessly until the veins were sealed off by the improvised tourniquets. Then she knotted it and left it there.

Through the red shades of pain that shrouded my eyes, I watched her go wild. Even as the blood-maddened sharks spun their muscular forty-foot lengths, she picked up the lance and met the first one head on. She rammed the knife blade into its tender snout.

There was no hope of stopping it. But as it rolled with blood running down its nose, and opened its mouth to strike at the raft, a second shark neatly and insanely bit the entire jaw away from its brother. Then a third lunged for a bigger gulp and swirled away with a huge piece of still living shark meat. The other killers snapped at the dangling intestines. The wounded shark, tried to swim away, but the whole pack was on him, ripping, slashing, tearing, eating him as he tried to escape.

In the mad slash of rending teeth, other sharks received wounds and were devoured as they tried to devour the others. The sea frothed with blood as the monsters ripped one another to pieces.

I roared with insane laughter. My body had gone into shock and I didn't feel pain anymore. I steadied the automatic on the side of the raft and poured bullets into the wild mass. Wherever a bullet struck, ripping jaws would follow.

Black fins flew past us—newcomers to the feast. Sharks were coming from everywhere, drawn by the scent of blood. They threw themselves into the melee and died in turn.

And gradually we were drifting away from the slaughter. I fired until there were no rounds left to fire. The sharks completely ignored us as they attended to the more urgent business of cannibalizing each other.

I laughed and laughed, more and more insanely. Irene threw herself on me to hold me down. I was still laughing as I slipped into blackness.

I BECAME conscious once in an airplane. Irene was there. And when I became fully conscious in the hospital my legs had been expertly trimmed at the knee. Irene was there to tell me what had happened.

A patrol plane had been attracted—not by us, the pilot didn't even see us—but by the red and white fury as the blood crazed sharks thrashed around over a wide area.

The astonished pilot had dropped down close to look at it. Then he saw our raft—with Irene madly signaling.

It takes a long time for leg stumps to heal. The Sullivan Gold Mining Exploitation Company told me to take all the time I wanted—I'd always have a job. They even provided me with a private nurse—Irene. It's going to take a lot of effort to readjust, but with Irene around I think I'll make it. ▼

BRYAN KELLER, PHD: It's funny; the term *circling* isn't demonic in and of itself, yet it is usually portrayed that way when sharks are doing it. Circling can be threatening, but sharks are social animals, they're curious animals, and they're inquisitive. Circling is the best way for them to keep their distance and still keep something in their line of sight. But it's always, *"Oh my God, the shark is circling you, you're doomed!"*

The narrator first identifies the species in this story based only upon a fin. That's not easy to do, even if you have a good idea of what species are around. So a *pilot* identifying the shark based on a fin is pretty impressive. Maybe not likely. Even more unlikely, they say the animal is 35 feet long, which isn't possible for the suggested species.

I've never been stranded on a vessel before (*knocks on wood*), but I've tracked sharks, following them for 50+ hours without ever getting off a small boat. And he's totally right about the sun and how brutal it is. The reflection off the water is so much worse than the sun actually coming down on you; you can't really hide from it.

Calling sharks indiscriminate eaters is largely untrue. To say the vast majority of species have some sort of preferred diet is an understatement. Certain animals, like tiger sharks, are considered generalists and feed on a wider variety of prey, but they're still generally eating within a selected *range* of prey. And there are numerous species out there with very specialized diets. I've worked at an aquarium where some sharks wouldn't eat unless you gave them their favorite type of fish.

Sharks are demonized as maneaters, but think of all the people who go swimming each day. If sharks really had people on the menu, we'd be getting wiped out by the thousands! The fact that so few people die as a result of shark encounters each year *worldwide* is a testament to how sophisticated these predators are and how evolution has honed their abilities. They've evolved to target specific stimuli and go after specific animals, and people aren't really on that list. Attacks are rare, and most can be attributed to mistaken identity.

The end of the story really gets crazy, with all the sharks attacking each other—that is utterly ridiculous. The social behavior of these animals is really advanced; there's a social hierarchy to their feeding regime, which makes it difficult for me to imagine a scenario like this one. If sharks all ganged up on each other and started killing each other when feeding in an aggregation, there probably wouldn't be too many sharks left. And obviously the fight to kill another shark puts them at greater risk than going after a whale carcass, or a school of fish. It's just not an evolutionary standard to put yourself at such high risk when unnecessary.

FROM THE PAGES OF PERIL, AUGUST 1960

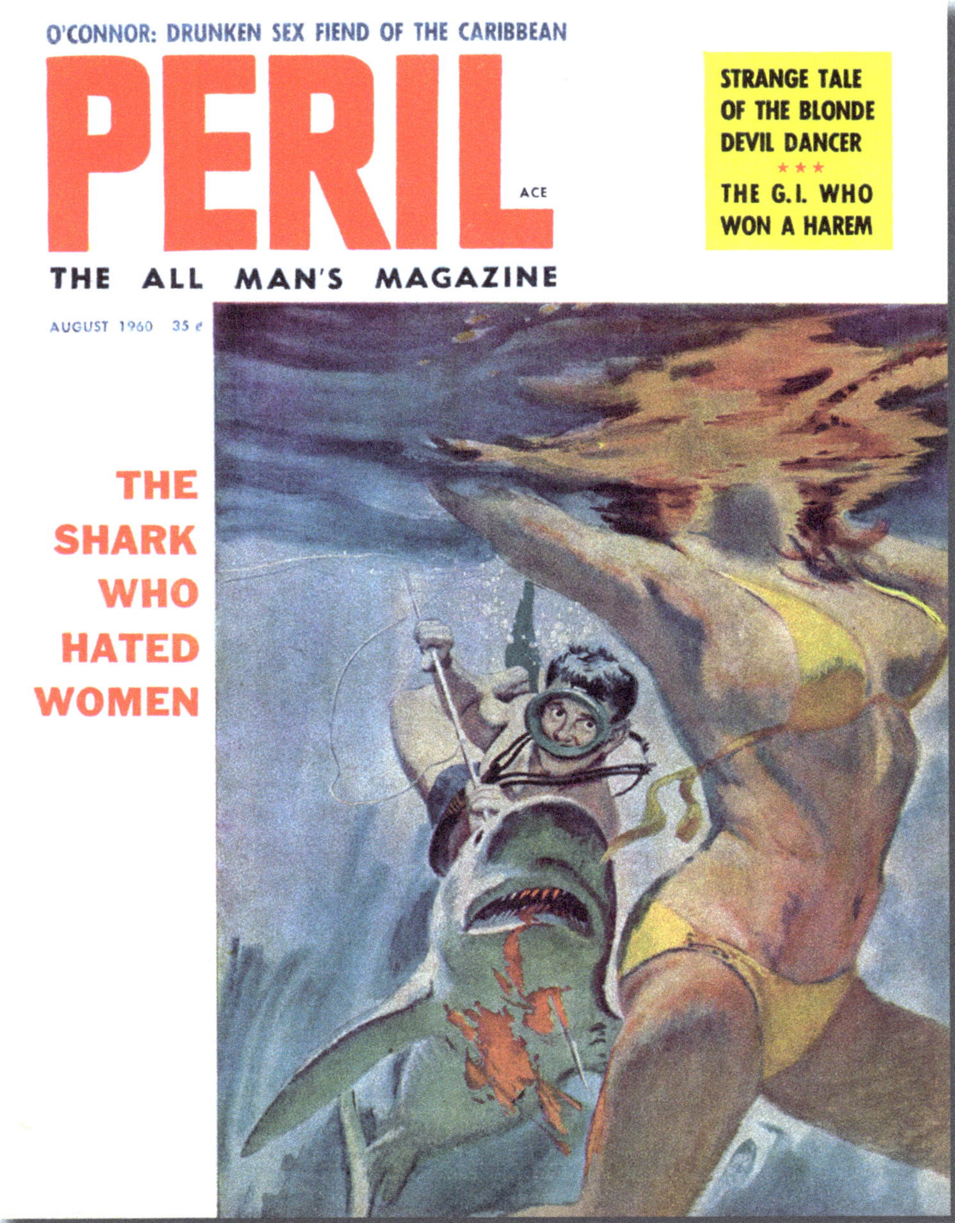

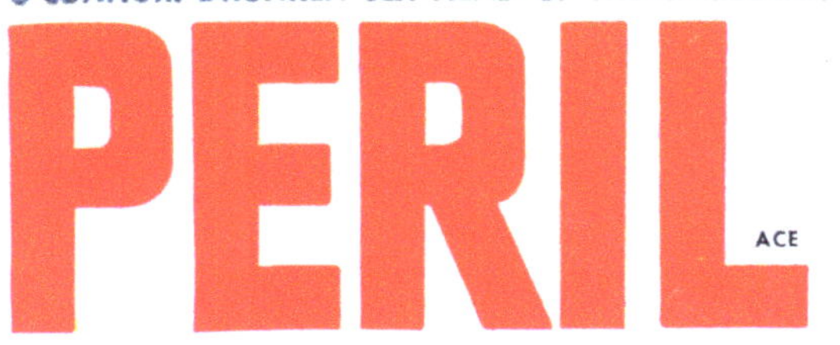

"The Shark Who Hated Women"

STORY BY S.P. FREE

COVER ART UNCREDITED

BY S. P. FREE

THE SHARK WHO HATED WOMEN

IN ONE DAY MY PARADISE BECAME A LIVING HELL

MY BEAUTIFUL Polynesian bride of one day lay beside me on the empty beach. We were naked, and as my hands roved dreamily over her lovely tawny body, I could not help congratulating myself. I had never been happier. Yet eight months before I had been living on a treadmill in the dirty, choking life of a big city.

One day in a fit of rebellion I had gone down to the docks, untied my boat not giving a damn where I was going, and started out to sea. I hadn't many provisions, or much money, but anything was better than working as a hack marine biologist eight-een hours a day in a dreary little west coast research station. I set sail south and west.

I made it to the Hawaiian group and dawdled awhile then worked down through the Marshalls. Weeks later I happened onto a little uncharted island south of Ebon Atoll. It was the kind of place every man dreams about, but never really finds. There I met Marina. She was the most beautiful girl any man could hope to see. There are no women in the world who can equal the Polynesian ones when it comes to beauty and kindness —and love-making. They are taught from childhood to make a man happy in every way. I married Marina. Now, alive once more in the free air, I basked in the sun in pure sensual pleasure the day after the great wedding feast.

I leaned over and kissed Marina. Her arms came up around my neck, and I was kissing her again when the wildest sound I'd ever head—a low half-human whine cut through the warm air. A chill ran through me. I felt Marina stiffen in my arms. My head shot up.

"My God, what was that?" I asked her.

She did not answer. Her eyes were filled with the fright she

9

My beautiful Polynesian bride of one day lay beside me on the empty beach. We were naked, and as my hands roved dreamily over her lovely tawny body, I could not help congratulating myself. I had never been happier. Yet eight months before I had been living on a treadmill in the dirty, choking life of a big city.

One day in a fit of rebellion I had gone down to the docks, untied my boat not giving a damn where I was going, and started out to sea. I hadn't many provisions, or much money, but anything was better than working as a hack marine biologist eighteen hours a day in a dreary little west coast research station. I set sail south and west.

I made it to the Hawaiian group and dawdled awhile then worked down through the Marshalls. Weeks later I happened onto a little uncharted island south of Ebon Atoll. It was the kind of place every man dreams about, but never really finds. There I met Marina. She was the most beautiful girl any man could hope to see. There are no women in the world who can equal the Polynesian ones when it comes to beauty and kindness—and love-making. They are taught from childhood to make a man happy in every way. I married Marina. Now, alive once more in the free air, I basked in the sun in pure sensual pleasure the day after the great wedding feast.

I leaned over and kissed Marina. Her arms came up around my neck, and I was kissing her again when the wildest sound I'd ever heard—a low half-human whine—cut through the warm air. A chill ran through me. I felt Marina stiffen in my arms. My head shot up.

"My God, what was that?" I asked her.

She did not answer. Her eyes were filled with the fright she felt when she prayed to her pagan devil-gods.

"Black Devil," Marina gasped out. She jumped, twisted on her sarong, and started running down the beach, pulling me with her.

Natives were scurrying to the water's edge and falling to their knees, moaning as though in supplication. Marina sprinted after them.

I called to Marina's cousin. "Kapo, what is it? Why are they crying?"

"Black Shark," he hissed through his teeth.

I looked at Kapo's face. It was contorted with all the wildness of the most primitive man in the world. I wondered what had suddenly become of the effort I'd spent trying to civilize this man so he could make a better world for his people when he became their chief?

I'd heard the terrible tale of a black shark who ate women years ago stateside. It was told by a drunken old sailor in one of San Francisco's waterfront dives. There was such a shark, he said, and he'd seen it leave three men and take a woman off Mili Island in the Marshalls. But no one would believe his gin-soaked story.

Then one day on this island I had met a native with a stump of an arm scarred with enormous teeth marks. He had lost his arm defending his wife from the Black Shark, he said. The shark got him first, but wounded him only to put him out of action. Then it went for his wife, imprisoned her in its mouth and dove down out of sight. Well, no man-eating shark had ever been recorded in any book as preferring women. And I went by the book. Though I knew this was the season when the dreaded Black Shark was supposed to appear, I still couldn't accept any such talk.

"Kapo," I said, "no shark acts like a human being."

"Maybe, but I see it myself."

I looked out to sea. A giant black shark's fin circled through the lagoon. But it still proved nothing about the tales I'd heard. "You're wrong," I said, "but we'll settle it once and for all. I'll kill the Black Shark just like I would any other." I raced up to my hut, and got my skin-diving equipment.

As I came back down to the water, Marina ran up to me and burst into tears. "No, no," Marina cried, "please no go."

"Look," I said with a reassuring smile, "if he likes women, I've got nothing to worry about." I put on my tank, mask and flippers. "Don't worry Marina, this is all a myth," I said. I picked up my spear gun and waded into the water. I could hear the natives imploring me to return.

I swam out until I reached the deepest part of the lagoon, without seeing him. Then I suddenly felt I was being followed. I turned, spear poised, expecting God knows what. It was Marina behind me. She was wearing my second set of equipment, which I had taught her to use. Her hand was outstretched holding my knife. In my rush I had forgotten it. I took it from her and waved her back. *Go back*, I signaled. Then I realized how dangerous it would be if she started back alone with any kind of shark in the water. They may not eat women as a specialty, I thought, but she would be fair game for any other sharks. I pulled her to me and signaled her to stay close behind. I started around the lagoon.

Suddenly a black shadow cut the water ahead. I stopped cold. It was a monstrous black shark, larger and blacker than any I'd ever seen or read about. It passed twice around us, stalking. I cut in front of him as he swam back nearer. I readied my spear gun. Suddenly he whipped into a frenzied, erotic dance in front of us as if in a sexual challenge of my prowess. Then he turned over on his back. He came in at a diving pass. I waited for him to draw closer. I let go with my spear straight at his head. But the gun was faulty. The spear went wide and the Black Shark kept coming straight in, his jaws open. At least he was coming for me first, I thought. The wild cry that could actually be heard under water came from his guts as he charged.

Suddenly he veered downward. From out of nowhere Kapo was on his belly cutting at him with his knife. Yet the razor-sharp blade made little difference to the shark. He whipped over. Kapo fell off. A crack of the Black Shark's tail sent him nearly out of the water.

It was my turn. I went after the shark with my knife. He turned, circled away and then back before I could get set. Suddenly I knew what it was to have an arm caught in a meat grinder. There was a searing shock of pain. The flesh was ripped from shoulder to elbow. I was losing blood fast and sinking. There was whirling darkness in my head. Then through the haze of my own blood I saw the most horrible sight I will ever know in my life.

In an orgiastic dive with his jaws open, the Black Shark went for Marina. She swam from him with all her strength.

Marina turned and twisted as the shark closed in. He did not go for her soft flesh, but grabbed her whole between his teeth.

Beating at his head with her hands, Marina thrashed in agony. But as the shark sank out of sight, her body went limp. The Black Shark, wild and frenzied, dove.

Before losing consciousness, the last thing I did was pray she was dead.

When I came to on the beach, Kapo was binding my wounds. Then I remembered, and began screaming. "He got her… He got Marina. He did…but I'll get him," I sobbed. Kapo held me down.

"No," said Kapo. "Lie down. You bad hurt."

Finally my hysteria subsided and Kapo let go. He tried to help me to my feet but I pushed him away and stumbled forward. Perhaps I did not want to live after Marina's end. But one thing I did want to do. I wanted to get that Black Shark. I could not rest until I equaled the score. I could not think again until I had my knife deep in the guts of that ugly monster.

Kapo had me by the waist and was forcing me to the hut away from the sea.

I relaxed in his grip. "Perhaps you're right after all." I said. I fell in step with him as we walked slowly toward the hut. Then I faked a stumble. Kapo bent over to help me up. At that moment I hit him as hard as I could with my right. But my strength had all but left me from the shark attack. He staggered back. I ran past him toward the sea.

He chased me, and tackled me on the fly. I rolled him off, then gave him another very hard right. For a moment he stared at me with a silly grin then fell back unconscious.

I dragged my equipment into the water then swam toward the deep center of the lagoon. There wasn't much oxygen left in my tank. The memory of Marina and all the happiness I had lost welled up in me as I swam. I wanted only to kill or be killed.

The salt in my deep wound was like fire. I swam slowly. I didn't want to tire myself. I finally reached the place where I had seen the Black Shark disappear. The sea was empty. I waited, treading water, turning slowly so I wouldn't be caught unawares. Would he come out of his lair?

An idea hit me. Taking my knife I opened up the wound in my arm again.

Soon a little trickle of blood oozed into the water. There was a possibility that it might bring the wrong sharks. I didn't care. I only wanted to live long enough to get that Black Shark.

The red blood spread out along the current.

Suddenly a shadow made a patch upon my path. I tightened my arm bandage and took a grip on the knife.

He circled once and then again. Evidently he was disappointed at not finding a woman. He began to swim off making a wider circle. He was like a bull in the ring not wanting to fight and I was the toreador using my red blood to taunt him on.

I chased him. Could I get him to fight? He circled once more to see why this man was rash enough to bother him. Was I dangerous to him? Evidently he didn't think I was worthwhile touching.

I waited, keeping close after him. He made a pass below my legs. I felt his body scrape my flippers. I turned around as he came back. Suddenly he was on his back, teeth agleam, his eyes lighted fires. He came slowly closer, to test my bravery.

I let my arms hang, staring at his eyes. He swam up, mouth open and gently glided by. He had never met a man who hadn't returned his challenge, hadn't flailed about or run off, or tried to ward off his passes with a weapon. What man in the sea had ever been insane enough to calmly invite his threats before? But his mistake was in not recognizing how deadly this mad enemy was.

Suddenly I lunged at him with the knife, aimed directly at the eye nearest me. The blade skidded off his thick skull.

In a rage he ripped at the wounded arm, taking it off completely. More blood spurted out. I sank in pain and weariness toward the bottom.

The Black Shark circled about, dropped the wretched limb and closed in again toward me. Though he wanted women first, I knew now he wanted to finish me off in hatred. I waited helplessly.

This time he came in high. He wanted to take off my head.

With my last strength welling up I lunged as we met. This time I got him deep in the eye.

He did not even thrash. His whole body gave one great monstrous, volcanic heave. Blood poured from his eyes, mouth and nose. His tail went stiff and he started dropping straight down like lead. Again I experienced the weird phenomenon of hearing sound come from the fish underwater. It was indescribable—something I can never forget, like a cry of terror from a stricken baby dinosaur. If he could have cried "mother" it might have come from his mouth. His mouth opened once more as his black figure continued dropping, down and down below me—into the bottom of the great, terrible sea.

Suddenly I was choking. I looked at my indicator. The oxygen was gone. I dropped the tanks quickly and went upward.

On the surface Kapo was paddling about in an outrigger. He had expected to find the mangled pieces of S.P. Free, marine biologist, but I was still in one piece and breathing—though plenty mangled. I had lost an arm and much blood. But with Kapo's help, I did stay alive—as alive as a man can be who has lost paradise and discovered hell all in one day.

Today, twelve years later, I am still a sad man, but a wiser man, who understands the meaning of natural wisdom of other kinds of people, even if it's not always scientific. ▼

Tyler Bowling, marine ecologist: The racism and sexism aside, this story is full of wild fantasies. The main issue is that the shark prefers women. Currently the International Shark Attack File (ISAF) has recorded a gender ratio of 8 men for every 2 women bitten. Meaning, more than 80% of recorded shark bites in history happened to men. This reflects a historic pattern of more men engaging in marine aquatic activities. This doesn't mean sharks prefer to bite males; rather, men had a greater historical chance of being around sharks. Recent data shows more females are being bitten; this is attributable to more women gaining equality and engaging in water sports.

The story's shark is all black, but very few sharks are black, and most have countershading coloration (dark top, light bottom), a form of camouflage. If seen from below the shark's ventral side (bottom) is lighter and blends in with the surface water, while when viewed from above the dark dorsal (top) blends in with the darker depths or bottom material. *Hypermelanism* is a condition where animals have an over production of skin pigment (the opposite of *albinism*), however this has never been documented in any large predatory shark species. This story's shark was likely inspired by the Mexican legend of *El Demonio Negro*, a supposed 50ft black great white shark.

The next stretch of the truth comes from the story's shark roaring. Sharks can't vocalize, because they don't even have vocal cords.

Lastly is the issue of this tale's "rogue shark," a single shark responsible for recurring attacks because it now craves human flesh. ISAF has never found any data to support this fear-mongering hypothesis.

Most confirmed cases involve test bites, where the shark is investigating and immediately releases. Unfortunately, even a single bite from a large animal can cause significant physical harm, and in some cases, be fatal. Considering the millions of people that go into the water each year and only several clusters of shark bites where a single shark was suspected have ever been documented.

This rogue shark hypothesis does not hold water.

"The Giant Shark That Guarded Rommel's Treasure"

STORY BY PETER FALL   COVER ART BY PHIL RONFOR

Gen. Rommel's treasure
disappeared without a trace.

The fabulous plunder of Rommel's Afrika Corps lay 40 fathoms deep. It was there for the taking — if anyone had guts enough to fight the huge monster that guarded it.

THE GIANT SHARK THAT GUARDED ROMMEL'S TREASURE

by PETER FALL

There was a marker buoy floating 10 feet below the surface, and from it a thin steel cable led into the murky green depths further down. Frank Hutchins followed the cable in a long, slow spiral, down out of the light, stopping every few yards to rest and let the pressure equalize.

The water was soupy-warm until Hutchins got down about 20 fathoms, where the hot Arabian sun no longer penetrated. It began to grow dark. Hutchins, clinging to the cable, unhooked the underwater floodlight from his belt and aimed it downward as he continued his dive.

A couple of convict-striped saupes and a whole school of sarguses came gliding over to investigate the light. Some of them poked up to Hutchins' glass face mask and stared in at him. But the American skin diver wasn't interested in fish. He was interested in what he would find at the base of the cable.

Then he saw it, a square-looking shadow among the sea-fans and

(continued on page 59)

Below him, Frank saw the glittering gold and platinum bars that spilled from the sunken chests. Above, between him and the surface, loomed the gigantic bulk of the biggest shark he ever saw.

25

ART BY PHIL RONFOR

There was a marker buoy floating 10 feet below the surface, and from it a thin steel cable led into the murky green depths further down. Frank Hutchins followed the cable in a long, slow spiral, down out of the light, stopping every few yards to rest and let the pressure equalize.

The water was soupy-warm until Hutchins got down about 20 fathoms, where the hot Arabian sun no longer penetrated. It began to grow dark. Hutchins, clinging to the cable, unhooked the underwater floodlight from his belt and aimed it downward as he continued his dive.

A couple of convict-striped saupes and a whole school of sarguses came gliding over to investigate the light. Some of them poked up to Hutchins' glass face mask and stared in at him. But the American skin diver wasn't interested in fish. He was interested in what he would find at the base of the cable.

Then he saw it, a square-looking shadow among the sea-fans and coral of the bottom, 40 fathoms down, half obscured by the waving dark-green fingers of ocean foliage. Hutchins cut loose from the cable, his rubber-flippered feet thrashing out to propel him down over the last few fathoms. Then he was crouching by the squarish object, which was covered with a light crust of barnacles and young coral.

He drew the short crowbar from the sheath at his belt and banged the object with it. Some of the crust came loose. Underneath was rusted metal, about the size and shape of a GI footlocker. It was one of the chests.

This was deep water, deeper than Hutchins had ever tried before. He sucked evenly at the plastic mouthpiece of the flexible hose drawing oxygen from the tank on his back, and peered around him, trying to spot the remaining two chests. He couldn't see them. Never mind, they'd be nearby.

He jammed the crowbar into the padlock that fastened the chest, and yanked. The lock broke open. The lid was stiff, and he pried it loose all around with the crowbar. Then he lifted.

This was really it! Bars of gold, stacked in neat piles within, more than he could count. They shone dull-bright in the dim light that filtered through 250 feet of water from the surface above. Jammed between them, Hutchins could see some flat gold plate, some canvas sacks and a couple of oblong shapes also wrapped in canvas—probably the platinum bars.

So it was true. Here he was, at the bottom of the Indian Ocean somewhere in the Gulf of Aden between Arabia and Somaliland, and he had found the lost $10,000,000 plunder of Field Marshal Rommel's Afrika Korps!

Hutchins stared through his face mask at the contents of the chest. One-sixth of this was his—a cool $1,500,000—give or take a few thousand for expenses and the cost of illegal marketing. As for the rest, it belonged to Dr. Hans Frobel and his four fellow Germans, who were waiting up there on the surface.

Hutchins grinned. He could just see them, hanging over the edge of the boat, peering down into the green depths, nervous as a bunch of mother hens.

The diver shut the lid, made a few brief circuits around it, and soon discovered the other two chests not far away. He didn't bother opening these.

He had a long way to go back to the surface and he would have to come up real slow. It was time to get started.

A dozen fathoms from the bottom, clinging to the buoy cable for a guide, Hutchins began to make out the dim shadow of the boat, floating on the milky green surface above. He kept his eyes on it, moving steadily upward.

And then suddenly, he couldn't see it any more. In its place was another shadow, a lot closer to Hutchins, a shadow easily as big as the boat. It was moving, drifting softly and deliberately with the characteristic slow, lazy motion of a big fish that's just nosing around.

Frank Hutchins froze on the cable. He knew that kind of shadow very well. He had seen it many times before, since he first began skin-diving in the Persian Gulf back in 1948. But he'd never seen one as big as this. For a second he thought he could be mistaken, that the huge shadow might be a cloud moving across the sun and the sea.

But then it moved again, nosing down, and came into sight—a monstrous, sinuous shape, glowing dirty white in the dim light, a hulking ton of lightning-quick muscle, with a cavernous mouth that looked four feet across. This was no cloud. Frank Hutchins was trapped, over 100 feet down, by the biggest damned mako shark that ever lived!

The road that led Hutchins to a sharkguarded, $10,000,000 sunken treasure began in the US Navy during World War II. That was where Hutchins—a rangy redhead from Missoula, Mont.—first crammed his six-foot-three frame into a rubber frogman's suit and began to learn the fine points of imitating fish.

In the Underwater Demolition Teams, Hutchins also learned a good deal about explosives. After his discharge, he put this knowledge to use, working in the Texas oilfields. In 1948, he signed up as an explosives man with an oil company in Kuwait, and shipped out for the Middle East.

Kuwait is a chunk of desert about the size of Rhode Island up at the head of the Persian Gulf. It is the richest petroleum area in the world, but also the hottest, and veteran oilmen shun the place. Only novices like Frank Hutchins sign up to work in Kuwait; novices and old-timers who can't work elsewhere—like Dr. Hans Frobel.

Frobel was a crack petroleum geologist with an Austrian passport and Heidelberg-type dueling scars. He had lost a hand somewhere between Tobruk and El Alamein in World War II. That was all anyone in Kuwait knew about his personal history. Frobel wasn't very friendly.

Between working shifts, Frank Hutchins spent a lot of time swimming in the tepid waters of the Gulf, mostly because there was little else to do, and because even the lukewarm, oil-stinking seawater was just a little cooler than the furnace-like air onshore.

When the former Navy frogman got the idea of sending to France for a skin-diving outfit, he soon became one of the wonders of Kuwait, attracting crowds of camel-borne Arabs who came to watch him cavorting in the water in his flippers, face-mask and twin, shoulder-slung oxygen tanks.

Another interested spectator was Hans Frobel. He was not a swimmer, because of his missing hand. But Hutchins noticed that the Austrian was a constant observer whenever he went skin-diving. Frobel also began to grow more friendly toward the young American.

One day in March 1950, in the bar of the Oilmen's Club, which overlooked the Gulf, Frobel revealed what was on his mind, over a round of cooling drinks.

"You are going on leave soon, aren't you?" he said casually. "Back to France again?"

Hutchins nodded. Since coming to Kuwait, he had spent all his two-week leaves in Paris and the Riviera, as a welcome change from the barrenness of the desert.

He said. "All I want is an air-conditioned room, cold oysters, and iced champagne. Nothing hot but the blondes."

Frobel laughed. "A worthy ambition. But I know a place much closer than Paris where you can have all these things."

"Where's that?"

"Djibouti." The capital of French Somaliland, Frobel explained, lay at the southern entrance of the Red Sea, and was a favorite port of call for many ships passing through the Suez Canal. "It is a place where anything goes, Hutchins. Gambling, fine hotels, many European girls, elegant restaurants. I'm going there myself in a few weeks. I have friends in Djibouti. Why don't you come along?"

It sounded fine to Hutchins. At the time, he had no reason to wonder why frozen-faced Frobel had suddenly turned so friendly. And the American didn't find it suspicious when his newfound friend suggested that he take his skindiving gear along to Djibouti. It seemed like a reasonable suggestion in view of his known fondness for the sport.

DJIBOUTI was all the Austrian had promised, and more. His "friends" turned out to be a quartet of stolid, desert-bronzed Germans, who were introduced as Helmut, Franz, Dieter and Paul—no last names. They were getting into early middle age, but looked remarkably fit, and seemed to know everyone worth knowing in Djibouti.

For Frank Hutchins, their most important acquaintance proved to be a saucy-eyed blonde named Suzette, with a mouth like Brigitte Bardot and figure to match. She took charge of the American, on his first evening in Djibouti and stuck with him, day and night, for the next six days.

Hutchins found it no sweat. He was having all he could handle of air-conditioned rooms, iced champagne, oysters, and Suzette. Frobel's friends insisted he was their guest, but the American realized that the krauts weren't *that* friendly. There had to be a gimmick, and he wondered when it would show.

A week after they arrived in Djibouti, Hans Frobel came to the point.

"How would you like to spend the rest of your life living like this?"

Hutchins looked at him carefully. Frobel wasn't joking. "What d'you mean, Hans?"

"I mean there's a way for you to make over a million dollars, if you want to.'"

The American laughed. "Oh sure! Me and Onassis."

"I'm serious, Frank. There's a reason I invited you to Djibouti. You can become a rich man—all of us can be rich—if you'll cooperate."

"Like what?"

"You would simply have to find something for us underwater."

Hutchins lit a cigarette to hide his excitement. "I'm listening, Hans."

Dr. Frobel leaned forward earnestly. "Frank," he said in a low voice, "have you ever heard of the lost Afrika Korps treasure?"

"Sure," said Hutchins. "Who hasn't?"

"Tell me what you know about it," Frobel said.

IT WAS a well-known story, Hutchins said. Back in 1943, when Field Marshal Erwin Rommel's Afrika Korps was beating a hasty retreat out of North Africa, a special detachment called the *Devisenschutzkommando* (DSK) systematically looted the homes and bank vaults of wealthy Tunisian and Algerian civilians.

Every major German military grouping had an attached DSK, charged with "protecting" all valuables found in occupied areas for the glory—and wealth—of the Third Reich.

The *Devisenschutzkommando* of the Afrika Korps was more successful than most. It appropriated gold bullion, platinum, jewels, coins and precious art objects estimated at between $15,000,000 and $20,000,000. This plunder was shipped out to Italy as the Germans retreated from Africa.

The Allies invaded Sicily and the Italian mainland. On September 16, 1943, having landed at Salerno, they were fighting their way toward the important German naval base at Castellammare di Stabia, south of Naples. The Germans began to evacuate Castellammare.

One torpedo boat was commandeered by a certain Colonel Dall, who appeared at the dock in a truck carrying four large and obviously heavy crates. With Dall were four other officers of the DSK.

The crates—which contained the bulk of the DSK's African plunder—were loaded on the torpedo boat. An enlisted boatswain, Peter Fleig, was the highest-ranking crew member aboard at the time, and Colonel Dall ordered him to cast off and make for Corsica. There, he said, the crates would be transferred to a convoy heading for safety in Genoa.

The torpedo boat reached the Corsican Port of Bastia on the morning of September 17, just as the departing convoy was being blasted by American bombers. As an alternative, Dall told Fleig to put into a sheltered cove. There, after taking bearings on certain landmarks to determine the site; Dall had the crates dumped overboard. When it was done, the boat proceeded toward La Spezia in northern Italy.

Hardly had they landed there when the Gestapo arrested the five DSK officers and the crew of the torpedo boat, including Peter Fleig. All were closely interrogated and tortured, the Gestapo believing that Dall and the rest had dumped the crates in a conspiracy to recover them for themselves after the war.

When the arrested men refused or proved unable to disclose the location of the sunken booty, Dall and the DSK officers were shot by a firing squad. Fleig and his fellow crewmen were court martialed and sent to the Russian front.

Only Peter Fleig survived the war. He was arrested by the French—who had found official German records of the whole affair—and taken to Corsica, where he was ordered to help divers recover the treasure. For weeks, Fleig stalled bis captors, claiming be didn't remember the exact bearings or that landmarks had disappeared. Finally, Fleig himself vanished.

A few years later, from a secret hideout somewhere in Europe, Fleig contacted a Marseilles lawyer, Charles Cancellieri. The German offered to lead an expedition to the treasure and split the proceeds if Cancellieri would finance the arrangements. The lawyer agreed, but he died a few weeks later, and so the last link to Fleig and the multi-million-dollar Rommel booty was lost.

This was the story as Hutchins had heard it, and as he recounted it to Hans Frobel that day in Djibouti. When the American finished, Frobel was grinning.

"A marvelous story, even if I say so myself," he exclaimed. "Too bad it isn't true."

"How do you know?" Hutchins asked.

"Because I *created* the Fleig story," Frobel said. "The Rommel treasure was never sunk off Corsica. It's right here in the Gulf of Aden!"

"What about Col. Dall and Fleig?"

"They never existed. Here is what actually happened..."

IN 1943, Frobel said, he was a *Devisenschutzkommando* lieutenant colonel stationed in Libya. When the British 8th Army routed the Afrika Korps at El Alamein, Frobel and four friends—the same four who were now their Djibouti hosts—conspired to desert, taking with them some of the loot which had been collected by the DSK in Africa.

On the night of March 20, 1943, they commandeered two half-tracks and started southwards across the trackless Libyan Desert. With them in the half-tracks were three crates containing nearly $10,000,000 in plundered gold bullion, coins and platinum bars.

"We traveled only at night, both to avoid the heat and escape detection. The Allies were flying constant patrols over the desert, and we were sure that our own Germans would be looking for us."

It was a harrowing journey, over 650 miles of waterless, treeless dunes, until the five Germans finally arrived in the remote Tibesti Mountains, on the frontier of French Equatorial Africa. There they ran out of fuel.

The Tibesti Mountains have long been a refuge for Arab slave-traders and gun-runners, and these outlaws welcomed the five Germans. There were no Allied forces for thousands of miles. In the safety of the impassable mountains, the millionaire deserters settled down to wait out the war.

In 1947, posing as Swiss Red Cross workers, the German quintet started out again, traveling from the Tibesti nearly 1,600 miles to Asmara, on the Red Sea. There, they chartered an Arab sailing *dhow* to take them down the coast to Portuguese Mozambique, where they hoped to sell the DSK loot without attracting attention.

In the Gulf of Aden, just off the island of Abd-al-Kuri, the *dhow's* Arab lookout sighted a British patrol boat heading toward them. These were slave-running waters, and the British were certain to stop and search any suspicious vessel.

"We knew we couldn't let them find the gold on board," Frobel recalled. "There was only one thing to do—dump it."

The three chests, too heavy to be stowed below, were lashed on the *dhow's* deck. Working swiftly, the Germans attached a length of cable to one of them, with a small buoy at its upper end, and dumped all three crates over the side.

"From a marine chart, we saw that the bottom was about 40 fathoms at that point. We deliberately shortened the cable so that the buoy would float below the surface, to guide only those who knew where to look for it. Then, just as the British launch came alongside to search us, we took three visual bearings on Abd-al-Kuri island. That marked the site for us."

The British left, having found nothing. But, since the *dhow* carried neither diving nor hoisting gear, the Germans could only return to Asmara.

Hutchins was silent awhile after Frobel finished this account. Then he asked:

"Have you tried to recover it since?"

"No. It's taken us this long to raise cash for a suitable boat and equipment. And we had to find a diver who could be trusted."

"Me?" Hutchins grinned.

"You."

"You haven't explained the story about Fleig and Corsica. I've heard it a half dozen times in France. What was that all about?" Hutchins asked.

The French government knew, Frobel explained, that most of the Afrika Korps loot from North Africa had never been accounted for. To throw the French off the trail, he had invented the whole Fleig story.

"In Rome two years ago, I met an American newspaperman. He printed the Fleig story verbatim, and several magazines picked it up."

"Weren't you afraid he'd check it?"

The Austrian laughed heartily. "What could he check? Col. Dall was supposed to be dead, the mysterious Fleig was in hiding. The only character who actually existed was Charles Cancellieri—and I knew he had died a few months earlier. It was a story which sounded authentic, but which could not be traced."

Hutchins nodded. "And now you're ready to go after the loot?"

"The question is: are you ready to dive for us?" Frobel replied.

"For a million dollars?" said Hutchins. "When do we start?"

Three days later, Hutchins and the five Germans—in the boat they had bought for the expedition—approached the southern shore of Abd-al-Kuri. There was a good deal of jockeying back and forth as Frobel stood sighting through a pelorus at some point on shore. Finally, the Austrian was satisfied he had the proper bearing.

Maintaining a steady, slow course, the boat inched out on that bearing, while Frobel swung the sighting instrument around to another heading.

"*Langsam*, slowly, slowly" he crooned. "Now, stop!"

He swung again, to find the third bearing. "Good, this is the place."

Frank Hutchins stood on the fantail, the oxygen tanks on his back, the glass face mask poised on his forehead, flippers on his feet.

Now, AS the huge mako drifted slowly nearby, Hutchins froze to the cable, praying the big fish hadn't spotted him. As long as he remained rigid, there was a chance the shark would glide on past and go on about its business.

A minute or two went by, but the white, ghostly hulk was still there. It was not attacking, but seemed fascinated by the cable and the indistinct form of the man who clung to it. Again and again, it passed within inches of Hutchins, swam past, then suddenly swerved and came back.

It was as if the fish were really patrolling over the sunken treasure, guarding it with deadly efficiency.

Hutchins swore. He couldn't stay here forever, with his precious oxygen being used up. Nor could he risk shooting to the surface and dying of the bends. He had to get going, and slowly. Yet, if he moved…

The big mako was back, so close that its rough skin grazed Hutchins' leg. The American fought to maintain his steadying grip on the cable. If the shark came any closer, its sandpaper-like hide could rip his skin open like a knife. When that happened and the blood began to flow, the shark would go kill-crazy. He had to get away from there!

Suddenly, the water overhead seemed to explode in a burst of movement and muffled sound. Involuntarily, Hutchins jerked his head upwards, in time to see the shadow of the boat move away in a mass of propeller-churned wake. The boat was leaving! Something was wrong on the surface.

The man's movement aroused the shark. It came barreling in towards him, swerving suddenly, inspecting this strange object. Then, recognizing an enemy, the shark turned once more. Horrified, Hutchins watched it twist over on its back. The gigantic mouth came open—and the mako charged!

There wasn't time to think. Hutchins reached up and snatched the oxygen hose from his mouth. Turning to face the shark, he reached for the petcock on the tank behind him, twisted the valve.

The oxygen shot out of the mouthpiece, burbling up in a stream of large, violent bubbles as it passed through the water. It looked like a silvery arrow that reached out to meet the big mako shark, even as the brute lunged in on its back, deadly mouth poised to rip the man apart.

It was fantastic. The shark seemed to brake in mid-lunge as it saw the bubbling oxygen stream. It twisted violently and turned in its own length, the huge body flailing in a paroxysm. Then it turned tail and fled, disappearing in the murk.

Hutchins could hardly believe it. He thrust the mouthpiece back between his lips, gulping the life-giving gas as he watched the shark retreat. It had been an impulse, out of a half-remembered legend that sharks were afraid of bubbling water or violent movement. But it had worked. The mako was gone.

The American, fighting his anxiety over the disappearance of the boat, began his slow ascent up the cable. He forced himself to maintain a slow, steady pace. But Hutchins had no illusions. He knew the mako would be back, as soon as the fish realized he was unhurt. The oxygen gimmick might work once more, or twice. After that, the big fish would get smart—or the oxygen would give out. It was a race.

The skin diver managed to gain three more fathoms before the mako made its second charge. This time, he was ready for it—sensing rather than seeing the sudden onrush of the gigantic hulk as it lanced at him out of the murk. Hutchins waited until he could see the gaping, voracious maw. Then he again lashed out with his stream of oxygen.

It was almost laughable, to see that tremendous shape turn and run from the harmless bubbles, but Frank Hutchins didn't laugh. This could be his life.

The mako did not return again as Hutchins, increasing his pace, passed the buoy and broke through to the surface.

He was alone. The boat was nowhere in sight, although—from the distance—he could hear the faint roar of diesel engines. What had scared them off? He didn't know, but he did know he couldn't hang around here waiting for the Germans to come back. Not with that great shark-mouth down below.

And suddenly Hutchins realized that he faced still another enemy—exhaustion.

He had been swimming for hours at depths he'd never tried before, and he was getting tired. Ahead of him, on the horizon, he could see the tantalizing shore of Abd-al-Kuri, about five miles away. Five miles wasn't much for Hutchins normally, but now it seemed an enormous distance. He would never make it, unless he could find something to help him float.

Then he remembered—the buoy! He took a deep gulp of oxygen, turned end over end and headed down. In a few seconds, using the crowbar, be had pried loose the cable, and the buoy floated to the surface. Hutchins went up after it, slipped out of the oxygentank harness and started toward the distant shore, using the seaweed-covered buoy for support.

By nightfall, he could no longer move his legs, but clung limply to the buoy, dimly wondering why the shore seemed no closer. Afraid that he would lose the buoy if he lost consciousness, Hutchins forced his wrist through a ring on the metal bell. All through the night he floated, half-conscious, exhausted. He never knew when he blacked out entirely.

A BRITISH patrol boat found Hutchins the next morning, still clinging to the buoy, nearly 15 miles at sea, where the strong offshore current had carried him. Taken to a hospital on the island of Socotra, he recovered consciousness to find himself under arrest.

It developed that a British boat had surprised Frobel's craft, while Hutchins was on the bottom. The Germans fled and led the British on a long chase out to sea. Finally, in an effort to stop the suspect boat, the patrol boat opened fire. Its second shot apparently hit Frobel's fuel tank, and the German boat exploded. Four bodies were recovered.

Hutchins told the British the true story. For several weeks, efforts were made to locate the spot where he had found Rommel's treasure, but they were fruitless. The American couldn't know on which landmarks Hans Frobel had taken his bearings, nor what those bearings were. Without that information, and without the marker buoy—which Hutchins had cut loose to save his life—the hunt was useless.

Frank Hutchins was released by the British and returned to Kuwait. A few years later, he moved down to Bahrein Island (later Bahrain), also in the Persian Gulf, where he was last reported working for an American oil firm. He has given up skin-diving for safer sports. But the memory of the gigantic mako shark that may yet guard the golden $10,000,000 treasure of Field Marshal Rommel haunts him to this day. ▼

MAM fiction can be a Dagwood sandwich, piled high with a little of everything that's in the fridge—familiar flavors with proven appeal that, in theory, should combine well. It might fall apart on the plate, unsteady under the weight of its layers. Or it might end up something delicious, excessive, and wholly satisfying—like this big, hearty MAM sandwich by Peter Fall.

The ingredients here are familiar to any MAM reader's palate, and any two would be enough for a less ambitious tale: A blue-collar (1) WWII veteran (2) is working abroad (3) in an exotic locale (4) when secretive Germans of dubious intent (5) propose a partnership (6) to reclaim a lost Nazi (7) treasure (8). But a near-lethal encounter with a giant shark (9) and his partners' betrayal (10) leave him alive but haunted by his experience (11). Heat and serve!

Even Phil Ronfor's harrowing illustration is a tasty lefttover from an issue of *Adventure* a few years earlier. But despite its cover art, no shark story appeared in that issue.

ADVENTURE July 1957

The Godfather MEETS JAWS

MORT KÜNSTLER'S BIG BLUES AND GREAT WHITES

"Every experience you have, you file away. Painting underwater scenes, I had to get an underwater effect. I had done some scuba diving and fishing in Florida and in Mexico…on Long Island, even. And that's where I came up with many of the underwater effects I utilized; I'd seen them first-hand.

"So you'll never see true white in underwater scenes; what's white underwater is going to have a tint to it: blue-to-green, gray, green-gray, blue-gray….

"There were some great underwater displays at the Museum of Natural History in New York; I remember taking many reference photos there. But most of the time

Adventure, August 1956 (*detail*)

you had to make it up, because [reality] never fit the way you wanted it.

"What it amounts to is, you take a photo that's basically gonna help you do the picture. The guys that just take a photo, trace it up and then render it? It looks like it. What it has to be is an *aid* to help you get to the end result. You take advantage of what technology there is, but you don't let the technology rule you.

"I think it probably helped that I was active myself. I'd even been in the water with sharks. (I was scared to death.)

"At times I was my own model. *Adventure*, August 1956? That's me. Aside from the fact that he looks like me (you don't see my face, but that's my body, my hands), the guy is a lefty—and I'm a lefty.

ADVENTURE, August 1956

"My attitude was, it's not realistic to begin with. Sharks, you made about three times bigger than they were, so they would look vicious, etcetera. Not that they don't look vicious already! But the shark is pretty easy. There's not an awful lot

Below: FOR MEN ONLY, October 1968   *Right:* MALE, April 1968

you can do with them, you know? I mean, you can have their mouth open, you can do them sideways, then you can do the *other* side, full-front…. Each time I did one of these, I tried to do a different angle on the shark, so it didn't look like the last painting.

"For the 1975 *Mad Magazine* cover *(overleaf)*, they showed me the *Jaws* poster and said they wanted to do a take-off on that. It was pretty easy. You make it funny, with the tongue hanging out on the shark, and Alfred E. Neuman…. Apparently they'd had a difficult time finding artists who could paint Alfred. They wanted him exactly the same every time; you weren't supposed to have him in profile or anything like that. Norman Mingo was the artist who'd established the character, and it's almost always the same angle and the same head. How other artists had trouble with it is beyond my comprehension. That's the easiest part of the job! And that's what they really loved: my rendering of Alfred. The shark was no big deal!

"They wanted me to take over their covers, and do every one. I felt at the time it was, I don't know, *beneath my dignity*. Ha! That's why I signed it *Mutz*. (My father didn't like the name Morton. He told my mother, "If you call him Morton, I'm gonna call him *Mutt*," and *Mutt*—then *Mutz*—it's been, ever since.)

"It was pretty foolish when I think back; it would have been fun. But I was doing a lot of work in advertising then, and I'd think, *"No advertiser's going to want to be associated with* Mad Magazine*!"* Which is sort of silly, but what did I know?

"I did keep busy, though!"

As told to Wyatt Doyle

Left: MALE, October 1958   FOR MEN ONLY, April 1968

Mad, January 1976 Art by Mort Künstler, as "Mutz"

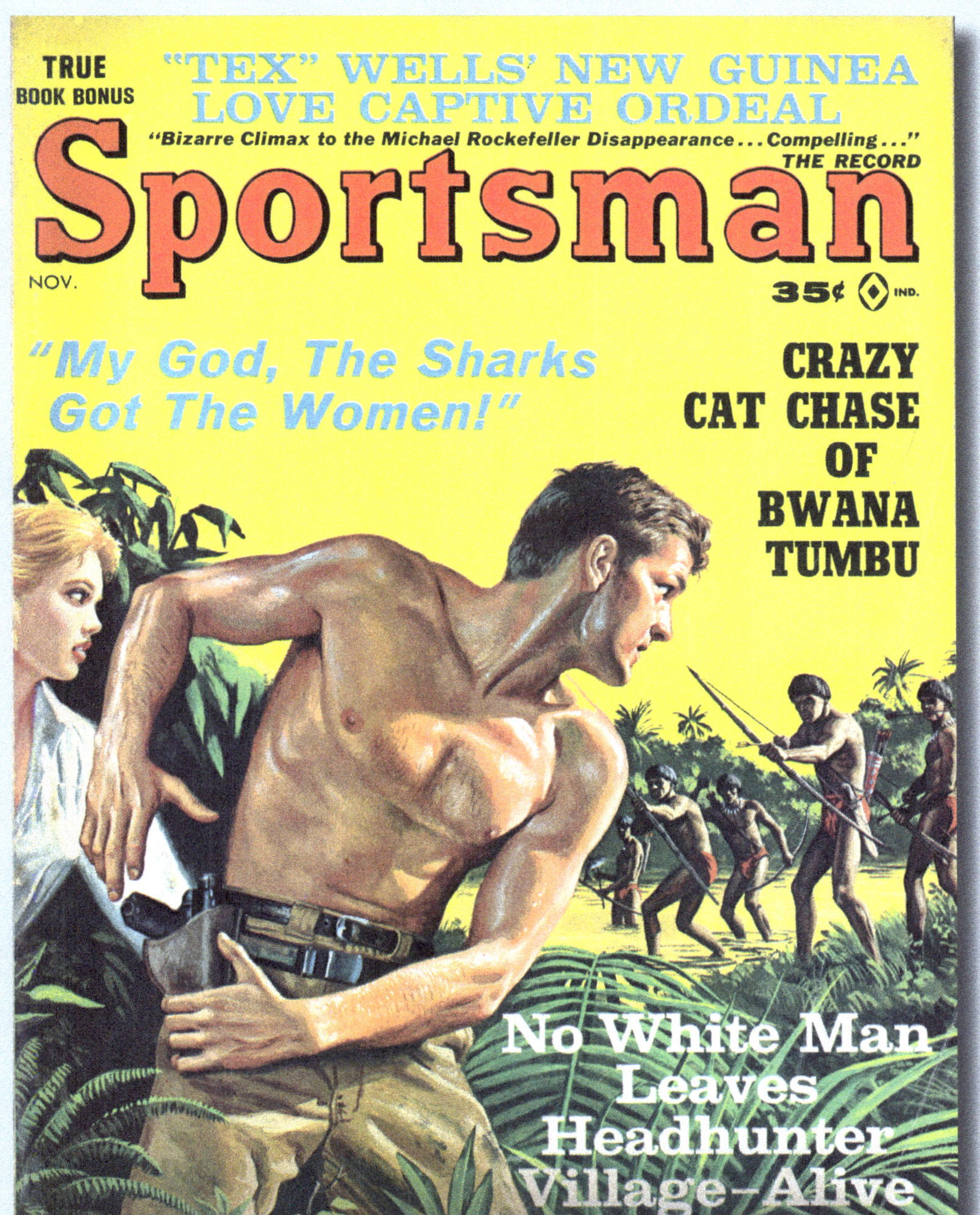

"My God, the Sharks Got the Women!"

STORY BY CAPT. KURT FRIHOLM   COVER ART BY MORT KÜNSTLER

Everyone aboard the craft went tumbling into the shark-filled waters. "Pretty soon they eat good," Andreas said.

A big gray dorsal fin came around in a quarter circle and was right next to the girl who seemed too tired to fight.

"MY GOD, THE SHARKS GOT THE WOMEN!"

by CAPT. KURT FRIHOLM

It was odd, I guess, how I'd been seeing sharks for years without giving them much thought. I accepted them just like part of the sea itself as their gray dorsal fins cut water around our tanker *Estrella de Cabimas*. That is, I did until that day when they suddenly began getting in my hair.

I don't think you'll find as many sharks anywhere else in western waters as you do on our Maracaibo-Aruba run. Bigger, maybe. Perhaps in Cuba off the foot of Morro Castle where in the old days the Spaniards threw prisoners to hem. Or beyond the green shallows offshore of Kingston Jamaica, where the sea darkens to purple-blue. . . . But not more numerous. Which is why the lads around the oil fields of Maracaibo and the refineries of Aruba call our run *Pasillo de Tiburon*—shark alley.

Like everything else, there's probably a reason for it. Maybe it's because our route lies over a natural deep-sea jungle. Or maybe the word spread around in shark circles that the lads on the lake tankers ate well and hearty and our cooks heaved more garbage over the stern than anywhere else in tropical waters.

Whatever the reason, we never make a run that we don't pick up a heavy escort. And the sight of their ugly fins didn't register with me one way or another until the day after Hurricane Carol swept through, leaving a heavy ground swell to kick up the Gulf of Venezuela.

We were coming on a line with Castilletes, opposite the Paraguana Peninsula, when Borkman, the second, called me to the bridge.

"I've been watching that little Dutchman off to port, Skipper," he said as he pointed. "She acts like she's in trouble."

I stared at the white sails silhouetted against the blue haze of the distant shore. It's hard to tell about these Dutchmen that freight fresh vegetables and other truck to Aruba from the mainland. Sometimes they haul a few passengers too. They're so jammed with stuff that it's piled up to the boom. Outward bound, it's damn near a miracle they don't capsize long before sighting Oranjestad.

"She's riding lower than most of them," I admitted as I reached for my glasses.

There were four people aboard, two men and two women. Through the glasses I saw that the men were bailing like hell and the women were waving at us frantically.

"Carrying a couple of passengers," I commented, "and maybe plenty of sea water."

We were less than half a mile astern of the Dutchman when I saw the activity aboard her increase. One of the men quit bailing and began throwing things, sacks of potatoes it looked like, over the side. One of the girls was helping him.

The Dutchman was rolling loggily in the heavy ground swell now. Not rising to it at all. (*Continued on page 54*)

It was odd, I guess, how I'd been seeing sharks for years without giving them much thought. I accepted them just like part of the sea itself as their gray dorsal fins cut water around our tanker *Estrella de Cabimas*. That is, I did until that day when they suddenly began getting in my hair.

I don't think you'll find as many sharks anywhere else in western waters as you do on our Maracaibo-Aruba run. Bigger, maybe. Perhaps in Cuba off the foot of Morro Castle where in the old days the Spaniards threw prisoners to them. Or beyond the green shallows offshore of Kingston, Jamaica, where the sea darkens to purple-blue… But not more numerous. Which is why the lads around the oil fields of Maracaibo and the refineries of Aruba call our run *Pasillo de Tiburon*— Shark Alley.

Like everything else, there's probably a reason for it. Maybe it's because our route lies over a natural deep-sea jungle. Or maybe the word spread around in shark circles that the lads on the lake tankers ate well and hearty and our cooks heaved more garbage over the stern than anywhere else in tropical waters.

Whatever the reason, we never make a run that we don't pick up a heavy escort. And the sight of their ugly fins didn't register with me one way or another until the day after Hurricane Carol swept through, leaving a heavy ground swell to kick up the Gulf of Venezuela.

We were coming on a line with Castilletes, opposite the Paraguana Peninsula, when Borkman, the second, called me to the bridge.

"I've been watching that little Dutchman off to port, Skipper," he said as he pointed. "She acts like she's in trouble."

I stared at the white sails silhouetted against the blue haze of the distant shore: It's hard to tell about these Dutchmen that freight fresh vegetables and other truck to Aruba from the mainland. Sometimes they haul a few passengers too. They're so jammed with stuff that it's piled up to the boom. Outward bound, it's damn near a miracle they don't capsize long before sighting Oranjestad.

"She's riding lower than most of them." I admitted as I reached for my glasses.

There were four people aboard, two men and two women. Through the glasses I saw that the men were bailing like hell and the women were waving at us frantically.

"Carrying a couple of passengers," I commented, "and maybe plenty of sea water."

We were less than half a mile astern of the Dutchman when I saw the activity aboard her increase. One of the men quit bailing and began throwing things, sacks of potatoes it looked like, over the side. One of the girls was helping him.

The Dutchman was rolling loggily in the heavy ground swell now. Not rising to it at all.

As she took a big one over the starboard bow we could see it was a losing fight. As the boat took a second wallop, the other girl tore off her wet pink blouse and stood there, naked to the waist, waving it at us frantically.

"Ready a boat," I told Borkman, "looks like we may be needing it."

He was about to leave the bridge and start aft when I thought of something and called him back.

"Better break the rifle out of the locker. And send the bo'sun to the stern. I want a report on the shark situation."

We had one rifle aboard for emergencies, a .30-06. It hadn't been fired for years—not since some marine insurance inspector got bored on a trip over to Aruba and took pot shots at our shark convoy.

"Five cartridges, Skipper," Borkman reported, "no others in the locker. We never did reorder after that guy's target practice."

"Remind me to get some next time we're in Maracaibo," I told him and promptly forgot about our lack of cartridges.

Then Andreas, the bo'sun came trotting up on the bridge.

"*Muchos tiburones astern,*" he reported. "I count now 21, maybe even 25. They wait for Pepe to throw more *basura.*"

Damn, I thought to myself, why couldn't the cook have waited awhile before he chucked the garbage? Now the whole pack of sharks'll be following us right into Aruba.

It wouldn't be the first time of course. They probably followed us on every voyage. But it was the first time I really had occasion to think about it. And the more I thought, the less I liked it.

And then it dawned on me. The *Estrella de Cabimas* was leading all those sharks straight toward the Dutchman. If the little schooner was in trouble now, she'd have it in spades when the sharks started nosing around.

I cussed out that marine insurance lad good and proper then. And I also threw in a few choice words about myself. If only we had enough cartridges, I thought, I could put a man aft with the rifle to pop at those hungry devils and—

"*Por Dias, mira!*" Andreas called out. "Now she catch it good!"

I followed his pointing finger. The Dutchman was in the trough of a long swell that looked as though it was going to roll right over her. For a second or two she seemed undecided. Then sluggishly she went up and over its crest and slid down into the next one. The men aboard struggled frantically to bring her bow about but she didn't respond.

The next impact caught her broadside. She keeled over on her side, knocked flat as a pancake. The four aboard tumbled into the water like oranges dumped out of a market basket.

I signaled to the engine room for more speed as I saw them start floundering in the heavy sea. The half-nude girl caught hold of the mast. The other three managed to make it to the vessel and hang on to the almost submerged rail. A man and the second girl close together, the other man farther forward. I figured that we'd rescue them all right if they just held on—and the sharks didn't get to them first.

We were about a third of a mile from her and I decided to bring the *Estrella* in as close as possible before launching a boat. And then I thought again about that damned shark escort astern. Andreas read my mind.

"Pretty soon they eat plenty good," he told me. *"Mira!"*

I saw a big gray dorsal fin off the port, moving rapidly ahead. Our deadly escort was beginning to leave us for food more to its liking.

I whistled down the tube. Donovan, the chief, answered.

"You signaled more speed and you got it. All our old cement mixer'll grind out."

"Now I want oil," I said. "Plenty of it. Rig a hose to the tank and start pumping it over the stern. Maybe the crude'll discourage some of the blasted sharks."

"You're daft, Friholm," he told me. "It's a waste of good crude. The damned sharks will just sound."

Well, maybe they would. But there were so many of them that if we laid a screen of heavy, stinking crude oil on top of the water it might keep some of them away. At least it was worth a try.

I saw another dorsal fin cleave swiftly through the ground swell to port. And still another. We were coming on, less than 1,000 yards from the four people. In the light, hot breeze fanning back I could hear the women screaming to us for help. Through the glasses I saw the slim one let go with one hand and at first I thought she was about to give up. Then I saw her wave the hand at us, urging us to hurry.

Grab hold with both hands, sister, I muttered, save your strength, we're coming as fast as we can.

"More to port," I ordered Felipe. "I want to pass them at 100 yards."

"Pass them?" he asked.

Maybe I'm nuts, I thought to myself. I didn't know if a screen of crude oil was going to work. But one thing for sure, I'd never heard of it being tried before.

Donovan whistled into the tube.

"We're pumping cargo as ordered," he growled. "Many an oil-soaked sea gull will not be flying again because of it. How are we doing astern?"

I stepped out to the wing of the bridge for a quick look: The thick, oily stream was spreading out in a black wake, and a lot of it was drifting to port where I wanted it. What, if anything, it was doing to that bunch of sharks I couldn't tell.

We were 500 yards from the Dutchman and the four of them were still hanging on. Felipe was edging the *Estrella* in closer.

"Tell Mr. Borkman to ready the boat crew," I told Andreas. "And stand by to help him."

My hand was on the telegraph. I had just signaled half speed when the first shark struck. It must have been at least 12 feet long. It made a swift half-turn and I saw the sunlight glistening on its wet, white belly. Then I groaned as it hit the leg of one of the men who had been holding on farther forward.

His scream of fright came to us above the cries of the women. Suddenly he was jerked backward and down as if he had been snapped out on a rubber band. It was horrifying. I expected to see the victim thrashing wildly about, trying to fight the shark off—like I had read and heard about. But it wasn't like that. The man simply disappeared from sight, his scream drowning in his lungs as he was pulled beneath the surface of the water.

For a few seconds the swiftness of the tragedy numbed me. I couldn't speak or move.

"Madre de Dias!" Felipe muttered, awestruck. *"Un monstruo!"*

I signaled, "Stop all engines," and stared down on the Dutchman from the wing of the bridge as we passed. The slim girl looked up at me with a pleading look. The man near her yelled something at me I could not under-stand. He was white-faced, his reddish mustache plastered under his nose like an ugly wound.

The other girl, the half-naked one, was kicking out in the water with her legs. Like a kid learning to swim.

"Hold on," I shouted. "Keep kicking to scare 'em off. We'll have a boat right out to you."

Some 30 yards beyond them I saw gray dorsal fins converging. There must have been at least half a dozen of them. Suddenly the water was churned to fury. A long gray shape leaped forward as though shot from the rolling ground swell. It plunged downward into the trough, twisting as it went. I could see the vicious jaws open as it dived. It came up again fast and there was something hanging from its jaws. Something that looked like a bloody mess of tattered rags.

"What's left of the body," I muttered to myself. "They're fighting over it. Now every last shark in creation'll be heading this way."

I glanced aft and saw that the crude was beginning to drift towards the Dutchman and I prayed that it would do some good. Borkman and his crew of four were lowering the boat now. He squatted in the stern with the rifle across his lap. He looked up at me once, pointed at the rifle and shook his head grimly. Just five cartridges.

His boat got away neatly. He let it drift a bit towards our stern before rowing for the foundered Dutchman just ahead of the spreading pool of crude. Then the boat was riding in it.

Two gray dorsal fins cut water about ten yards ahead of his bow. That made a total of eight or nine sharks in the vicinity of the Dutchman. There might have been triple that number but for the screen of crude oil. Plainly the sharks didn't care for it at all.

Looking down I saw a shark heading in the direction of the half-nude girl. I shouted to Borkman and pointed. He had seen it too and raised his rifle.

The shark veered away, probably frightened by the threshing of the girl's legs. Borkman held his fire. A cool head, that one. He was going to make every cartridge count.

Keep right on kicking, sister, I breathed to myself. Then I saw them.

"Kick your feet!" I yelled to her. "Sharks behind you! *Tiburones!*"

She made a half-hearted attempt to kick out as the man near her shouted and beat the water. She seemed very tired.

If I only had another rifle, I thought to myself helplessly as the two killers shot towards her, I could get both of them from here.

Our ship's boat was still about 50 yards away when Borkman fired. His rifle cracked again and again. I saw the trailing shark slow up and then churn water in an agony of death. The lead shark kept right moving. Borkman fired his fourth shot and hit again. But wounded as it was, the shark flashed in and twisted. It got the slim girl's lower arm.

She screamed in terror. What remained of her severed arm came upward, as though it was all still there and she was trying to motion to the boat crew to hurry. It was gone above the elbow and I turned sick inside as the blood spouted.

She'll bleed to death before we even get her back aboard ship, I thought, and felt my stomach turn over. The stump came down and the other arm let go its hold. As she started to go under the man near her reached out and grabbed her, pulling her towards him. Then he shook his head and let go. She was already dead.

As she disappeared beneath the water, another shark dashed in towards the man. He saw it coming and threshed out wildly, yelling at the top of his lungs. I heard the crack of Borkman's rifle. His fifth and last cartridge. The shark sheered off and in panic the man began swimming the 25 yards to the ship's boat, his arms flailing like windmills.

Another shark started after him and I held my breath. It was very close. For about 15 yards the big gray killer gained rapidly before the man swam frantically into the crude. Then the thick, blackish oil on the surface seemed to scare the shark. Or perhaps it was the stench.

The giant fish veered off as Borkman arose with clubbed rifle. In another few seconds, Peterson, the seaman in the bow, leaned over and grabbed the man by the belt. He was hauled in, looking black as one of our Jamaican oilers, choking and spitting crude.

"One to go," I muttered as the boat headed in to rescue the remaining girl.

It looked as if Borkman was going to make it all right. There were 20 yards, and though I could see several fins cutting water farther away, the immediate area appeared to be clear. I could hear him shouting encouragement to the girl. And she kept screaming back to him. From the bridge it sounded as though she was totally hysterical.

The boat could not have been more than eight yards from her when another shark suddenly appeared. A big gray dorsal fin broke surface almost under the bow. So close that Peterson took a jab at it with the blade of his oar. It got out of the way in a hurry and sounded. Then the boat was alongside the girl and Savona, on the starboard side, reached down to haul her in.

The big shark broke surface again, right beside the boat, hellbent on getting its intended prey before she could be pulled to safety. Borkman saw it first and moved swiftly forward behind Savona. His rifle went up and then came down with all of his 220 pounds behind it. The shark had started twisting. I could see its ugly white belly as the rifle stock thudded hard just above those cruel, gaping jaws.

The girl screamed then. Terribly. And for the moment, as she was pulled into the boat, I thought she'd been bitten.

I swore to myself and I reached for the glasses. Then I saw that Borkman was looking toward me with one upraised hand. His thumb and forefinger formed a closed circle signaling okay. After which he removed his shirt and personally wrapped it around the girl. I sighed to myself as the ship's boat was rowed back. We'd managed to save half of them at any rate, probably a damn good average for survivors in Shark Alley.

After they had come aboard I turned my cabin over to the girl. Despite her terror and shock, she made a very attractive sight. But she had taken a rather nasty wound on her right leg. All the way from ankle to thigh it appeared as if it had been scraped by a nutmeg grater. The hide of the attacking shark had done that as she was being pulled into the boat. At that it could have been a lot worse.

The man was in much better shape. After some of the oil had been scraped off him I had Borkman bring him up to the bridge in a dry shirt and pair of pants. He was a native of Aruba and, as I had surmised, skipper of the little schooner. He spoke in Papiamento which is the official patois of Aruba. It is a bastard mixture of Spanish, Portuguese and Dutch with a dash of French thrown in for utter confusion. Neither Borkman nor I understood.

"No use taking notes for the log until we get ashore," I said "'The harbor captain can interpret for this chap."

"I can tell you this much, Skipper," Borkman grinned. "The name of the dame in your cabin is Dolores. She was an entertainer in La Guaira and she's going to do the same in Oranjestad—at that pink-colored joint with four *divi-divi* trees in front."

"Thanks," I said, "that'll make good reading in the log." ▼

BITING BACK   commentary

SARAH FAE TORRE, MARINE FISHERIES BIOLOGIST: The author describes an area between Aruba and Maracaibo as one of the more highly populated shark waters in western waters. While it may be true that this area is home to numerous sharks, within Atlantic waters, the southeast coast of the United States in general is known to be home to some of the most densely populated shark habitats. However, given that this was published in 1964 and theoretically occurred in 1954 (the author references the story's events as occurring the day after Hurricane Carol), it is likely that research on shark populations in different areas had yet to be conducted.

In my personal experience and in documented research, it is not common for large numbers of sharks to follow vessels for long periods of time. But there is anecdotal evidence of sharks following fishing/shrimping vessels looking for a free meal. (This has also been observed with dolphins.) While anchored and actively chumming the waters in efforts to tag a shark and identify the population, I have personally witnessed the appearance of many sharks—at times, more than 25. The narrator mentions repeatedly that their vessel dumps waste overboard, and that would be reason for any animal to follow for freebies.

There are repeated mentions of "big gray dorsal fin" or other aspects of the shark being large, in addition to references to a "white belly," which leads me to think they may have been describing a great white shark or potentially a bull shark, although white sharks are more widely known for and specifically described mentioning their white bellies. I have witnessed large numbers of both white sharks and bull sharks, on separate occasions and in separate locations, surrounding chumming vessels.

The injury sustained by the female survivor in the story is an accurate description of what could happen to skin if it rubs along the shark the wrong way. The hard denticles that make up the shark's skin are a protection element, and also assist with hydrodynamics in the water. When rubbed the wrong way, the skin is very rough and is known to cause "shark burn" or "shark rash" on exposed skin.

Sharks tend to be labeled as mindless killing machines, when they actually have complex sensory organs to help aid them in identifying smells and movements in the water. As the author documents the sharks "fighting over" a body in the water, they may have been simply scoping out the situation. At that point in the story, there is now waste, food, and blood in the water, all triggers for the fish to continue to hunt in that area. Humans have very little nutritional value to sharks in comparison to seals, tuna, and other large fish they may hunt. It is likely that if a shark "attacks" a person, the fish will release them nearly instantly, realizing that this is not their intended meal. With the number of other things in the water, and the splashing of the individuals in the water, more sharks may be trying to "test bite" whatever the panicked animal is in the water, human or not.

In addition to description of the sharks, the behaviors mostly jibe with what published literature states and how my own personal experiences with sharks have been. Although numbers of sharks and sizes may be exaggerated for the entertainment factor (and owing to lack of knowledge of shark behavior), this story overall is a fairly accurate description of possible interactions with sharks in that type of disastrous situation.

I strongly urge the public to continue to educate themselves on sharks, their declining numbers on a global scale, and the health of the ocean ecosystem as a whole. The health of the ocean ecosystem relies on balance, from the smallest phytoplankton to the largest apex predators.

Humans have been detrimental to the health of the ocean via overfishing, exploiting resources, coastal development, offshore dumping, pollution from fishing, and pollution from regular communities like yours. Nearly 80% of pollution found in the ocean comes from what we throw away on land, such as food packaging, bottles and cans, tires, etc. Ill-conceived waste management solutions end up allowing more trash to pollute the ocean we rely heavily on for survival, even in landlocked areas of the globe. It is up to us to do better.

FROM THE PAGES OF ARGOSY, JULY 1968
ARGOSY
JULY 50¢
JOHN DOWD'S OWN STORY—
ADVENTURE AT $1.00 A DAY FROM THE ROCKIES TO THE ANDES
HOW YOU CAN ESCAPE FROM MONOTONY TO EXCITEMENT ON A HANDFUL OF MONEY AND PLENTY OF COURAGE
"E Mao Ariki"
STORY BY ROBERT EDMOND ALTER

Beyond the pass, the lagoon of Iliate glimmered like a turquoise mirror enclosed in an oblong frame. The atoll consisted of three long, curving islands, each standing separate from its brother by a short stretch of reef over which the sea washed at knee-depth. Iliate was not large for the Paumotus; its lagoon was only eight miles in length and five in width. It was a sand-covered, sun-flooded, palm-dotted outpost of primitive life, a back-of-the-beyond paradise — if viewed from the surface. But it contained, so legend said, the age-old horror of the world in its sunken blue bowl — E Mao Ariki, the king of sharks, the Shark God.

Dave Phillips pulled his eyes away from the atoll with a fixed look of concern. He wasn't a superstitious man, merely cautious. He didn't believe there was anything supernatural about the shark in Iliate lagoon, but he had fought a shark once (continued on page 56

E MAO ARIKI

FICTION by ROBERT EDMOND ALTER

Illustration by Walter Richards

ART BY WALTER RICHARDS

Beyond the pass, the lagoon of Iliate glimmered like a turquoise mirror enclosed
in an oblong frame. The atoll consisted of three long, curving islands, each standing
separate from its brother by a short stretch of reef over which the sea washed at
knee-depth. Iliate was not large for the Paumotus; its lagoon was only eight miles
in length and five in width. It was a sand-covered, sun-flooded, palm-dotted outpost
of primitive life, a back-of-the-beyond paradise—if viewed from the surface. But
it contained, so legend said, the age-old horror of the world in its sunken blue
bowl—*E Mao Ariki*, the king of sharks, the Shark God.

Dave Phillips pulled his eyes away from the atoll with a fixed look of concern.
He wasn't a superstitious man, merely cautious. He didn't believe there was
anything supernatural about the shark in Iliate lagoon, hut he had fought a shark
once in the Celebes Sea, a ten-foot whaler, and he had no desire to duplicate
the encounter.

Still, a thousand dollars for one dive wasn't the type of proposition one
thumbed one's nose at. Not, he thought, when one has nearly reached the "on-the-
beach" state, as he had at Papeete.

I'm just going down to act as a guard, he told himself for the hundredth time that
day. *I'm just going to stand by and cover Ricky, that's all. Simple.*

He looked aft to the cockpit of the schooner-yacht and saw that Ricky Hare
and Captain Jarvis were still arguing. It had been going on for twenty minutes now.
Jarvis was an old-stager and he had definite ideas about men and the sea.

"I got thirty-eight years time in on this sea," he had told them, "from Singapore
to Callao, and there ain't never been a minute of it spent under the water. Man was
given legs to walk decks with. If the Lord had meant for him to spend his time
under the sea, He would have slapped a pair of gills in his head instead of a pair of
ears. What are you two, anyway—a couple of freaks?"

What are we, indeed? Dave now wondered. Well, in a way, he was like Jarvis—a
professional from Singapore to Callao. The only difference was that he did his
work under the sea, while Jarvis floated along in the sun and wind and spray. And
Ricky Hare?

Ricky was the boy from Hollywood, the money man, the kid with the camera
and with the hot glints of boyish ambition sparking in his forty-year-old eyes. But
he was all nerve, Dave realized. You had to say that. Though perhaps people with
ambition didn't have time for indecision or caution; they couldn't risk a pause along
the way to ponder, *"Is this safe? Is that wise?"* but had to charge straight ahead like a
train on a schedule.

Dave turned back to the atoll wondering if that was what he needed, a little ambition. Their voices drifted to him on a soft zephyr.

"Mr. Hare, I don't give a diddly-damn what you want. You didn't buy this schooner, you know. You only hired her. And as long as she belongs to me, she ain't going through that pass! Why, damn it, man, that's shoal water. You want to sink us?"

"Oh my, oh my," Ricky muttered exasperatedly, voicing a word habit that was incongruous to his bluff, driving manner. "I'm not asking you to sink your stupid scow, Captain. I'm asking you from bended knee to bring her in where we can use her as a base of operations."

He shouldn't have said that to the old man, Dave thought. And then he looked aft again, he saw a deep stain of anger flood Jarvis's florid face. Jarvis stared at Ricky for a count of five, then turned his head to bellow at the Kanaka boys waiting in the bow.

"Let go!"

The anchor chain ground its peculiar scream and the hook struck the water with a *splamp.*

The captain turned back to Ricky with a stiff face. "Is there anything else you want from your bended knee, Mr. Hare?"

Ricky came away with a shake of his head. "Dear, dear, sweet boy," he muttered as he came up to Dave. "Don't you think he's a dear, dear, sweet boy, Dave?"

Dave smiled. "Forget about him. He knows what he's doing. Tell me more about this shark."

Ricky clapped his hands together and his eyes went upward with supplication. "Please, Lord, just this once let the legend be true. Just this one legend for poor, long-suffering, patiently waiting Ricky." Then, the seizure of emotion over, his eyes sparked on Dave.

"A shark out of the past, baby! A shark so rare, he is known only by his Latin name: *Carcharodon rondeliti.* A species of nearly extinct man-eating sharks of great size, relics of prehistoric times. His ancestors, Dave—take a grip on the rail—grew to be *ninety feet long!* They came from the Tertiary seas."

"But you don't believe that this one—"

Ricky flapped his hands in the air. "Oh my, no. This one is reputed to be about forty feet long." Again his eyes rolled toward the sky. "Please, Lord, let him be only *thirty* feet. That's not much to ask."

Then he looked at Dave and winked. "Underwater, he'll magnify to more. Some fish, huh?"

It was an annual game that the youths of Iliate played with the shark god. At the northern end or the lagoon, not more than eleven fathoms deep, was an oyster bed that an obscure Dutch speculator had cultivated years before. The bed was curious in that the oysters were of the gold-lipped variety, a species more at home in the Celebes and Sulu Seas than in the Iles Tuamotu. The bed lay before a rising wall of coral and there was a cave at its foot that was reputed to be the home of the shark god. Each year, the elders of the lliates chose two of their most promising young men to dive down into the purple depths and fill two pearling baskets with the shell.

The game was to get the shell without being caught by *E Mao Ariki*, and unlike most games, you could only get caught once. That was the shark's ruling.

Ricky Hare had heard of the annual test and he had come more than three thousand miles to see and capture the event on film.

Now it was the right day and the right hour, and Dave and Ricky were being rowed by a Kanaka youth across the polished surface of the lagoon. Ricky was still looking over his shoulder at the *Para* riding her anchor westward of the atoll, still grumbling about Jarvis's obstinate nature.

"The old fool could have brought his damn bucket of bilge in here if he'd wanted to. I don't like working out of a loving rowboat. With the schooner, a man can go aboard and flake out when he wants to."

Dave smiled absently, but his mind wasn't on Ricky. He was thinking of the shark. Thirty feet, maybe more. The largest he had ever seen had been a twenty-foot tiger in the Indian Ocean. Thirty feet…

The trouble was he had too much imagination to be a good diver. He was wholeheartedly enamored of the underwater world, but every time he activated the imagery of its hidden dangers, something went out of whack in his solar plexus.

He looked at Ricky, at the cigar in the pouty, baby-lipped mouth, the tinted glasses sparking rose-gold in the sun, the smooth, white swell of stomach that bulged over the tight, floral-print trunks, the stocky, black-haired legs, and thought: *Look at him. No imagination. At least not for human emotions, only for making money. The shark isn't a horror or a man-eater to him in a physical or mental sense, only a spectacle of danger.*

FIFTY yards within nature's mending wall of coral drifted a group of fifteen hibiscus-wood canoes. Five or six natives waited in each canoe for the white men to join them. As the rowboat knifed into the pack, the natives all tried to come alongside in order to inspect Ricky's underwater movie camera.

The two youths who were about to make the annual attempt sat apart from the others and looked slightly contemptuously at the white men and their wonderful metal fish. They were eighteenish—lithe young gods in breathing bronze. Their skins glowed with life; you could almost see it burning in their wide-apart, intelligent and daring eyes.

Looking at them, Dave wondered why they were willing to gamble their lives for a basket of shell. He turned to the Kanaka oarsman.

"Jo-Jo, why do they make this dive?"

The Kanaka looked politely startled, as if he couldn't believe that the whole world didn't know why. He answered Dave in *beche de mer.*

"That fella lagoon belong *E Mao Ariki*, big fella marster. Long time him stop. Long time little bit one fella Metua belong *marae* write Word: say two fella Kanaka belong Iliate take'm fella pearl belong *E Mao*, make'm too much *mea maitai roa* for all fella Kanaka diver."

"Oh, for crysake, Dave!" Ricky complained. "What's all that about?"

Dave grinned. "Long time little bit—which probably means sometime this century—a Kanaka priest called Metua gave out the word that if, at the start of each pearling season, two divers would go down and snitch the shell from under the shark's nose, then all the divers would be guaranteed good luck."

"Yeah?" Ricky was interested. "He said something about this witch doctor writing it, didn't he? Is it a book or something? Maybe l can use it."

Dave shook his head. "Jo-Jo uses the term 'write' loosely. Probably this Metua sprinkled some pebbles and twigs at the foot of his *marae* and made mumbo-jumbo over them. But as long as it's a legend, they have to believe it. They're just made that way."

Ricky winked and began strapping on his scuba. "Makes it nice for the shark, don't it? I hear he's picked off dozens."

Dave looked down at the translucent water. "Yeah. Makes it real nice."

It was a blue room at first, then a green one, and finally a land of purple twilight. Ricky and Dave hovered ten feet above the coral bottom, Ricky angling the fat bat-wing camera upward to catch the divers descent, Dave suspended upright just behind his back with a speargun in his hand. He ran his eyes along the duralumin and steel length of the gun to the small gas-pressure tank in the butt. The barrel held a hollow arrow which was blasted out by the gas and which gained in speed as it traveled, due to the discharging gas in its hollow interior. The harpoon contained a vial of curare poison. Like the camera and the scuba gear and the schooner and Dave, too, the gun had cost Ricky a pretty penny. But money was nothing to the man from Hollywood. Only the picture counted.

The two Kanaka youths came down on shot lines, bare except for their pearling baskets, knives and their horn-andglass diving goggles. As the thirty-pound bulbs of lead they stood on struck the bottom, they let go of their lines and began swimming in a strange, slow-motion rhythm toward the submerged coral wall. Ricky panned the camera with them and started finning, keeping fifteen feet in their rear and a fathom above.

Dave, hitch-kicking along in Ricky's wake, turned his head from time to time to stare uneasily at the shadowy coral surrounding them. Maybe the big bruiser would be away from home. Maybe not.

The lagoon bottom reminded him of a beautiful graveyard. Sepulchral chambers without roofs rose toward the surface, garnished with lacy clusters, ribbed with wicked sawtooth edges, and everywhere the madrepore lay like giant corrugated skulls in the crannies and crevices.

Carcharodon rondeliti. Dave spoke the name in his mouthpiece. His imagination suddenly sideslipped and he saw an absurd picture of a little fuddie-duddie German professor standing before his students, tapping a drawing of a shark on a chart with the end of his lecture stick, saying. "*Carcharodon rondeliti*—the largest, most ferocious, least-known shark in the world." And here he was playing in the monster's front yard!

Suddenly the oyster bed spread out below them as far as the circular horizon of wan pink light would permit. They could see the shells now—fat, coral-encrusted, roundish lumps, fully eight inches across—and looming before them was the pitted and castled wall of coral. The shell bed sloped up to the coral rampart like a beach shelving to a sea cliff, and at the top and shaped like a black heart turned upside down was the cave, the so-called home of *E Mao Ariki*.

The shadows of the divers settled over the bed, and the two youths went to work wrenching the *mararitifera*, the pearl oyster, free from its hold on the bottom.

Ricky circled them once, pausing to catch a close view of the cave's mouth, then drifted on to get the divers at their work from different angles. Sparkling haze of small reef fish appeared without warning and veered off sharply for the open lagoon just as they were about to break over Dave.

He turned slowly in a tight circle, wary and tense. He had that something-is-coming feeling in his nerve center. The reef fish might have been the vanguard of something big.

He saw the shadow first. It was like a gigantic ink blotch spilled over the slope. He looked up and felt his heart lurch. The shark was hanging in the water two fathoms above the bed, its curiously myopic eyes extended and startled. The eyes looked angry. They seemed to be asking: *What the hell is coming off here?*

Absently, Dave realized that the Lord had been good to Ricky Hare. The shark was all of thirty feet long, maybe more.

He turned his head quickly and saw Ricky's eyes behind the face mask, wide and staring, and then saw him aim the eye of the Kodak on the shark with the Latin name. But his legs had swung up under the camera and he was already backfinning, as if death and violence had suddenly become a very personal thing.

"*Run, fat boy,*" Dave said, under his breath. But it was childish to try to restrict fear to Ricky. It was a personal thing with all of them, and each man was on his own.

The Kanaka divers abandoned the shell and their baskets and swam off awkwardly for the crevices in the coral. There they turned, crouched in the wavering shadows—and waited.

God, Dave thought. *How long can they hold their breath?*

The shark made up its mind and gave a flick of its tail and shot forward in a long brown streak of color. One of the Kanakas raised to a somewhat standing position, with his knife in the tight square of his fist, and faced the onslaught. *David and Goliath*, Dave thought. But this time the stone would miss.

You have the gun, he told himself. *Use the damn thing!*

He started forward. A hand caught his shoulder and pulled him back, and he looked up and around. Ricky was holding him and was squeaking a high-pitched, distorted sound into his mouthpiece and shaking his head urgently. Abruptly he let Dave go and started finning upward, his stocky legs chopping at the water.

Dave was suspended in a little glassy ball of shock and indecision. He couldn't believe what he saw.

The shark rolled slightly and took the first Kanaka by the middle, not giving a damn about the piddly little knife trying to dent his hide, and peeled off across the roofless coral rooms shaking the forward part of his body as a dog shakes a rat, the Kanaka's arms and legs kicking and reaching and grabbing at nothing. And then the shark let the body go—and you could hardly even call it a body by then—and curved around in a smooth, quick turn, his jaws working on what he had taken and spitting out fragments of it as he came, and Dave couldn't guess if he was coming back to hit him next or the other boy, and he wasn't going to wait to see. He got out frantically.

WITH Jo-Jo's excited help, he piled into the boat and sagged into a soggy heap of nerves in the stern. He spat the mouthpiece out and pushed the mask onto his forehead and that was all he could do. Ricky had already shed his lung and was now pawing among the litter at his feet for a cigar. His hands were trembling badly.

"Oh my, oh *my*, have you *evah* seen anything like that?" Ricky looked at the rocking water where the blood was beginning to stain the surface. "Too bad l lost my nerve," he said (and his tone seemed to hint that he was surprised he had), "or I could have caught a few feet of the action."

Dave got his eyes off the scarlet water and put them on Ricky. "That's a damn shame. Shall l have one of the boys put his leg over the side for you? Maybe you can get a shot of the shark taking it off. Go on. Rick, slip one of them a few bucks. Money buys anything, you know."

Ricky looked at him sharply. "Take it easy, baby. I didn't ask the kid to go down there. This is a business to me…"

"How was your business when you first saw that Carcharodon of yours? Did you see all of him, fat boy? Did you get all thirty feet in your damn camera? What did you run for? You missed the best part. You bunged out just when he chopped the kid in two."

RICKY hunched forward, his hands grasping the gunwales. "Close your goddamn mouth, sweetheart. Or maybe you want me to reach out and do it for you?"

"Why don't you suck some courage through that cigar or yours and come try it?" Dave snapped.

"*A haere!*" Jo-Jo suddenly shouted to the canoes. "Go on! *E Mao Ariki!*"

Dave forgot about Ricky and looked over the side. The giant shark was rising like a tossed shadow toward the keel of the boat. "Pull, Jo-Jo!" he shouted.

No one had to tell the Kanaka. He was already on the oars and his arms seemed to swell as if injected with air. But he was frightened and rattled. and he brought the bow of the boat into the cluster of outriggers.

Instantly, there was mass confusion a, cries of *"Aue!"* *"A hio!"* and *"Ho viti-viti!"* ripped the air around them, and men were moving everywhere, waving paddles, reaching for balance. Then the shark struck the boat and propelled it farther into the jumble or outriggers, starting a dozen seams in the planking.

"Hey! What that the hell?" Ricky cried, his eyes leaping wildly in his white face.

"*Tapea maitai!*" Jo-Jo shouted, and Dave yelled, "Hang on!" at Ricky. "That bugger is going to kick us out of the water… *Hoe!* Paddle, Jo-Jo!"

The shark was at the surface now. Swimming in a swift zigzag, its tall dorsal fin like a tan jibsail knifing through the water. Dave crouched in the stern with the gun. his eyes fixed on the rushing fin. He raised the gun and started panning it with the shark.

And right then, a crew of frantic natives shoved their outrigger between the boat and the shark, and as Dave shouted at then, to get the hell out of the way, the shark sounded. Then he saw two of the Kanakas leap to their feet and point down at the water. *"Aue!"* they cried.

For a split second. he couldn't understand what was wrong—why all six natives were rising from their haunches and springing into the air at him. Then be heard the crash as the outrigger went over and the Kanakas came spilling down willy-nilly into the rowboat, and felt the bow going up and sliding off at the same time as the boar canted crazily to port. And he saw the camera spin into the air, like a fat stubby airplane heading for a crash, and Ricky's wide-flung hand snatching for it, and then he was caught in a human kaleidoscope of gleaming brown arms and legs and a paddle blade and the swift shock of crashing water.

He began finning as soon as he was underwater, kicking his way through the wiggling tangle of Kanakas and equipment. At two fathoms, he leveled off to adjust the mask over his eyes and nose. Then he turned on the two-stage regulator mounted on lop of the aluminum cylinders and brought the bubbling mouthpiece up to his mouth. as if he were taking a drink from a garden hose, and swallowed some godawful briny water; and then he started to breathe.

He cleared the flooded mask by exerting air pressure through his nose and took a quick look around. All he could sec was the empty blue of the water. He jackknifed and started down again.

While the others were struggling in the confusion above, the shark wouldn't bother him. With the scuba, he could cut back across the bottom and reach the coral wall again and go on up. Once he was safely on the island, he had merely to wait for an outrigger lo take him off.

But there was a catch.

Ile looked at his right hand. The jet-propulsion gun was still clutched in his greenish fist. Out of a possible seventy-five men in and on the lagoon, the gun was the only weapon that might stop the shark. And he was running away with it.

He closed both hands on the gun and stopped finning. His mind jammed in a jumble of fear and contrition and he tilted his head up toward the surface. The depth diffused color, distorted objects. He saw only the silvered whorl of the sun-struck surface, broken by black shapes treading and thrashing around.

The camera was drifting down like a pregnant manta ray. He watched absently, then spotted something else descending in a loose spiral. It was the shark, dragging a dead Kanaka in its razor-rimmed maw, shaking the body angrily.

The camera passed through the shark's limited field of vision and the monster braked to a stop all at once and eyed the gliding object curiously, the dead Kanaka dangling abjectly from its mouth. Then it spat out the torn-up body and shot after the metal fish.

The tickling finger of terror that traced its cold path up Dave's spine ran out in his hairline and left him. It was suddenly inconceivable to him that this amoral, cold-blooded, witless freak was going to continue to gut and eat and kill living men. Then he knew that he could no longer accept the existence of this man-eater who was turning the lagoon into a blood bowl.

Almost without a conscious will of his own, Dave started toward the shark.

The shark snapped at the camera, just before it touched bottom. But he was disappointed. He shook his blunt snout and let the Kodak go. Then he made a sweep with his great heterocercal tail and nosed up for the surface.

Dave hooted into his mouthpiece.

The shark turned off course and eyed the skin diver.

Dave backfinned, rolled and then jack-knifed for the bottom. Seven quick flips of his fins brought him into the coral wonderland. It was like a romantic youth's dream of lost Atlantis. Chambers and corridors and vaults and courtyards, castles and spires and turrets. He darted here, there, under and around and over and through, and every time he looked back, he saw the damned shark coming like a dirigible in a purple sunset.

A collection of parrotfish and nailfish were startled at their dinner plates of coral and madrepore as he came charging toward them. *Run, you damn fools, run!* he said. And they did, spattering themselves into little separate dabs of color fleeing down the shadowy alleyways. And he only hoped that Ricky and all the Kanakas had been as wise, had regained the canoes and made for the safety of the island. Because the chase had run out of time.

The coral city seemed to shrivel in on itself and fall away beneath him. The slope was rising to the shell bed, to the looming wall and the cave. He looked back to see if he'd lost the monster in the coral jungle, and if he had time to reach the surface. But he hadn't and he didn't. The big boy cruised sleekly through a fluted archway, opened its mouth and came on.

Dave hooted wildly and the exhaust shot up a fat cloud of air bubbles. The shark spread its pectorals and came to a graceful halt. It eyed the wobbling, elongated bubbles and the skin diver.

Dave turned and suspended upright in the water, holding the gun horizontally. *Don't come yet, fish,* he said. *Think about what might happen to one of us.* But he knew it was hopeless because the shark had tasted blood and the red fever was in its brain.

The shark opened its mouth and burst forward from a full stop like a bolt of crooked lightning.

Dave yelled all his air into the hose, leaned into the gun and squeezed the trigger. He felt the spear take off through the barrel and heard the gun go *taaznnng*, and the last thing he saw clearly was that damned gaping mouth with the double row of jagged teeth like tall, white, peaked hoods. Then there was a burst of darkness in front of his mask, the lens smashed into his nose and cheekbones. and his arms jerked up as though he'd gripped a high-voltage wire. Then the backwash displaced by the shark's rushing passage struck him full front and bowled him over backward.

He spun off in a loose somersault, vacuum-packed and helpless, the accordion-like flexible hoses whipping uselessly above his head and spewing out great bulbs of silver, For one vivid moment. he saw again the fuddie-duddie German professor's face staring at him aghast, and distinctly heard the little fellow cry: *"I said, the most ferocious shark in the world!"*

He drifted across the top of a giant coral mushroom in a glassy, shimmering ball of shock. His fins scraped the coral and something stirred in his brain and started to work. It didn't attempt to dictate to his legs, arms or fingers; that was hopeless. Instead, it teletyped a thin, rapid message clown to his lungs: *Don't breathe…You've lost the hose.* All right. That was good advice, but how long was he supposed to slob around without breathing?

Just as long as it takes you to reach for the hose.

So he did it and the glassy ball popped and he was all right again.

The shark was twisting off across a staghorn bed, bending its great body into one violent S-shape after another as it whipped through the crumbling, brittle branches. Its erratic passage painted livid streaks of crimson along the way. And then it was swallowed by the shadows.

Dave hitch-kicked for the surface.

RICKY helped him over the gunwale and then lit a cigarette for him and placed it in his mouth. They were alone in the drifting boat. The outriggers had reached the island and all the Kanakas were standing in a jabbering line along the shore, pointing at the lagoon.

"Why didn't you beat it ashore with the others?" Dave asked. "Did you stick out here with some wacky idea of helping me?'"

Ricky made a face and shrugged. "Hell, that's nothing. Look at old man Jarvis. He's risking his precious schooner to get in here to us."

Dave looked toward the distant pass and was somehow pleased to see the *Para* working its way into the lagoon on auxiliary power. "The old boy must like us, after all,'" he said. Then he turned to Ricky. "You lost your camera. I saw it on the bottom."

Ricky robbed at his face wearily. "Yeah. Will you get it for me, Dave? It's worth an extra hundred to you." His voice trailed off and left a painful silence behind. He lowered his eyes.

"That's all right. Rick. I'll get it for you later. You going after more sharks?"

Ricky shook his head slowly. "Nope. No more sharks. When I got knocked into the water, I saw that damned thing take the boy who was right next to me. Right next to me. I saw it that time—saw those jaws take… No, I don't want any more of that sort of thing. The story's finished for me."

Dave said nothing. He looked at the red water reflectively. The story was finished for all of them, for good. He had written the last chapter. ▼

BITING BACK   commentary

There *was* such a creature as *Carcharodon rondeliti* (more commonly, the *mackerel shark*), but its last swim was a little over 65 million years ago, in the Cenozoic era. A huge prehistoric shark species similar to Megalodon, the prehistoric giant shark that became famous in novels and movies decades after this story was published, *Carcharodon* is long extinct, with no sightings, official or otherwise, reported outside the pages of *Argosy* circa 1968.

And while the people of Tahiti *did* originally refer to the Polynesian island chain now known as the Tuamotus as the Paumotus, the name used in the story, that about wraps up the story's factual elements. The notion that *Carcharodon rondeliti* may have survived the centuries? The daring ritual ceremony, and the disastrous attempt to document it? Pure MAM hokum.

Author Robert Edmond Alter had a short life and writing career. He didn't become a professional writer until his thirties, after brief stints as a farm worker, soldier, and movie extra. He died at age 40. However, during his final decade, he penned several novels that have become cult classics, including *Carny Kill* and *Swamp Sister* (both published 1966) and the seminal post-apocalyptic science fiction novel *Path to Savagery* (1969), later adapted as the 1979 movie *The Ravagers*, starring Richard Harris and Ernest Borgnine. Alter also wrote scores of short stories for mystery and crime digest magazines like *Alfred Hitchcock's Mystery Magazine*, *Manhunt*, and *Mike Shayne Mystery Magazine*, and for MAMs like *Adventure* and *Argosy*. The luminous art below by Jack Hearne illustrates an earlier shark tale by Alter published in *Argosy* in 1960, "Monster of the Madrepore."

ARGOSY July 1960 Art by Jack Hearne

The July 1969 issue of **For Men Only** brought readers the same harrowing scene interpreted by two of the most admired illustrators of the MAM era. **Bruce Minney** works in vivid colors for the cover *(right)*, while **Samson Pollen** applies his trademark dynamism to the monochrome interior spread *(original artwork below)*.

For Men Only July 1969 Cover art by Bruce Minney

For Men Only July 1969 Art by Samson Pollen

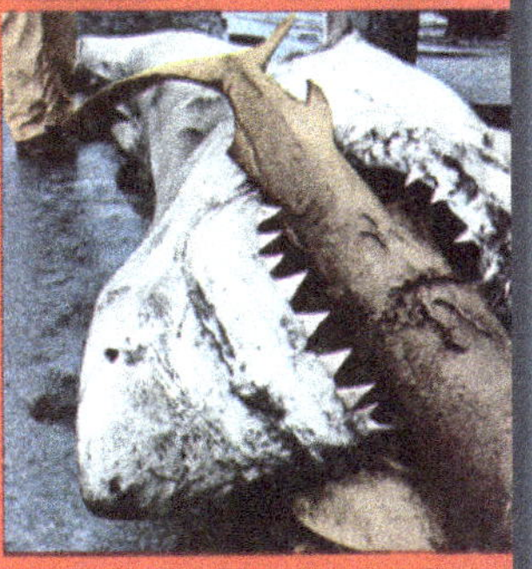

"US Shark Epidemic Coming This Summer!"

STORY BY PETER COURTNEY   COVER ART BY BRUCE MINNEY

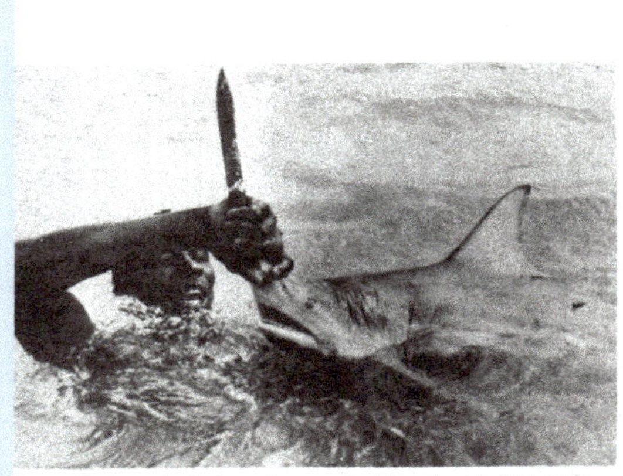

A sharp knife is useless against the shark's thick hide as a wound in a vital area only makes them more vicious.

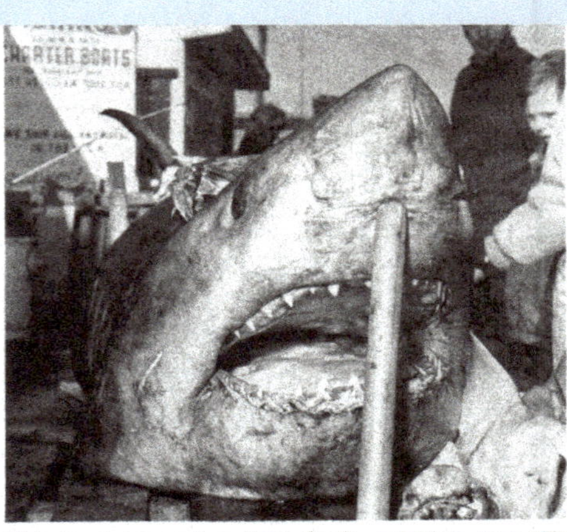

This huge man-eating tiger shark, weighing over 1500 pounds, was caught in fishing nets off Maine's coast.

Top Oceanographers' Alarming Report:

U.S. SHARK EPIDEMIC COMING THIS SUMMER!

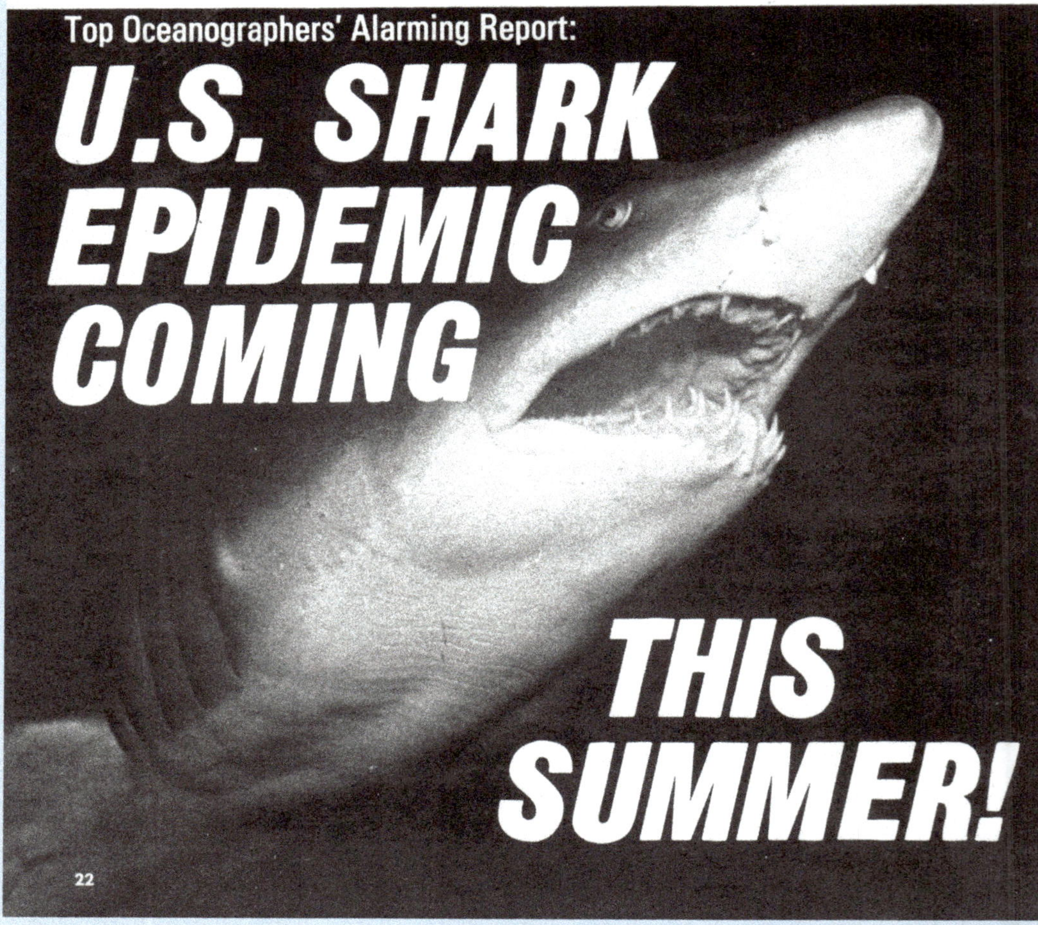

22

By PETER COURTNEY

FRANK Phillips stood waist-deep in the crystal blue surf of the Gulf of Mexico, enjoying his casting, but unaware of the fish blood that dotted the water from his latest catch.

Suddenly, something slammed against his thigh—something hard, cold and heavy.

Phillips was thrown under the water. The wind knocked out of him, he gasped for breath. Dazed, he managed to right himself, but suddenly he felt searing pain that started somewhere below his waist. Within seconds it felt as though his whole body was being torn apart.

All at once he realized what had happened. He'd been attacked by a shark! Phillips let out a scream of pain and terror that shattered the serenity of the summer Sunday at the beach. The sunbathers and swimmers frolicking on Padre Island, a thin spit of land that runs all along the Texas Gulf Coast, watched with horror as Phillips thrashed in the water.

Meanwhile, as the silent killer of the deep prepared to strike again, Bob Lauer of Harlingen, Texas, who was swimming in the surf reacted swiftly when he heard Phillips' screams. Without a thought for his own safety, he stroked to the injured man's side.

The water, stained bright red with Phillips' blood, was churning all around the critically injured fisherman and his eight-foot-long attacker.

Again and again, Phillips struck at the shark with his flimsy fishing rod. Again and again, the shark struck back, digging his razor-sharp teeth into Phillips' leg.

"The water was boiling all around him," Lauer said afterward. And even while I was pulling him to the shore, the shark hit him once on the leg—and then again."

Lauer managed to pull Phillips to shore, and grabbing a towel he rigged up an improvised tourniquet on what was left of the fisherman's right leg. Much of the flesh had been ripped away and the severed arteries squirted bright red (Continued on page 40)

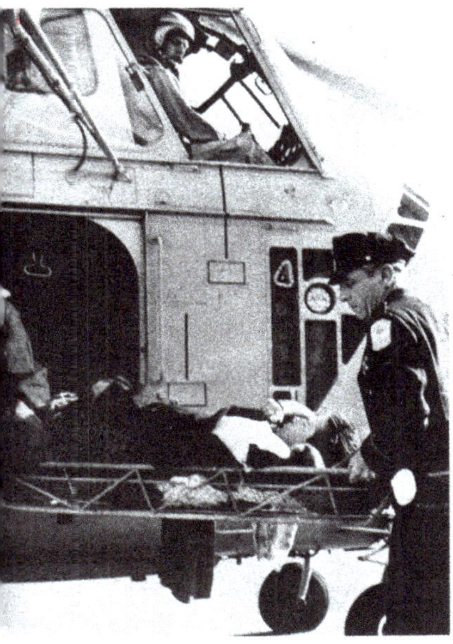

This young man was mangled moments before in a shark attack 26 miles west of the Golden Gate.

Because of the rising frequency of shark attacks, authorities have warned cruise parties not to swim in shark infested waters.

From Long Island Sound to California beaches, sharks, the most vicious of creatures, are now on a wild rampage for human flesh.

23

Frank Phillips stood waist-deep in the crystal blue surf of the Gulf of Mexico, enjoying his casting, but unaware of the fish blood that dotted the water from his latest catch.

Suddenly, something slammed against his thigh—something hard, cold and heavy.

Phillips was thrown under the water. The wind knocked out of him, he gasped for breath. Dazed, he managed to right himself, but suddenly he felt searing pain that started somewhere below his waist. Within seconds it felt as though his whole body was being torn apart.

All at once he realized what had happened. He'd been attacked by a shark! Phillips let out a scream of pain and terror that shattered the serenity of the summer Sunday at the beach. The sunbathers and swimmers frolicking on Padre Island, a thin spit of land that runs all along the Texas Gulf Coast, watched with horror as Phillips thrashed in the water.

Meanwhile, as the silent killer of the deep prepared to strike again, Bob Lauer of Harlingen, Texas, who was swimming in the surf reacted swiftly when he heard Phillips' screams. Without a thought for his own safety, he stroked to the injured man's side.

The water, stained bright red with Phillips' blood, was churning all around the critically injured fisherman and his eight-foot-long attacker.

Again and again, Phillips struck at the shark with his flimsy fishing rod. Again and again, the shark struck back, digging his razor-sharp teeth into Phillips' leg.

"The water was boiling all around him," Lauer said afterward. "And even while I was pulling him to the shore, the shark hit him once on the leg—and then again."

Lauer managed to pull Phillips to shore, and grabbing a towel, he rigged up an improvised tourniquet on what was left of the fisherman's right leg. Much of the flesh had been ripped away and the severed arteries squirted bright red blood over the yellow sand.

Onlookers stared in horror. Mrs. Phillips, frantic and frightened, tried to shield her children from seeing the grisly sight. When the telephoned ambulance arrived, Phillips was taken to the nearby office of Dr. J.A. Hockaday in Port Isabel. But it was too late. Twenty minutes after he was placed on the operating table, Frank Phillips had died from shock and the loss of blood.

Dr. Hockaday, who'd been practicing medicine in the Texas town for 43 years, had treated all kinds of injuries and had seen many men die all kinds of horrible deaths, but the Phillips tragedy was the most grisly of the lot. It was the doctor's opinion that the blood from Phillips' catch had attracted the marine killer. Every now and then, the doctor added, he'd treated persons who'd been bitten on the hands while trying to remove sharks from their fishing lines. "But this full bodied attack was something different."

According to the Shark Research Panel of the American Institute of Biological Sciences, unprovoked shark attacks along the nation's ocean beaches are becoming more frequent with each passing year, and it is generally predicted that the summer of '70 may produce more shark attack victims than that of any previous recorded year.

In one recent year, the Shark Research Panel received reports of attacks from all parts of the globe—in the waters off both coasts of the United States; off Hawaii, the Philippines and other Pacific islands; off Bermuda in the Atlantic; off both South and East Africa in the waters of the Indian Ocean; and in the Persian Gulf and Mediterranean Sea. In one case, a shark attack was recorded 100 miles upstream in the supposedly fresh and safe waters of the Limpopo River in East Africa.

Let's look at some more cases:

Mrs. Marion Leaf, 35, was fishing with her husband from a 36-foot cabin cruiser off California's Santa Catalina Island when she fell overboard. By the time Gordon Leaf managed to turn the boat around, she'd been devoured by sharks.

Raymond Short, 13, was swimming in the surf near Sydney, Australia, when an eight-foot shark dug its teeth into his leg. It took four lifeguards to carry the boy to shore, and four others to haul in the shark, which had to be beaten to death with an oar before it released its grip on the boy's leg. Raymond survived, but he may be crippled for life.

Michael Roman, 24, was attacked by a shark while swimming 20 yards off shore at Manasquan, New Jersey. "It didn't hurt at all—at first," he recalled from his hospital bed. "When it hit my thigh, there was no pain—just a thud, like how you feel when a man stealing base crashes into you. But when that shark got my wrist, I really felt it."

The examples are endless.

But all too often with shark stories, there's no account to tell, simply because there's no one left to relate it. This was the tragic case of nine fishermen whose 25-foot cabin cruiser capsized in shark-infested waters five miles off Newport Beach, California. The bodies of three were never found. The bodies of five others were mangled almost beyond recognition. The ninth died by drowning— presumably when a shark pulled him under the surface. "We'll never know exactly what happened in his case," said Coroner Eugene Miller.

Meanwhile, the main reason for the annual increase in shark attacks is the increasing availability of human bait. With more people in the world, more money to spend and more free time to spend it in, water sports have zoomed in popularity. When warm weather comes, millions of persons rush like lemmings to the water's edge—to swim or surf, to skin dive or spearfish, to paddle a kayak or sail a yacht, to sail the deep and troll for tuna, or merely to stand along the shore and cast a line into the surf like hapless Frank Phillips did.

And the sharks, millions of them, lie waiting. And if you think that figure's an exaggeration, consider this fact: in one recent year, the shark catch in US coastal waters alone was close to 2,000,000.

ONE NEVER knows where and when a shark will strike. And when one does, there's little or no hope of escape. The chances of survival are extremely thin. Some scientists speculate that only one out of three persons attacked by sharks lives to tell about it. And the "lucky" one is likely to be scarred or crippled for life.

That's why the cry of *"Shark!"* strikes terror into the heart of even the bravest or most foolhardy swimmer.

One professional diver, who often has occasion to plunge into dangerous shark infested waters, summed up his attitude toward sharks in this flip way: "I always carry a carefully honed 10-inch knife with me when I go under water. If a shark went for me, I'd pull out the knife, grit my teeth…then carefully slit my throat."

According to most marine biologists, little is known about sharks, and what isn't known about them would fill volumes. Shark research is still in its infancy, and it's only been in the last 25 years or so that the experts have gotten down to the nitty-gritty of finding out what sharks are like, why they behave the way they do—and, most important, what men can do to prevent or repel their attacks.

The great impetus to this research effort came in World War II when millions of American servicemen had to fly over or sail through shark-infested waters. A well-placed torpedo, machine-gun burst, or fresh bait was generally sufficient to drive off the vicious man-eaters; but for those unfortunates who survived a shark attack, it remains a grim and terrifying memory. Meanwhile, these cases have provided scientists with thousands of accounts of how sharks behave toward humans.

Typical of such war-time narratives is the account of Lt. (j.g.) A.G. Reading, who had to ditch his plane in the Pacific. 65 miles off Wallis Island. Reading was knocked unconscious by the impact of the crash landing, but his radioman, E.H. Almond, managed to pull him from the cockpit before the plane sank.

"After I came to," Reading later reported to Coast Guard authorities, "Almond told me the plane had sunk in two minutes and that he didn't have time to salvage the life raft. He pulled both our dye markers and had a parachute alongside of him. I don't know how it happened, but Almond was minus his pants. But he was wearing shorts.

"After a bit we soon lost the 'chute and began drifting away from the dye that stained the water. About an hour-and-a-half later sharks appeared, swimming around us. Since we were tied together by the dye-marker cords, it was difficult to outmaneuver the monsters.

"About an hour later, we heard aircraft. I suggested that we kick and splash— to do something to try to attract the pilot's attention. This failed. Suddenly, I heard Almond cry out, that he had felt something strike his right foot and it was beginning to pain.

"I told him to get on my back and keep his right foot out of the water. But before he could, the sharks—this time there were more of them—struck again and we were both jerked under water for a second. I knew we were in for it then, because I counted five more sharks and there was blood all around us.

"But they kept striking at us. Once, we both went under and I found myself separated from Almond. I also caught a number of wallops across the cheek by one of the shark's flying tails. Almond's head was under water, and I could see his body jerk as the sharks hit at it. As I drifted away, helpless to lend Almond a hand, the sharks continually swam about. Every now and then I could feel one with my foot. At midnight I sighted a (patrol) boat and was rescued after calling for help."

FROM the raw data of these harrowing accounts scientists have amassed a mine of material about shark behavior. Reading's narrative, for example, helped verify that sharks often circle their prey for hours before attacking, and that victims who are fully clothed are less likely to be attacked. Also, that the spilling of blood can excite the sharks to a frenzy, and that they tend to center on the weakest victim while often allowing the stronger to escape.

From thousands of such accounts, the scientists started compiling a pattern. of shark behavior—and ways to deal with the killers.

But, so far, no method of repelling or averting shark attacks has met with any major success. Still the earliest and most famous of these anti-shark devices is the shark repellent of World War II. It was nothing more than a mixture of copper acetate and a water-soluble black dye. The copper acetate supposedly carries an odor that's offensive to sharks. The dark dye works like an octopus' spray of ink, creating an unknown world where sharks fear to enter.

Originally, the dye was tested in a pool. As it spread through the water, the shark kept circling, retreating all the while until at last he cowered in the only clear untouched corner of the pool.

The dye also has another use—it tends to camouflage the swimmer. On the same basis, dark clothing may also obscure human prey from a shark's vision. But bright colors—especially reds and yellows—tend to attract a shark.

Still, sharks have been known to swim through dyes and chemical repellants. And such devices are of little use in rough water, when the concentration is too quickly scattered. And, as we have seen in Lt. Reading's case, the current may often carry a swimmer outside the dye-stained area.

Accordingly, other devices have been created to try to protect beach areas from sharks.

One of these was the "bubble fence" set-up at several New Jersey beaches. This was created after deep-sea divers noticed that sharks were afraid to swim through their own trail of air bubbles they leave behind. So pipes were run into the water, blocking off the swimming area, and air pumped into them bubbled to the surface through tiny holes. The manager of one New Jersey resort boasted that the bubble screen was "absolutely impenetrable by sharks."

But when Dr. Perry W. Gilbert, a Cornell University marine expert, tested such a screen on 11 sharks, ten of them swain right through it.

Another device, which has won wide use at Australian beaches, is a nylon mesh net hung from a buoyed line and completely enclosing a swimming area. This has proved fairly successful. But some sharks have been known to cut their way through the mesh, and in rough waters others have been lifted bodily over the barrier.

The newest shark-repellent device was developed last year by Dr. C. Scott Johnson of the Naval Ordinance Test Station's Marine Biology Facility at Point Magu, California. It consists of an inflatable black plastic bag which is carried in a small package on a sailor's life jacket. It expands to a container five feet long and three feet wide which completely envelopes a cast-away.

In addition to keeping shark-attracting human scents safely inside, the bag also helps keep its user warm by conserving body heat, in much the same manner as a scuba diver's wet suit. Also, Dr. Johnson added, "The man is relieved of the mental and physical strain that accompanies the expectation of a shark attack."

Tests of the bag were made at the Hawaiian Institute of Marine Biology. Two bags were anchored in a shark tank, which contained two gray sharks—one six feet long, the other seven. Pieces of fish were thrown into the tank near the bags and the sharks went into a feeding frenzy. But the sharks avoided the bags, doing little more than grazing against them.

As RESULT of the tests, the Navy rates Dr. Johnson's bag "far superior" to any other known shark repellent.

But it's a bit awkward for the average swimmer, skin-diver or fisherman to carry Dr. Johnson's bag around with them. Few who wallow in the water for pleasure would want to be burdened by such a device, no matter how safe it is.

Meanwhile, what can an individual do to protect himself in the event of an attack?

The Shark Research Panel suggests the following rules:

1. Always dive with a companion.
2. Don't spear, ride or hang on to the tail of any shark.
3. Remove all speared fish from the water immediately, since blood attracts sharks.

Dr. Gilbert adds the following bit of advice if sharks come into close range: "A shark can be run off by a sharp release of bubbles. Shouting under water may discourage it. A clout on the snout will often repel a shark, but use your bare hands only as a last resort."

But one shark expert says all such instructions are for the most part ineffective. "You won't be able to follow them," he explains. "You won't have a chance to slam a rampaging shark on the snout and still leave the water. It also won't do much good to straight-arm a rogue shark with your best Sunday punch, because sharks don't retreat that readily if aroused, Besides, you'd only offer your arm as an appetizer."

The expert offered some other reasons to avoid close-in clashes with sharks—even with a knife: "A friendly arm thrown over a shark's back will cause its owner to lose a lot of blood, because sharkskin is a lot like sandpaper.

"Stabbing a shark in its vitals with a handy sheath knife sounds marvelous, but I've tried to dissect sharks when their bodies were stretched out harmlessly on a dock, and their hearts were difficult to find even under these ideal conditions. And they're also capable of biting off an arm or a leg even after their stomach organs have been removed."

In short, even the experts agree, all the rules can be boiled down to one—and one which doesn't even have to be memorized and remembered:

When you see a shark, forget the rules and just do what comes naturally.

Run!

Get out of the water and get out fast.

Remember, sharks are killers and you don't want to be their next victim. ▼

BITING BACK commentary

CHUCK BANGLEY, PhD: There's a mix in this article of things that have changed and things that have (somewhat) stayed the same. One thing that has definitely changed is the state of knowledge about sharks. In 1970 when this article was originally published, the field of shark research was still very much in its early stages. Shark research really took off in the wake of World War II and was largely focused on helping shipwrecked sailors avoid the attentions of sharks as they waited for rescue. Fortunately, this led to the early research on shark sensory capabilities, behavior, feeding habits, and habitat use that has expanded into the much wider field it is today.

Sadly, one thing that hasn't changed as much as one would think is the perception of sharks as inherently dangerous, and this article *really* leans into it. While one named shark expert, Dr. Perry Gilbert, gives well-reasoned advice that mostly still holds up today, another (suspiciously unnamed) "expert" is quoted to provide the counterpoint that a swimmer is basically doomed the second a shark notices them. While this correctly rings as ridiculous hyperbole, it's not too far off from what can be heard in the more sensationalist Shark Week installments of the last few years. That said, the general attitude of people towards sharks has shifted in a much more positive direction. The diver quoted as saying that he would rather slit his own throat than face a shark underwater (yeesh) would be very surprised to see the number of divers traveling from across the world to places like the Bahamas, South Africa, and Australia to dive with sharks on purpose.

Previously unpublished reference photos from Mort Künstler's archives show the athletic artist as his own model circa 1956, posing for shark encounters in the safety of his backyard.

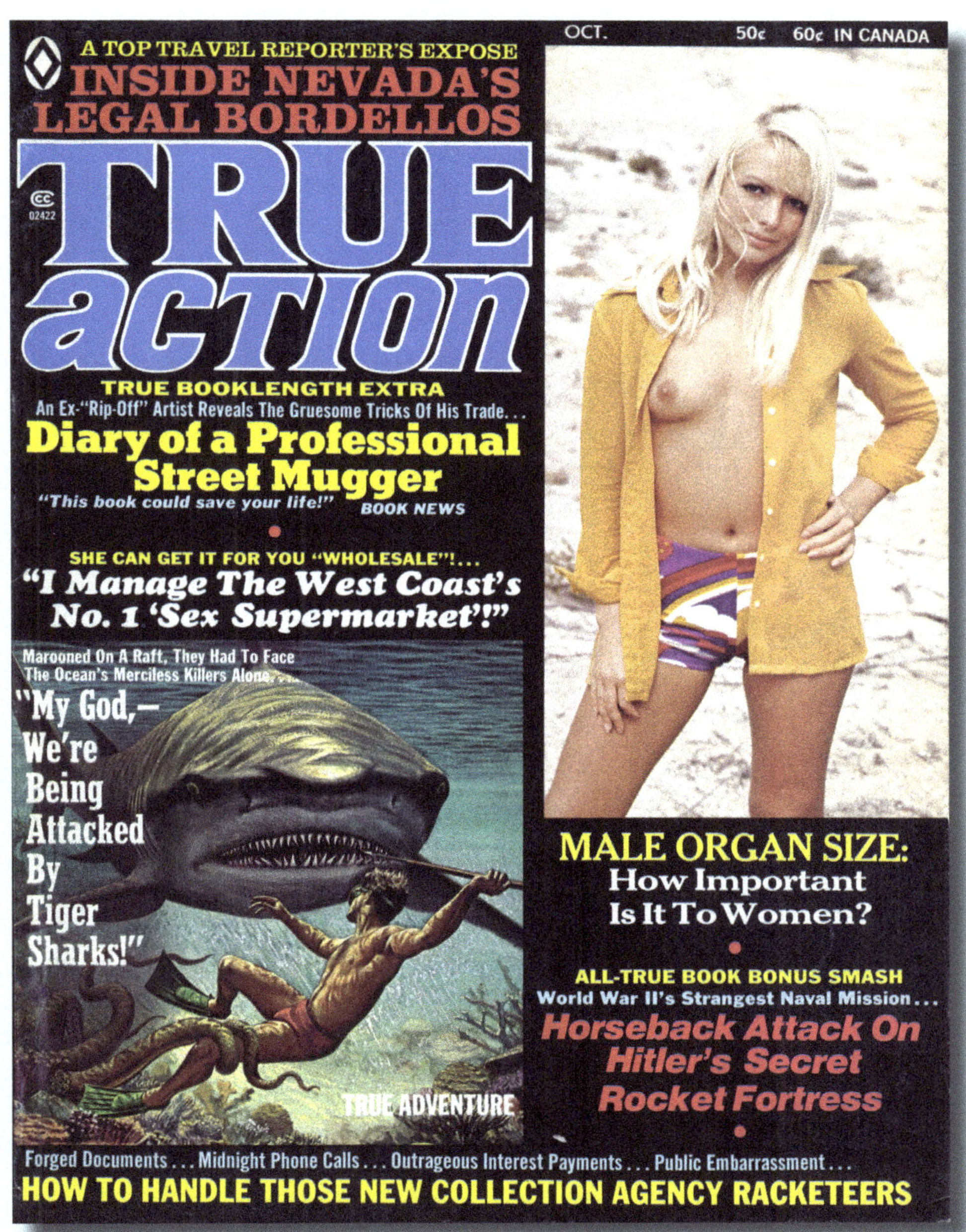

"My God—We're Being Attacked by Tiger Sharks!"

STORY BY TOM CHRISTOPHER   COVER ART BY MORT KÜNSTLER

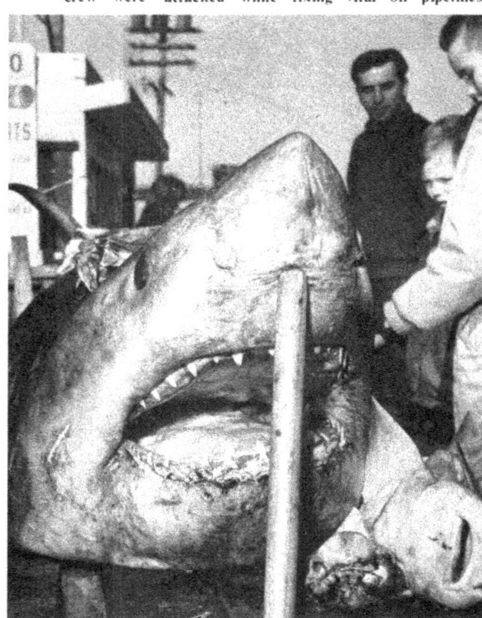

BY Tom Christopher

Marooned Under Tons Of Water, They Had To Face The Ocean's Most Merciless Killers Alone!

Frenzied by the sight or smell of blood, sharks will attack with blind fury, their double rows of razor-sharp teeth instantly mutilating anything in their path *(above)*. Shark below had been terrorizing swimmers at a beach on Gulf Coast, only a few miles from the spot where Sturges and his crew were attacked while fixing vital oil pipelines.

The blood-thirsty sharks could massacre them all in seconds—but they had to repair the pipeline or go to their oily grave . . . !

16

J ack Sturges braced himself on the heaving deck of the barge, shifting his weights from leg to leg to maintain his balance, as the two men lifted the aqualung cylinder and fitted it to his back, carefully adjusting the webbed harness until the cylinder fit tight over the gleaming, black, rubber wetsuit he wore, Sturges clamped the rubber mouthpiece between his teeth and released the air valve. He sampled

"MY GOD-- WE'RE BEING ATTACKED BY TIGER SHARKS!"

the oxygen supply until he was satisfied with the aqualung's performance, then shut the valve off and removed the mouthpiece.

Three other divers, also outfitted in wetsuits and aqualungs, stood a few feet away from him on the deck, waiting for him to give them the word to go over the side. Before he did, Sturges crossed to the bow and, using a pair of binoculars, scanned the surface of the water for any sign of the dark dorsal fins of the two tiger sharks that had been circling the barge earlier. He didn't spot thé sharks, but he still felt uneasy.

"I don't want any slipups down there," he told the waiting divers. "If you spot a shark, no hesitation. Get in the damned cages."

The barge crew had already lowered the four huge iron counter-shark *(Continued on page 44)*

17

131

Jack Sturges braced himself on the heaving deck of the barge, shifting his
weights from leg to leg to maintain his balance as the two men lifted the aqualung
cylinder and fitted it to his back, carefully adjusting the webbed harness until
the cylinder fit tight over the gleaming black rubber wetsuit he wore. Sturges
clamped the rubber mouthpiece between his teeth and released the air valve. He
sampled the oxygen supply until he was satisfied with the aqualung's performance,
then shut the valve off and removed the mouthpiece.

Three other divers, also outfitted in wetsuits and aqualungs, stood a few feet
away from him on the deck, waiting for him to give them the word to go over the
side. Before he did, Sturges crossed to the bow, and using a pair of binoculars,
scanned the surface of the water for any sign of the dark dorsal fins of the two
tiger sharks that had been circling the barge earlier. He didn't spot the sharks, but
he still felt uneasy.

"I don't want any slip-ups down there," he told the waiting divers. "If you
spot a shark, no hesitation. Get in the damned cages."

The barge crew had already lowered the four huge iron counter-shark cages
into the water and Sturges knew they'd provide some protection for the divers if
they got into trouble with the sharks.

"Any last questions?" he asked.

"No questions, Jack," the man nearest to Sturges answered, and the other two
shook their heads. That was the reply Sturges had expected; all three were, like
himself, seasoned divers and experienced oil-field troubleshooters.

"Let's go," Sturges said. He replaced the mouthpiece between his teeth and
gave a brief wave of his hand to the crewmen on the barge. His fins slapping
the deck, he led the way across the barge and climbed down the rope ladder
slung over the side. He went down slowly, the water lapping up over him until,
submerged, the only trace left of him was the trail of tiny bubbles which rose and
popped on the surface of the sea. One by one, the other three divers followed him
over the side and into the dark waters.

The heaving barge, which rode the choppy surface of the Gulf of Mexico
that day, was anchored ten miles off the coast of Louisiana. It was located
approximately halfway between land and the giant oil rig which stood its four
steel legs securely anchored in the ocean floor, about ten miles farther out in
the Gulf. For the past two years, the rig, which was operated by Petroco, an
independent oil combine, had been dredging up oil from the depths and pumping
it through the twenty-mile-long pipeline to shore.

A COUPLE weeks earlier, the Gulf and the Louisiania coast had been hit by
a sudden tropical squall which, while it contained nothing like the fury of
Hurricane Camille of the year before, still sank several fishing boats and small
yachts and buffeted the offshore oil rig. Soon after the squall, the pipes carrying
the oil onshore sprang a leak, spewing huge quantities of oil to the surface. The
rig had been immediately shut down, and Petroco officials, after visiting the site in
a helicopter, had sent for troubleshooter Jack Sturges.

Jack Sturges, a tall-rawboned man with sandy hair which he kept cropped
close to his skull, was 29 years old. He had been literally raised in the oil fields of
Oklahoma, put to work there by his father, "OK" Sturges, a wildcatter, when the
boy was 14 years old. "OK" had made and lost several fortunes by the time he died
when his son was 20. Jack Sturges enlisted in the US Navy after his father died,
became a top deep-sea diver and, after he got out of the service, began to work as
an oil-field troubleshooter, capping runaway gushers, repairing underwater pipe
leaks, shooting out well fires.

Once the leak in Petroco's pipeline had been pinpointed, the oil combine had
had a repair barge towed out from shore and anchored at the spot. Meanwhile, of
course, the rig had shut down its drilling and the men on the barge had to wait
several days for the oil slick that had formed on the surface to break up and float
off before Sturges and the other three divers could make their descent.

Each of the other three divers had been hand-picked and trained by Sturges,
and while none of the three possessed the nerve and skill of Sturges, each knew
his job. The three were Ed Cole, from La Jolla, California, Mike Grolich, from
Glen Burnie, Maryland, and Cliff Spina, from New Orleans, Louisiana.

Sturges swam head first down the guide-rope, which was anchored to the sea
bottom, illuminating the way ahead with the narrow beam searchlight he held
in his hand. The searchlight was attached to a power cable, and crewmen aboard
the barge unreeled the cable as Sturges descended. In addition to the searchlight,
his equipment consisted of a belt of hand tools and a sheathed knife. When he
reached the end of the guide-rope, Sturges stepped into the mucky sand and
played the searchlight up over his shoulder as it picked out the dim, wavering
forms of the three divers coming down behind him. He waited until all three men
had reached bottom and were grouped around him.

FROM here on, the men moving around at the bottom of the soundless sea would
communicate through hand signals like a gathering of deaf mutes. Sturges
signaled to the others at that moment and swept the beam of his searchlight
around until he had picked out the four iron cages resting on the sand. The cages,
which had been lowered by winches from the barge above, were large enough for
a man to stand upright in and had a small trap opening just wide enough to let a
man slip in through but too small for any except lesser-size sharks to enter. One
by one, he pointed to each man, then to a corresponding cage, so each would know
his place in case of shark attack.

Once that had been established, Sturges directed the searchlight at the sandy

bottom and Spina and Grolich began digging with their small shovels to uncover
the pipeline. It took them about fifteen minutes to sweep away about a twenty-foot
length of sand and expose the pipe. Each man then swam along a couple of feet
above the pipe, examining it for the break.

Sturges was so intent on finding the leak point that he didn't at first realize
what was happening when the beam from one of the other searchlights kept
hitting him in the face. He finally realized that one of the other divers was trying
to signal to him and flashed his own light back. Ed Cole was waving frantically at
Sturges to join him so he swam over quickly and Cole immediately aimed the light
at the dark, hulk of an object about five yards away.

Both men quickly signaled to the other two divers and as soon as Spina and
Grolich joined them, all four swam slowly toward the dark shape looming up in
the water. When they were close enough so that their four searchlights lit up the
dark object, they saw that it was the keel of a small yacht which lay on its side
on the sandy bottom. Sturges gave a quick kick of his flippers and swam up over
the top of the boat until his searchlight's beam picked out the name on the bow:
WHIRLWIND II, NEWPORT NEWS, VA.

Must have been one of the yachts sunk in the squall, Sturges thought, and swam
up over the side, followed by Grolich, Cole, and Spina. In the beam of his probing
searchlight, Sturges saw that half of the hull had been crushed in like the shell of
an egg. The men swam on and when they reached the slanting deck. they saw that
the yacht's deck house had been completely demolished and swept away.

It took another quarter of an hour for Sturges and the others to locate the
break in the pipe. It was almost directly under the stern of the yacht and Sturges
guessed that the boat's propeller had busted the oil line open when the yacht
had first settled to the bottom. The pipe was coupled in four-foot lengths and
the break overlapped into two separate sections of pipe. The four divers worked
as rapidly as they could to unbolt both broken sections, replace them with new
lengths, and bolt them securely into place.

Sturges was relieved when the job was finished and he was able to give the
three men a "thumbs up" signal. He was weary now and almost languid as he
swam to the guide-rope and gave it a tug to alert the crew on the barge that they
were coming up. He had actually grabbed the rope and started up hand over hand
when he caught the warning flash of a frantically waving searchlight out of the
corner of his eye and turned his head just in time to see Cliff Spina swimming
furiously for one of the iron cages as two twenty-foot tiger sharks came gliding
through the waving seagrass just off the bow of the sunken yacht. Sturges
rapidly calculated the distance from the guide-rope to the nearest cage, and
deciding to stay put, froze where he was.

Grolich and Cole were swimming swiftly for two of the other cages. The pair
of sharks, their bodies flashing silver as if they were encased in stainless steel,
cut clearly through the green underwater like twin, lethal torpedoes. They were
moving parallel to Spina and for a moment Sturges believed the predatory fish
might not have detected Spina's presence.

Sturges knew that sharks possessed very poor eyesight and that, while their sense of smell is highly developed, it is usually their ability to detect vibrations in the water that lead them to attack their prey. He was hoping that they still hadn't picked up the sounds Spina was making as he desperately swam for the cage. He knew that, for the moment at least, he, Cole, and Grolich hadn't been detected. In fact, Cole and Grolich had both made it to two of the counter-shark cages and were safe inside. Sturges himself was waiting to see what the sharks were going to do before he made a move.

Just at the moment that Spina reached the mouth of the protective iron cage, one of the sharks veered off and streaked incredibly swiftly through the water straight at Spina. Sturges caught a quick, fleeting glimpse of the shark's mouth gaping open to expose the multiple sets of jagged saw-teeth as it struck at Spina's left shoulder from the back. Sturges saw Spina's head turn as the shark hit. Then the tremendous impact as the shark struck and hurled Spina into the cage. Blood, black as smoke, drifted up in the water from Spina's slashed-open shoulder.

THE BLOOD sent both sharks into a maddened frenzy and, together, they rammed against the iron bars of the cage, trying to get at Spina who floated, dazed, just out of reach. Spina appeared to Sturges to be in a state of shock from the attack and the blood he was losing. He had both hands up to his oxygen mouthpiece to hold it in place. Each time one of the deadly fish slammed against the cage with its ugly snout, Spina was thrown back and forth inside. Sturges knew that as Spina continued to weaken he would, sooner or later, be thrown close enough to the bars for the sharks to finish him off. Or he would lose his mouthpiece and it would all be over.

Sturges hesitated for only a moment longer and then, pulling the knife from the sheath at his waist, kicked off from the guide-rope and began swimming rhythmically toward the thrashing sharks. He kept his light off, but Cole and Grolich, from their cages, saw what he was doing and directed their searchlights on Spina and the two sharks. Sturges swam just above the sandy bottom since he wanted, if possible, to come up underneath the sharks before they were aware of him.

He knew he couldn't battle both of the sharks at the same time, but he had a plan which he knew would work if he could just get in one good swipe of his knife. Seconds later he drifted in under the dark his feet on the bottom, gave a hard kick and started up, the knife held out in front of him aimed straight at the soft underbelly of one of the tiger sharks.

Sturges was but a few feet away from the nearest shark, about to make his final lunge and thrust the knife in, when the huge killer-fish suddenly swerved away from its attack on the cage and rolled sideways, one of its ugly milky-white eyes fixed coldly on Sturges. The diver back-pedaled very slowly in the water, watching those hideous scythe-like teeth working in the fish's powerful jaws. The shark turned almost lazily and, tail thrashing, dived for Sturges. Sturges jackknifed under the onrushing fish, clutching the knife in both outstretched hands, and jabbed savagely upward with the sharp blade.

For a split second, Sturges felt nothing and he thought he had missed. Then he felt the knife blade strike home, deep into the shark's gut, and received a shocking jolt from his wrists to his shoulder blades as the giant fish impaled itself on the knife point and, shuddering from teeth to tail, tried to twist free. Sturges could see the thick black blood of the shark as it gushed out of its ripped-open belly and floated toward him, almost in slow motion. Sturges let himself drift down. There was nothing more he could do now. His knife was gone, he was defenseless. All he could do was wait and see if his plan would work.

He felt the sandy bottom against the soles of his flippers and he crouched there looking upward. He didn't have to wait long. Suddenly as the wounded shark above him started thrashing upward toward the surface, the second shark dived like a bolt of silver lightning straight at its wounded mate, jagged teeth gnashing furiously in its gaping jaws as it homed in on the other fish's bleeding mid-section.

This was what Sturges had hoped would happen. He knew that one of the weirdest forms of shark behavior is what is called the "feeding frenzy." Blood, even a shark's own blood, triggers a manic response in the killer-fish and very often, as now, the shark will attack its own kind or even, on occasion, itself. Now that Sturges had succeeded in setting off a "feeding frenzy," he swam cautiously up and into the iron cage with the semi-conscious Spina while the two sharks tore at each other.

ONCE inside the cage, Sturges quickly signaled by several urgent tugs on the rope to the crew above that the cages were to be taken up as quickly as possible. As the cages, all four of them, were rapidly lifted to the surface, the divers watched fascinated as the two sharks continued to bite and slash each other to the death, the blood spreading rapidly through the water all around them and drawing a whole pack of other tiger sharks which closed in, fighting with each other to get at the two wounded sharks. As soon as the cages, dripping seaweed and streams of water, were out of the sea and being lifted aboard the barge. Sturges yanked out his mouthpiece and shouted, "Get the first-aid man on deck and radio for a helicopter!"

Spina was unconscious but still breathing when they lifted him from the cage and the first-aid man began working on him. He still hadn't regained consciousness by the time the helicopter reached the barge. Meantime, Sturges had instructed the radio operator to send a message to the Coast Guard to report the sunken yacht and the skeletons. When the helicopter returned to shore, carrying the still-unconscious Spina, Sturges, Cole, and Grolich went along. None of them left the hospital until the doctors had patched up Spina's shoulder and pronounced him okay, although he'd have to stay in the hospital a while.

NEXT day the three divers flew back out to the barge to watch as the oil rig went into operation pumping oil through the mended pipe. There was no leakage. Only then was Sturges satisfied with the job. Coast Guard divers had already recovered the skeletons from the sunken yacht and were in the process of trying to salvage the boat itself. They reported there was no sign of sharks in the area and when Petroco officials praised Sturges for his courage in going to Spina's rescue, the troubleshooter shrugged it off: "Danger, sunken shipwrecks, sharks, they're all part of the day's work," he said. As if to prove it, three months later, he, Cole, Grolich, and Spina, who had mended, were diving again in the Persian Gulf. ▾

GAVIN NAYLOR, EVOLUTIONARY BIOLOGIST: What's quite unusual is these sharks are 20 feet long, which would be a world record by about 6 feet. And there are two of them. The hero says quite modestly that he couldn't take them both on at the same time, but one shouldn't be too much! He uses these wonderful phrases such as *scythe-like teeth*, but tiger sharks don't have scythe-like teeth at all. They're coxcomb-shaped, recurved teeth with strong serrations, specially adapted to cut through turtle shells. They don't really have these scary, Hollywood-type pointy teeth, but we'll give him a pass on that.

One shark battles the other one, induced into a frenzy by the smell of the other shark's blood. The hero saves the day, and is very matter of fact about it. (I think he did lose his knife.) I don't think there's any evidence of tiger sharks getting into these frenzies. Schooling sharks, such as blacktips, will, and schools of two or three hundred gray reef sharks get quite excited by big spawning operations of bony fishes. It's an opportunity for them to feed, and they'll bite anything that is nearby. Occasionally one another, but once they've bitten one shark, it doesn't mean they smell blood and go after it or kill it.

Sharks *are* food for other sharks, and tiger sharks will routinely eat gray reef sharks. But the notion that there's this sort of cannibalism…? It's a myth that if one shark gets injured, the others will all turn on it and shred it.

These animals have been around for 400 million years, and humans have been around in some form for probably about 2 million years. Sharks have had a long time to adapt to their environment. Biologically, they are fascinating animals. They have weathered the bloody Permian extinction, for goodness sake, and the Cretaceous extinction! And they've done this despite being what we call *K-selected*: They don't have many offspring, and they live a long time. This is not a recipe for survival. If their numbers get wiped out, they can't rebound very quickly. They're poorly adapted, one would think, to survive. Yet somehow they have. They're obviously very resilient, and they can deal, we believe, with lots of different environmental perturbations. But if humans keep pulling them out of the water, for fins or for eating or whatever, they're not going to survive. It's a shame, because there's so much that we can learn about these animals that we don't yet know.

They've survived 400 million years, but they can't survive a bunch of monkeys that pull them out of the water.

ARGOSY Janurary 1957 Art by Fred Freeman

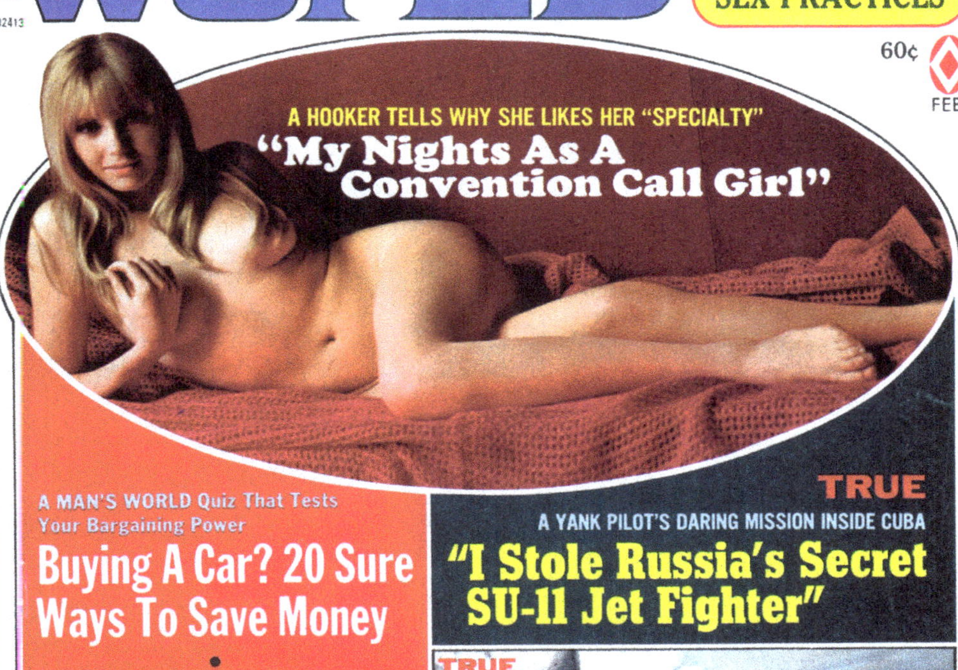

"Shark-Battling Dolphins Saved My Life"

STORY BY BILL ROSENBLITHE   COVER ART BY KEN BARR

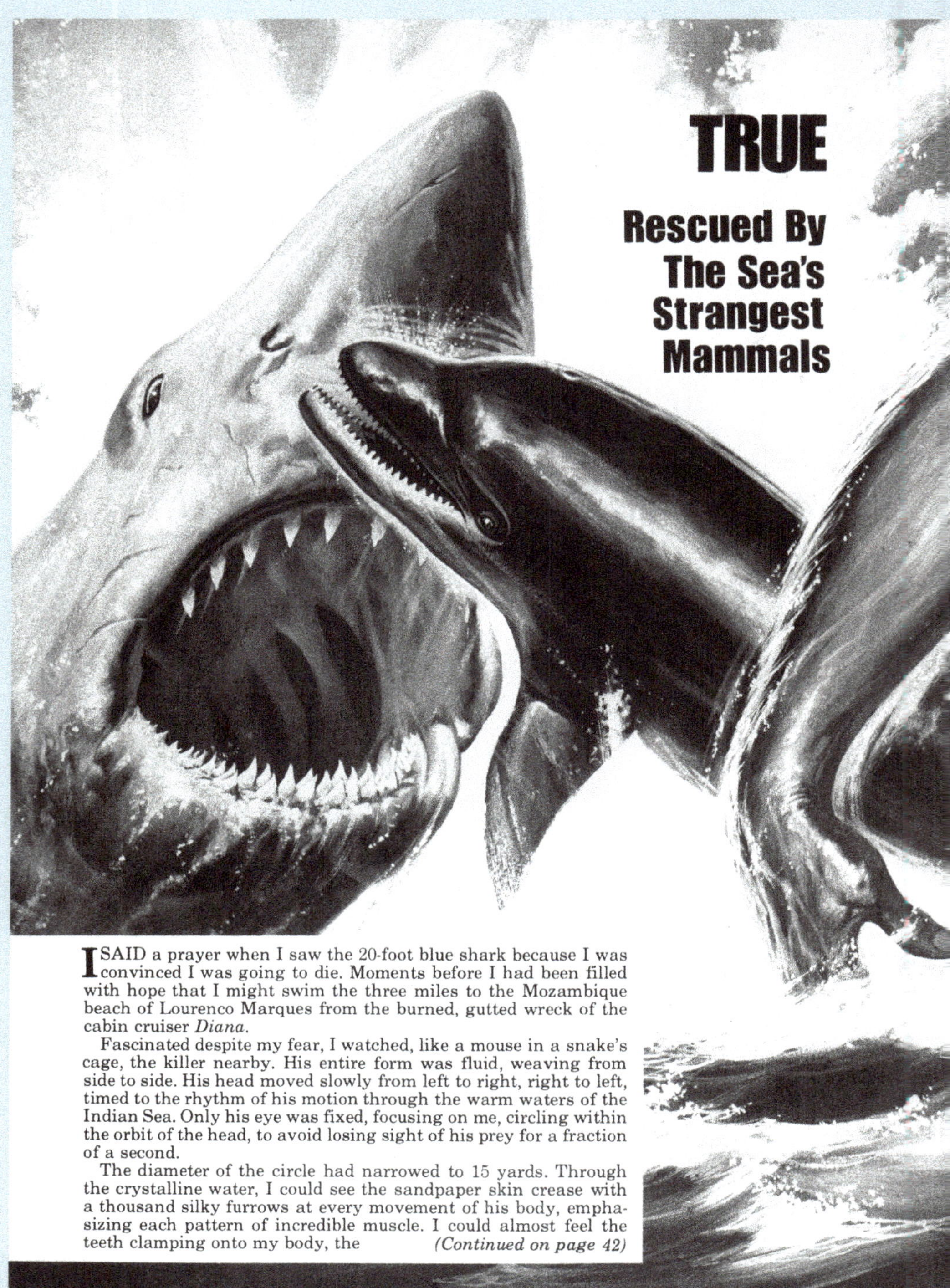

I SAID a prayer when I saw the 20-foot blue shark because I was convinced I was going to die. Moments before I had been filled with hope that I might swim the three miles to the Mozambique beach of Lourenco Marques from the burned, gutted wreck of the cabin cruiser *Diana*.

Fascinated despite my fear, I watched, like a mouse in a snake's cage, the killer nearby. His entire form was fluid, weaving from side to side. His head moved slowly from left to right, right to left, timed to the rhythm of his motion through the warm waters of the Indian Sea. Only his eye was fixed, focusing on me, circling within the orbit of the head, to avoid losing sight of his prey for a fraction of a second.

The diameter of the circle had narrowed to 15 yards. Through the crystalline water, I could see the sandpaper skin crease with a thousand silky furrows at every movement of his body, emphasizing each pattern of incredible muscle. I could almost feel the teeth clamping onto my body, the *(Continued on page 42)*

"SHARK-BATTLING DOLPHINS SAVED MY LIFE"

The New York Times

South African Reports A Rescue by Dolphins

Special to The New York Times

JOHANNESBURG, South Africa, Sept. 9 — A 23-year-old South African man who swam for 3 miles in the shark-infested Indian Ocean after a shipwreck off Lourenco Marques, Mozambique, says that he owes his life to two dolphins.

By KURT GIFFARD
as told to
BILL ROSENBLITHE

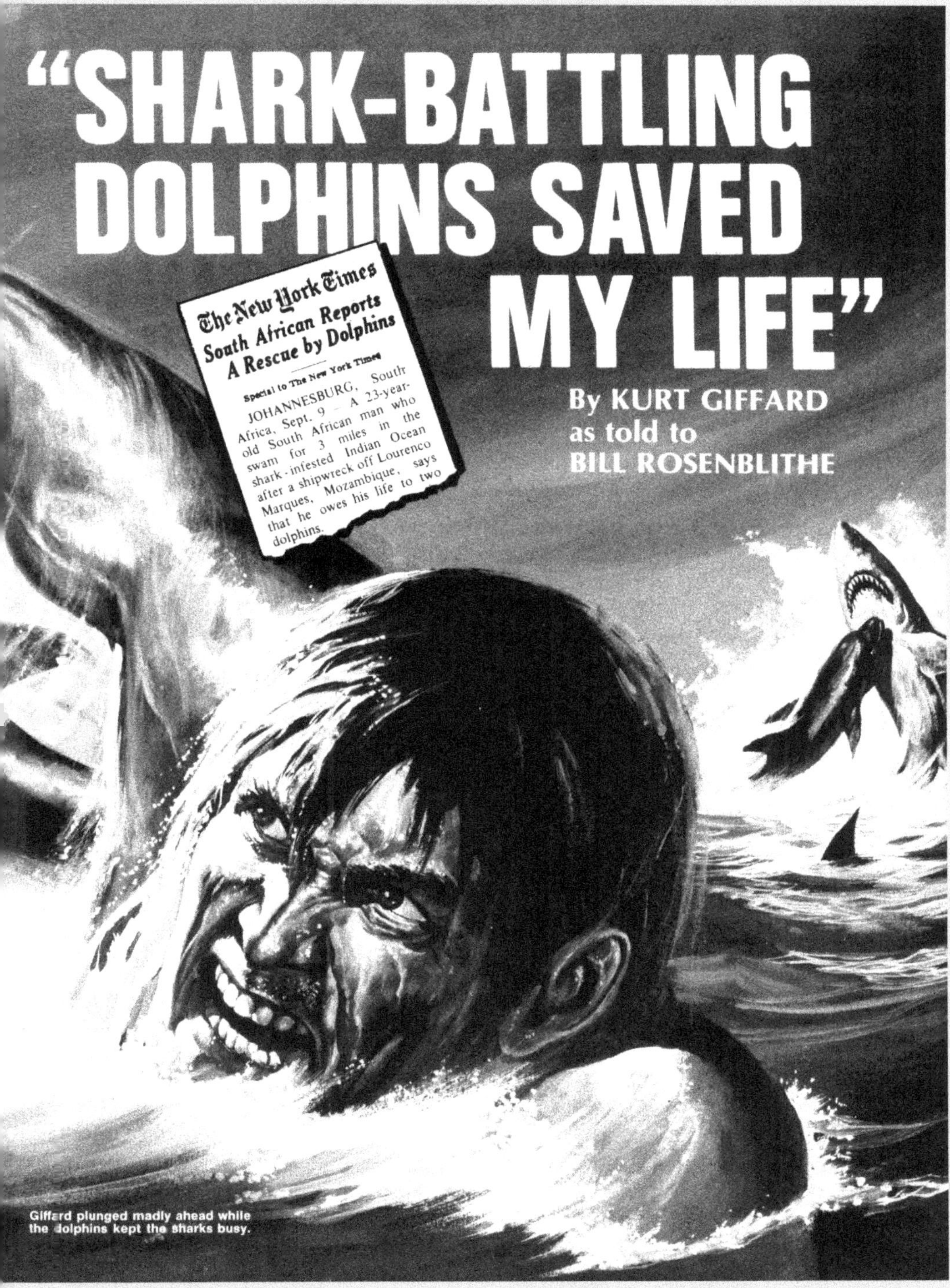

Giffard plunged madly ahead while the dolphins kept the sharks busy.

ART BY KEN BARR

I said a prayer when I saw the 20-foot blue shark, because I was convinced I was going to die. Moments before I had been filled with hope that I might swim the three miles to the Mozambique beach of Lourenco Marques from the burned, gutted wreck of the cabin cruiser *Diana*.

Fascinated despite my fear, I watched, like a mouse in a snake's cage, the killer nearby. His entire form was fluid, weaving from side to side. His head moved slowly from left to right, right to left, timed to the rhythm of his motion through the warm waters of the Indian Sea. Only his eye was fixed, focusing on me, circling within the orbit of the head, to avoid losing sight of his prey for a fraction of a second.

The diameter of the circle had narrowed to 15 yards. Through the crystalline water, I could see the sandpaper skin crease with a thousand silky furrows at every movement of his body, emphasizing each pattern of incredible muscle. I could almost feel the teeth clamping onto my body, the powerful turn, and the ripping away of my flesh.

The blue shark swam on. There was no threat, no movement of aggression. Yet never had I been filled with such terror. Swimming as slowly and steadily as I could, I tried to keep him constantly in front of me.

The huge marauder continued his approach, narrowing the circle another five feet or so. For the first time I saw that stupendous jaw lined with teeth, seven symmetrical rows of them. As he continued to circle, I drew my knife, but even as it cleared the sheath, I knew what a futile gesture it was. Even if I repelled the first attack, he would simply resume the circle of hunger, and then, without warning, attack again. Drawn by invisible signals, other sharks would soon appear. Then there would be the scramble for spoils, the frenzy. The bloody and swirling horror I envisioned brought cramps to my stomach.

For an hour the shark circled. The circle was down to a mere five yards now. There was no point in swimming further. Treading water, I waited. My strength was ebbing, and I wanted at least the satisfaction of cutting the beast so that its comrades would tear it apart, even as it had me.

Then the shark opened its jaws.

The lower jawbone jutted forward, the snout was drawn back and up until it made a right angle with the axis of its body.

Twice I struck out at the wolftrap jaws. And twice the knife missed as my knuckles scraped alongside the sandpaper skin of that enormous mouth. With a flick of its torso, the killer veered. But instead of resuming its circle as I expected,

it dashed toward me again, rolling its dorsal fin under to bring the great jaws to
bear. I braced myself for the second attack.

Bᴜᴛ ɪᴛ never came.

Because I had not taken my eyes off the beast for an instant, I never saw the
two bottlenose dolphins racing towards us.

The first dolphin to strike was the smaller of the two, perhaps ten feet at most,
but the point of its muzzle striking the shark's abdominal cavity sounded like two
ships colliding. The second dolphin struck inches away from where its mate had
impacted seconds before.

The shark was dead.

Though there was no trace of blood that I could see, the shark, doubled over
like a sucker-punched boxer, sank slowly out of the blue-green, into the murk below.
Its delicate insides were, I knew, totally destroyed. Had they not been, the dolphins
would have aimed their second attack at the gills, annihilating the beast's breathing
apparatus.

Looking at the two dolphins frolicking about me, grayish dorsal sections
shading into whitish underbellies and perpetually upturned mouths that always
seem to be smiling, I was tempted to say thanks.

But I stopped myself. It could be fatal to assume that all danger was past. The
encounter with the shark had worn me out, and I would have to float awhile to
regain my strength for the long swim to shore. Besides, the shark and the dolphin
are natural enemies. It was for that reason alone, and not out of any affection for
me, that the dolphins had attacked.

Or so I thought at the time.

Tᴀᴋɪɴɢ a vacation by cabin cruiser off Lourenco Marques was a bit unusual for me,
but my fiancée, Ingaret, thought it might be fun.

"Why don't we go inland?" I had complained. "I've never been to any of the
great Kenyan game preserves."

Ingaret had frowned. "Just because you're a sailor doesn't mean the ocean is out
for a vacation. I haven't been to the coast for over a year."

In the end I gave in. She lived in Johannesburg and I could understand her
desire for a few weeks at the sea. In the winter, the great gold mining center
is one of the most pleasant spots on earth. In the summer, it turns into a hot,
dusty, hellhole.

I was not, as my fiancée called me, a "sailor." Like my shipmates who sailed
aboard the *Thor Larsen* from Port Natal, I considered myself a whaler. For over 12
years, in fact, ever since my 18th birthday, I had sailed with the great whaling fleet
during the hunting season. For more than six months out of every twelve, we'd
criss-cross the Indian Ocean and the Antarctic in search of the *blah val (blue whale)*:
those immense creatures of more than 130 tons, able to swim hour after hour at
better than 15 knots.

Twelve seasons of hunting. You could understand why I thought cabin cruising
along the shore of Mozambique was a busman's holiday if ever there was one. But

1972 had been my most profitable voyage ever. Sailing as Second Mate for the first time, I had picked up an even bigger percentage of a full catch that included three sperms with rectums full of ambergris at $40 a pound. I figured I could well afford a cabin cruiser and a long rest.

It had been, by and large, an uneventful journey from Port Natal north to Mozambique. At night we slept aboard ship. By day we swam and picnicked among the hundreds of sandy coves that dot the coast. The days seemed to merge into one another, and the excitement I can remember is when we saved the porpoises' lives.

PORPOISES, as you may or may not know, are related to dolphins, but differ from them as a German Shepherd, say, differs from a Poodle. For one thing, the porpoise has a more rounded head without the pronounced beak of his dolphin cousin. For another, he has spade-shaped teeth instead of conical. Finally, he is smaller and generally stays farther out to sea than the dolphin.

It was the last fact about them that caused me surprise when I heard Ingaret screaming from the other end of the cove for me to come on the double.

I couldn't for the life of me figure out what was wrong as I caught sight of her about a half mile off. Like me, she was naked, for there wasn't much point on donning suits on those deserted strips of white sand.

"They'll die out of water," she was screaming as I reached her. "Hurry, Kurt."

"Don't panic," I said. "They're just porpoises. Probably driven ashore by a Killer Whale. And they're mammals, not fish. They drown in water not air. The only danger is their skin's drying out in the sun. From the way these are lying quiet, I'd say they've been struggling for some time. Let's get back to the boat and pick up some blankets. We'll wet the porpoises down, then carry them into the water."

They were all under five feet and none weighed more than 80 pounds, so it wasn't hard to get them the 20 feet to the water's edge.

"Don't put him in the water," I cautioned Ingaret when we hauled the first one to the wet sand. "The others will let out distress signals, and this one will come racing back and beach himself again. Let's get all three near the water and start them out together. Mind the skin, though, it's very sensitive."

Five minutes later, all three porpoises were poised near the water, giving off that curious, characteristic squeak which many scientists claim is their method of communication. At any rate, a few quick shoves and they were floating. Then they were racing out to sea.

If someone had ever told me that their kin would soon return the favor, I'd have had him committed.

IT WAS outside Lourenco Marques that the *Diana's* fuel injector conked out, so we put into port for repairs. I, for one, was pleased to spend the three or four days ashore that would be needed. For one thing, sleeping aboard the cramped cabin cruiser was fun only because Ingaret shared my quarters. For another, Lourenco Marques, a city of almost 200,000 people, was one of the most beautiful ports on Africa's east coast. I looked forward to a large bed in a room cooled by an overhead fan, charcoal-broiled steaks and lobsters in Portuguese fashion, and ice cold beer to wash it all down.

Three days later, I walked into the yacht basin to inspect the repairs. I had left lngaret reading in the hotel room. "I want to take her out for a trial run," I had explained to her as I shaved. "If everything's all right, I'll pick you up at noon and we'll head north again."

Everything seemed perfect as I eased her out about three miles where the clear green water becomes suddenly a brilliant blue. As I let her out full throttle I was even thinking that I'd have to tip the mechanic who had carried out the repairs.

A minute later, I smelled the fire. Then I saw the smoke billowing out of the engine. At that point, there was still hope. Leaping down the stairs into the cabin, I grabbed the extinguisher from the wall and rushed back on deck. I had read the instructions many times before, and only an idiot could have misunderstood them:

To Use
Remove Clip
Strike Knob on Ground
Keep Extinguisher Upside Down
Aim Jet at Fire

The only problem was, an idiot had made the thing because it dribbled once, then sputtered uselessly.

Cursing both extinguisher manufacturer and moron mechanic, I threw the useless hunk of metal overboard and started filling buckets. But it was too late. I would have needed a firetruck and power hose to put that blaze out. Already the floorboards were charred and crumbling. Giving it up, I rushed for the inflatable raft stowed in the stern.

I reached it at precisely the same moment the flames reached the gasoline tanks beneath my feet and the explosion tossed me 15 or 20 feet into the sea.

Stunned from the blast, I recovered myself in time to see a wave was carrying a fiery sheet of oil directly toward me. Throwing my hands above my head, I submerged and stayed down as long as I could before rising with aching lungs to the surface.

The wave of burning oil was safely past me, heading in for shore. I wondered if it could be seen from land. The sun was still behind me, in the east, so I suspected it couldn't. I knew they couldn't see the flaming wreckage of the Diana, because in the time I had ducked below the surface, the cabin cruiser had foundered and sunk.

There was no decision to be made. I had only one course of action, and that was to swim toward shore. The three miles didn't trouble me. I could swim before I was four, and had been a high school champion in both the butterfly and backstroke. Besides, the waves would push me toward the land when I was tired and had to float.

Treading water, I untied my plimsolls and let them sink. I was just about to remove my windbreaker when I noticed the sleeve was ripped. Then I realized that whatever had torn the jacket had also gashed my arm. Not bad enough to keep me from using it, but bad enough to bleed. And blood on the water in the Indian Ocean was a siren call to sharks—and violent death. Despite the time and effort it would take, I decided to try to shred my windbreaker and apply both a tourniquet and a bandage. When it was done, I struck out for shore, swimming an even 100 strokes, then floating on my back to rest. I guess I had swum close to 500 before I saw the fin of the great blue shark coming from shore to intercept me.

As I stroked away from the spectre of my death, the dolphins swam playfully alongside. I couldn't help admiring their enormous power, incongruous though it seemed, as they dashed around me like delighted children. Each turn they made brought them into my line of vision, and I watched their silhouettes, slightly blurred by the streaming water, skimming the surface like the best competitive swimmers, they limited their breathing period as much as possible, exhaling underwater and sending streams of bubbles to the surface.

Suddenly, completely, the watery play ceased. I had not far to look for the reason. Less than 100 yards to the north, I saw the tell-tale triangular fin. Not one this time, but four. I had—I told myself, with less than a mile between me and shore—had it. At any moment I expected my dolphin companions to flee.

I was wrong. One dolphin, the smaller of the two, continued to circle me while the larger suddenly charged the four approaching sharks as if to scatter them. Was he sacrificing himself? I'll never know. I began to swim furiously in the direction of land.

When I could no longer put one hand in front of another, I stopped and looked back. Three sharks were attacking the dolphin with incredible ferocity. He must have got one on his first pass. I knew that from the shattered chest of the creature a great black bubble of air was carrying away his life. I sucked in great gulps of air, turned my face toward the shore, and began to swim again. I knew that had it not been for that dolphin, it would have been me being torn apart. I had seen with my own eyes what a pack of sharks in a feeding frenzy had done to a wounded whale.

Would the 200 pounds of dolphin be enough to satisfy those enormous appetites and let me make shore? There was no way of knowing. I increased my stroke, trying to put as much distance between me and that frothing stain of blood as I could.

But even as I swam, I could feel the strength ebbing. All my skill as a swimmer wasn't going to save me if exhaustion paralyzed my body. Already black dots floated across my eyes. I had to rest.

How long I treaded water can't even be guessed at.

I was conscious only of an enormous fatigue spreading through my body.

It was at that moment, I think, that I felt the first bump propelling me upwards. Another bump. Adrenaline spurted through my system. My first thought was that the sharks had finished their bloody meal and had turned their attention to me. But when no attack came, I realized that the surviving dolphin was below me, pushing me to the surface, urging me onward.

Again I began to swim, slowly and deliberately. The rest had given me a second breath. Not enough to cover the distance that still lay between me and shore, but enough to continue. Had I stayed there much longer, I'm sure that other sharks would have appeared to finish the meal they'd had delayed.

And near me the dolphin swam, its pace slowed down to mine.

I must have been 400 yards from shore when the fatigue began to spread through me once more. I remember cursing that l was going to drown so close to safety. As I lost consciousness, I remember that last tremendous dolphin shove…

The enormous lifeguard, an African from the Bantu tribe, was hovering over me anxiously when l opened my eyes. "Are you all right?" he asked in Portuguese, and when a tourist standing nearby translated his question, I nodded that I was.

"Ask him how far out I was when he got to me," I told my translator.

"About 100 yards," came his reply.

One hundred yards! When I lost consciousness, I was four times that from shore. Somehow, the dolphin had managed to propel my body more than 300 yards toward shore, and from the way my ribs, chest and back ached, I knew he had been forced to exert a tremendous amount of energy. I stood up shakily in the sand and looked out toward the ocean. There was nothing but sea and sky. But I muttered anyway, "Thanks."

Editor's Note: In an effort to verify Kurt Giffard's story, we asked Chester Krone, author of *The World of the Dolphin* (Belmont, New York, 1972) if he would comment on some of the more important details. Mr. Krone's reply is as follows: "Thanks for sending me Kurt Giffard's account of his dolphin rescue. We have been receiving reports of dolphins saving the lives of drowning people for some time, the first as early as 1943 when *Natural History Magazine* reported that a dolphin pushed a distressed swimmer ashore in Miami. Two years later in an official report in *Airmen Against the Sea*, author George Llano recounts how a dolphin pushed a rubber raft filled with airmen to a beach. Accounts similar to Giffard's have been received from Australia, Brazil, Tunisia, and other places frequented by dolphins.

"What makes Kurt Giffard's report so interesting is that for the first time, the witness's reliability cannot be questioned on the basis of expertise. As a whaler with 12 years experience, he has had first-hand knowledge of both sharks and dolphins. Every detail in his story on dolphin behavior has been scientifically confirmed. It is, in my opinion, the most conclusive bit of evidence we have ever had that man does, indeed, have a friend in the sea." ▼

BITING BACK commentary

David Shiffman, marine conservation biologist: This is is one of my favorite myths to debunk. It comes up a lot, and as far as we know, there isn't any convincing evidence of it ever happening anywhere, despite scuba divers regularly having cameras with them, and despite lots of scientific research on both dolphin and shark behavior.

The more common story is, *"I was in the water and I saw a shark and I thought I was going to die, and then I saw a dolphin and the shark went away."* That can also be described as *"I went in the ocean and saw some marine life and had a pretty normal day."*

People interpret the presence of a shark to mean *the shark is about to eat me.* People interpret the presence of the dolphin as *intentionally scaring the shark away to protect me.* And there's no evidence of either of those things. I've been in the water with sharks a lot, and I have taken thousands of pictures of sharks. And most are of sharks swimming away really fast, because most of the time that's what they do when they see a person!

In this particular story, a dolphin kills a shark in one blow. Dolphins can't do that. Dolphins are capable of killing sharks, and it does happen sometimes, but it takes a lot of repeated blows. Sharks are pretty tough. But that sort of behavior *has* been described among dolphins. When there is a dolphin baby around and they're trying to discourage a shark away, they'll hit it pretty hard. But the goal is not to kill it necessarily, but to just say, *Hey, maybe you'd best be going on your way.* Some of the larger sharks do occasionally eat dolphins. But it's very unusual, because dolphins are big, dolphins are fast, and dolphins are pretty tough, too.

There's this myth that dolphins and sharks hate each other. But if you've ever seen videos of a bait ball (which is an aggregation of small bait fish), you'll see dolphins diving through it to get food, and sharks diving through it to get food, and they leave each other alone.

There have been documented cases of marine mammals like dolphins and whales mimicking altruistic behavior towards members of other species. That's fairly common among social, intelligent animals. Chimpanzees do this. There have been cases of dolphins pushing drowning sailors to shore, and stuff like that. But not many.

A big part of this belief has to do with the dolphin's face: It looks like they're smiling. It looks like they're happy when they see us. And maybe they are, I don't know—and neither does anyone else. People look for human-like behavior in animals, and dolphins *are* very intelligent—but they're intelligent in a different way than we are. Intelligence means different things to different types of organisms. It doesn't mean that they're basically humans that can swim. It means that they're really, really good at processing information in their environment, and communicating with each other, and making a plan. That doesn't mean they have a translatable-to-human language. It doesn't mean they know what the hell we're doing. People want to see human-like behavior in other animals, and it's not there. That doesn't mean other animals don't care about you. It doesn't mean other animals aren't interested in you. But they don't process the world and think about the world the same way we do. And I think that's good, because it makes the world a lot more interesting.

"A Man-Eating Shark Pack Against Scuba Divers"

STORY BY WALTHER STURM

It took the first two reports of maneater attacks to trigger Chuck Ramsey's scuba-diver army into action. What followed has come to be known as the "Underwater War of 1974."

By WALTHER STURM

The Strange 'War' Off New Jersey's Coast

A MAN-EATING SHARK PACK AGAINST SCUBA DIVERS

TOM REYNOLDS AND NINA TUCCI were clowning in the water. The Atlantic waters off the New Jersey coast were still chill on this Memorial Day weekend and it was just as well to remain active. Nina, not nearly as proficient in the water as Tom, was trying to swim back through the splashes he threw at her. Tom accompanied her by taking one stroke on his belly, flopping over to his back for the next, then to his belly, back, belly.

Then Tom screamed. Nina stopped and stared at him, half-wondering if he was still kidding. Then she saw the crescent-shaped fin swirling away from him, the torpedo shadow under it and the dark cloud of blood blossoming in the water. She screamed too and without thinking, lunged through the water to help him.

The crescent fin circled back and cut a vee towards Tom. Nina threw herself at it, hitting and kicking. She connected solidly and felt as if her hands and feet had pressed against a running grinding wheel. The crescent fin veered away.

The beach was alerted now and the weekend crowd of young people—the only ones willing to endure the cold water—came swimming to help them. Nina's scream cut into the shrill range when she saw the fin whirl and cone charging in.

Again she kicked and hit, was thrown backwards by heavy contact with the rushing body. Tom's scream was cut off as he bobbed under the water. He emerged slowly, hair plastered down, eyes bulging in shock, mouth opening and closing silently, his hair dripped red.

Many of the rescuers turned back when they saw the crescent fin—and you couldn't accuse them of cowardice. The remaining few calculated their chances. Tom and Nina were in fairly shallow water now, propelled both by the shark's lunges and Nina's pushes. They made a quick conerted rush, grabbed Tom and Nina, beached them. A number of those close by who saw Tom Reynolds either vomited or had stomach heaves.

His left leg was surgically severed at the knee. His right leg was off just below the thigh. His wounds were hemhorraging in great gouts, and despite desperate First Aid treatment he died seconds after rescue.

Nina Tucci had no skin on her hands nor below her knees. In those areas it looked as though she had (Continued on page 38)

By the time the shark had finished with Joe Polansky and he was hauled back on board, most of his right buttock was gone.

In a similar West Coast shark battle, skin diver Floyd Pair, Jr., was horribly mauled before being rescued by his buddies.

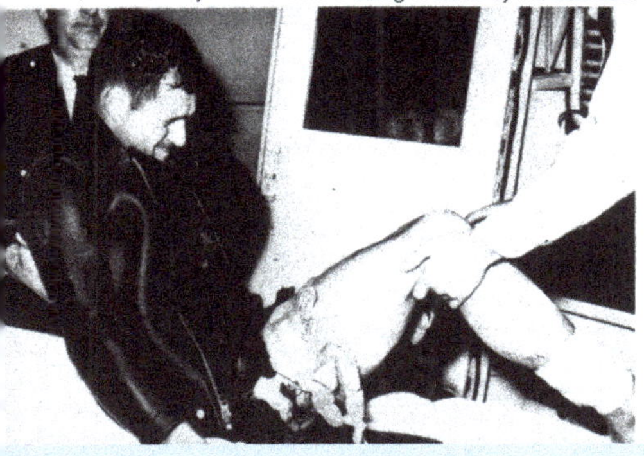

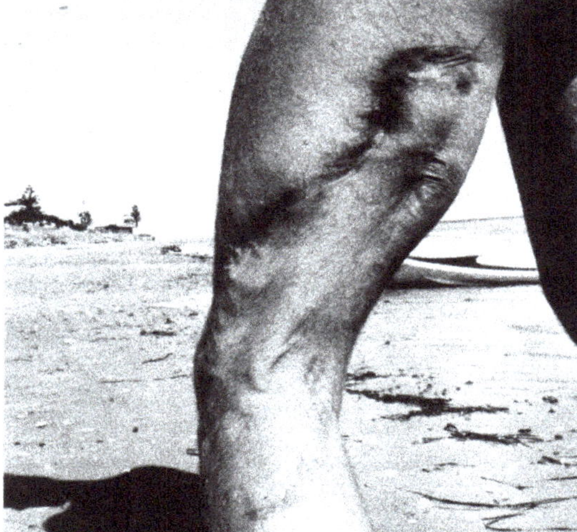

This man's leg is as healed as it will ever be. It took one crunch of a shark's massive jaws to rip his flesh to shreds.

Tom Reynolds and Nina Tucci were clowning in the water. The Atlantic waters off the New Jersey coast were still chill on this Memorial Day weekend, and it was just as well to remain active. Nina, not nearly as proficient in the water as Tom, was trying to swim back through the splashes he threw at her. Tom accompanied her by taking one stroke on his belly, flopping over to his back for the next, then to his belly, back, belly.

Then Tom screamed. Nina stopped and stared at him, half-wondering if he was still kidding. Then she saw the crescent-shaped fin swirling away from him, the torpedo shadow under it and the dark cloud of blood blossoming in the water. She screamed too and without thinking, lunged through the water to help him.

The crescent fin circled back and cut a vee towards Tom. Nina threw herself at it, hitting and kicking. She connected solidly and felt as if her hands and feet had pressed against a running grinding wheel. The crescent fin veered away.

The beach was alerted now and the weekend crowd of young people—the only ones willing to endure the cold water—came swimming to help them. Nina's scream cut into the shrill range when she saw the fin whirl and come charging in.

Again she kicked and hit, was thrown backwards by heavy contact with the rushing body. Tom's scream was cut off as he bobbed under the water. He emerged slowly, hair plastered down, eyes bulging in shock, mouth opening and closing silently, his hair dripped red.

Many of the rescuers turned back when they saw the crescent fin—and you couldn't accuse them of cowardice. The remaining few calculated their chances. Tom and Nina were in fairly shallow water now, propelled both by the shark's lunges and Nina's pushes. They made a quick concerted rush, grabbed Tom and Nina, beached them. A number of those close by who saw Tom Reynolds either vomited or had stomach heaves.

His left leg was surgically severed at the knee. His right leg was off just below the thigh. His wounds were hemorrhaging in great gouts, and despite desperate First Aid treatment he died seconds after rescue.

Nina Tucci had no skin on her hands nor below her knees. In those areas it looked as though she had been flayed. The denticles on the shark's skin, like thousands of miniature teeth, had stripped Nina's skin to the raw flesh.

Two days later, off Barnegat Light, the yawl *Sea Plume* was beating to the wind. Skipper Harry Andrews wanted to take a new tack and dutifully sounded the warning, "Coming about." Everyone ducked except Pete Kells.

The main boom came swinging around, hit him solidly on the side of the head, and flicked him overboard.

He floated face down in the water like a piece of soggy cardboard.

Joe Polansky went in after him while the skipper spilled wind. In a few powerful strokes, he was alongside Kells, hauling him back to the *Sea Plume*. Reaching hands pulled Kells from the water as Polansky waited, treading water.

Warning shouts. Joe turned partially to see what was wrong. A long, torpedoing body hurtled from the depths and struck. He screamed agony. The shark spun away in a right circle, trying for another bite.

Desperately, the crew pulled Joe on deck. His right side, below the belt line of his shorts was covered with blood. Most of his right buttock was gone.

The men stuffed towels in the ham-sized wound and applied pressure bandages but Joe Polansky hemorrhaged to death on the deck.

IN A housing development being constructed in Trenton, Chuck Ramsey read the newspaper account while sitting under a kitchen sink, waiting for his plumber's blow torch to pressurize. Like any ardent scuba diver, Ramsey considered shark attacks his business. And a rash of attacks, this early in the season meant only one thing—a killer had invaded the Jersey coastal waters. Chuck threaded pipe and sweat joints while he thought. In both instances there were sounds of trouble in the water. In the first, Tom Reynolds was clowning. In the second, Pete Kells was actually floundering. And to a shark, trouble means dinner on the table. Only thing wrong with Chuck's killer-shark theory was that just two species in these waters were potential man eaters—mako and hammerhead—and as far as he knew, the water was still too cold for either of them.

Ramsey eased his massive, 6'3" frame out from under the sink and scratched his red beard. Beards were OK, he decided, for maintaining a wetsuit hood's seal around your face, but for sitting under a sink on a warm day, they were a damn nuisance.

At his house on Long Beach, he got on the phone and called the scuba clubs up and down the coast. As president of the Allied Scuba Clubs, Ramsey was aware of the potential danger that this maneater was to all divers. Already, it had ranged 75 miles between attacks.

Evidently, the shark was willing to go to some effort to seek out human flesh. They had to get him.

All clubs agreed to cooperate the next day, Saturday.

Sunrise, Ramsey was in his beach truck, a former stand-up bread wagon equipped with stove, water tank, head, cold box, fold-up bed and air compressor to fill his Scott tanks. He was met by the Trident Diving Club and by ten they had formed a line out from the beach, boats placed about a mile or more apart.

Every man wore his wet suit as some protection against the flaying rasp of shark's skin. Shark guns, or "sticks," long tubes filled with blank shotgun shells, were loaded. They could be fired by pressing the working end against a shark's only vulnerable spot, his tiny brain. Since it could be used only during an eyeball confrontation, the most experienced swimmers were handed the stick, literally and figuratively.

On signal, buckets of cattle blood went over the side followed by hooks baited with over-ripe meat. Oars were placed in the water and wrists turned to make the flip-flap of trouble.

An in-shore boat got the first strike. It's tied-down hawser went taut and water droplets squeezed from its thinned length. The crew heaved and a six-foot hammerhead was jerked out of the water, thrashing its ugly length furiously. A husky man used a baseball bat against its skull repeatedly. Then, watching for signs of renewed life all the time, it was brought aboard. A shark stick pressed against its brain made sure.

CHUCK radio-phoned, "Good work. Don't throw that thing overboard." He was about to end it by telling everybody to go home, they had caught the killer, when another boat in relatively shallow waters got a hit. Another ugly hammerhead, a nine-footer, was yanked out and subdued.

Then Chuck's deep water boat got a hit. The crew heaved but they might as well have been trying to move a ton of lead with a cotton string. The bow of the anchored, 27-foot cabin cruiser shifted as the shark turned away from the hook, trying to escape.

Chuck went over with a mask and a shark stick. As soon as the bubbles of his entry cleared, he saw the streamlined shape fighting the hook. He glided towards it with controlled power, stick first. As long as the shark remained hooked he was safe. He could position himself beyond the line's reach, then dive down and press the stick against the shark's vulnerable brain.

The shark heard Ramsey coming. Whirling in a tight fighting circle, it opened its grin of a mouth and displayed rows of triangular teeth that could cut with the efficiency of a guillotine. The teeth headed straight for Chuck. Somersaulting desperately, he hoped to intercept the charge with a dive and a touch of his stick. He hoped, that's all. The shark, hooked or not hooked, could kill him with one thrash of its tail.

A loop of loosened rope fell into the shark's mouth. It bit down, wig-wagging its head and body. The hawser parted like a string cut with surgical scissors. But free, the shark did the unexpected; he turned and disappeared into the dark depths, carrying the hook and a long length of line.

That day the Trident Club alone brought in 14 hammerheads, 3 thresher sharks, 4 nurse sharks, and 1 sand shark.

Chuck Ramsey emptied his stick, boxed the shells, and looked up to the red, duskwarmed sky. Cursing softly, he got stronger and longer as he went on. "Goddamn the effing sunovabitching awkward whoring…" was his warm-up.

The group waited till he cooled off somewhat. "Think we got the killer?" they asked.

CHUCK closed his eyes, mentally counted, then roared, "How the hell do I know? I thought there was only one stinking shark in these waters, and now we're scupper deep in 'em.

"What do you want done with them, Chuck?"

"Save 'em…for tomorrow. Use shark to catch shark. We start at sun up."

Back at his beach wagon, Ramsey found a slender, fully bearded young man waiting outside. "You must be Chuck Ramsey. They told me I'd find you here. I drove down from Woods Hole to meet you. Name's Hal King."

"Belong to the Oceanographic?"

"Yes, staff. Marine biology."

Chuck grunted recognition and admiration. Any guy who could get on the staff of the Woods Hole Oceanographic Institute was top drawer; probably had a doctorate degree although he hadn't mentioned it.

Hal King indicated the binoculars hanging from his neck. "I saw the haul you brought in. Is there some place we can talk?"

Chuck waved him inside the truck. King went right to the point.

"My specialty is the elasmobranchs—sharks, rays, skates—that family. I want to find out if one particular kind of shark might be responsible for the recent attacks here and why."

"Would you know the species that attacked?"

"Called Nina Tucci, the girlfriend of the boy who was killed. She couldn't remember enough to provide a description, but I'm inclined to vote for a mako. We get them around here in August and September—even July if it's a warm summer and the water temperature is right."

"What fish are running now?"

Chuck opened a quart of beer. "Plenty of mackerel. Striped bass starting to come in."

King shrugged. "Sharks follow fish."

"Yeah, and men if they're floundering around."

Hal put a book on the table. "There're more than 200 species in there. Pick out the ones you saw today."

Chuck skimmed the pages. "This one here…and here. Mostly threshers, a sand shark, nurses… We hooked another shark today. Reminded me of a spiny dogfish; nice and streamlined."

Chuck stopped turning pages. "This looks like him. Would he grow to 7 feet?"

"Probably." King sat back and spoke thoughtfully. "Although that's a lemon shark and strictly a warm water species. Never heard of it coming this far north before and it's not generally considered a man killer." He sat up straight. "If you catch this one, I'd like to do an autopsy on the brain."

"All you'd get is scrambled eggs. We use a shark stick."

"Oh," there was disappointment in King's voice. "Do you still have him?"

"No. I hate to use the expression, but he was the one that got away. Bit through the line and took off with the hook. Not a barbed hook either. We don't use 'em. Don't like to stick our hands in a dead shark's mouth to remove the hook."

"Yes," King grinned. "I'm familiar with the way 'dead' sharks bite. He'll probably spit out the hook inside of an hour, which means he's still on the loose."

Chuck stood. "I have to check in with the rest of the clubs, see how they made out today."

"Want me to warn them about the lemon shark?"

"Yes. This shark is already out of his native waters. No telling what he might do… Oh, one other thing. Would it be possible to capture, or maybe not damage…?"

"No way," Chuck shook his massive head. "Even clubbing or using a shark stick is dangerous. A ten- or fifteen-foot live shark on board without the proper equipment is suicide. And we don't have the equipment."

The other clubs reported no lemon shark. They hadn't even *heard* of one.

Next morning, before sun up, Chuck woke Hal King and readied his equipment. King was satisfied with a ball of nylon netting.

"What do you expect to do with that?" Chuck demanded.

"Sharks have to swim constantly in order to breathe. If we can stop one from moving in the water with this net, he'd drown… And his brain would be intact."

"How'd you know he was dead?"

"You wouldn't," King admitted.

The boat Chuck used was *Wave Dancer*, owned by Jimmy West, a New York advertising man. Sharks caught the day before were chopped up, then either put through the chum grinder to get the scent of blood in the water, or placed on hooks as bait.

A half-hour later the *Jersey Viking* got a hit, pulled up, and found a three-foot sand shark grimly holding onto the bait.

Then *Wave Dancer* got a hit. Jimmy West and his crew started to haul, and found they were in a tug of war. They couldn't gain an inch and whatever was below wasn't giving an inch. Chuck donned his tank and mask and mouthpiece, went over the side to see.

HE SWAM through bubbles, waited for his vision to clear, followed the line down. At the end a spiny dog fish was fighting the hook. Chuck pulled his knife. A poke in the gills would take the bull dog out of that dog fish. He swam closer, then drew up sharply.

Dog fish, hell! That was the lemon shark!

He flew for the top, spit his mouthpiece, yelled, "Shark! Lemon shark! Give me my stick."

"No, no," King yelled. "Use the net! Don't kill him." And he threw the heavy-duty nylon.

Chuck felt the pressure rush of water from below, saw the rope go slack, cursed and dived. If he survived this he'd put that crazy King bastard through the chum grinder.

The shark was coming up. The crew of the *Dancer* hauled but the lemon shark had plenty of slack line. Its cold eye glared at Ramsey. There was no wary circling, no cat-and-mouse tactics. The shark was coming straight in, attacking from its favorite position—below.

Chuck went down deep, hoping the *Dancer's* crew could yank the shark out of the water. Slack line was being hauled in but not nearly fast enough. Chuck let go of his knife, the hollow handle buoyed it to the surface. The knife wouldn't do him a goddamn bit of good against a shark's skin, and if he got near enough to poke the shark in the eye or gill, it would mean he was being swallowed. His only hope was the *Dancer's* crew.

The lemon shark came level with him, swirled to the attack. The nose lifted, the jaw dropped, the thin lipped, tooth lined mouth opened like a tunnel. Chuck tried to get below, to make it more it more difficult for the shark to dive on him. Of course the shark merely had to dip to change course in an eye blink. Which is what it did and was making that slight upward attack.

The whole pointed head jerked as the *Dancer's* crew hauled him in. With powerful surge it sped upwards, much faster than the line could be taken in, turned, and lost the hook.

It came back down foaming fury.

Chuck realized he had the net, and as a last hopeless gesture spread it between himself and the lemon shark. It was a very fragile barrier.

The shark hit it like a falling building. Chuck didn't clear his fingers from the thin strands fast enough and almost had his powerful arm pulled from its socket. The surge of water threw him aside as the shark plunged past him.

It roared back, looking like a vicious lady wearing a veil. Chuck saw a glimmer of hope, two remote possibilities. If he could trap one of the pectoral fins, the shark might lose its ability to remain balanced.

The net was definitely bothering the shark. It kept thrashing to free itself, and all the time it kept an eye on Chuck. That was his lunch and he wasn't going to let it get away from him.

Chuck dove down, grabbed an edge of the net, twisted and pulled. The lemon shark rolled in anger and the flailing tail missed Chuck's leg by a hair.

He pulled the net again, and again the shark rolled. Somehow he was disturbing its balance. Vaguely he felt he was an underwater matador, except he needed a sword, his stick. He pulled again, and the shark writhed in irritation, plunged for the depths, whirled near the bottom, stirred sand and mud, came lunging from the cloud straight at Chuck.

WHETHER the eyes or the nose was bothered by the net, Chuck didn't know, but he managed to avoid the usually deadly charge, and as the lemon shark went past him he gave the net a pull. The nylon strands were in the mouth. The teeth came down like steel traps. The nylon parted and the shark was wearing a lace dress held in place by the pectoral fins.

It spun supplely, charged again. Chuck did a forward roll as a surprise trick, and the shark went under him. As it did Chuck grabbed the net and was sorry for it. The strands sliced into his hand; there was blood in the water.

Another shadow above him. The sharks were already closing for the kill.

He looked up.

Hal King was free diving, holding out a shark stick. Chuck grabbed it, dove to meet the lemon shark.

The shark came in again, cold-eyed fury, open from lips to stomach. Chuck jabbed with the stick. It slipped as the shark's snout rose, slid around. Chuck jammed desperately. If he didn't get a firing, he'd be chopped like an ear of com.

The stick fired into the gill structure. The lemon shark shook its head, turned away.

Chuck lunged, followed it, dived down on it. He poised the stick, aimed, slammed it down. Center head, just below the eyes. The brain was scrambled.

The lemon shark wiggled like a belly dancer, going deeper. Chuck kicked for the surface, seeing shadows of hammerheads closing in. The sharks were gathering.

Chuck went under the *Dancer*, came up the other side, using the boat as protection from the rushing hammerheads although they weren't after him. He crawled aboard, stared at Hal King.

"I wasn't going to let you die down there," King said.

"Thanks."

"Now I don't know if I'll ever have another chance to examine a killer."

Chuck Ramsey looked into the water. Crescent fins surfaced and disappeared; the water clouded with blood.

Soon the sharks would start to tear at one another in their fight for food.

He looked back at Hal King. "Would you like to go down and ask them?" ▼

BITING BACK   commentary

Yannis Papastamatiou, PhD: Shark attacks on humans, or *shark bites* as they are more accurately termed, are a very rare occurrence, with an average of 80 reported bites each year. We still don't understand the reasons for these negative interactions between sharks and humans, but this story gets several facts very wrong.

First, the author suggests that shark bites are mostly predatory in nature, with the sharks trying to eat their victims. While humans have been consumed by sharks, this is a very rare occurrence, even amongst species that may take large prey (e.g. white sharks). The number of shark bites worldwide are very low, and the number of attacks that result in consumption are zero most years (but there are certainly examples).

There is also a general misunderstanding of which species of shark are considered dangerous. For example, hammerheads are not a risky species, and while makos have bitten humans, the chance of finding them in shallow coastal water is extremely low.

Getting in the water with a shark that is hooked can be dangerous, as the animal is in a defensive state. However, once a shark gets free it will almost always flee and try to escape. The chance of it coming back to attack a human in the water is pretty minimal.

Interestingly, New Jersey is the site of one of the most notorious series of shark attacks, when in 1916 four people were killed within a 12-day period. The most likely culprit? A white or bull shark.

ARGOSY May 1953 Art by Fred Freeman

"The Headhunting Shark That Destroyed a Texas Family"

STORY BY BOB TROTTER

THE HEADHUNTING SHARK THAT DESTROYED A TEXAS FAMILY

By BOB TROTTER

ART BY DAVE CHRISTENSEN

ELVIN Slade had to blink five times to be sure he was awake. He was still locked into that dream. Something about riding Waimea with his brothers. Only in this dream there were three good waves for every set of three, instead of just one.

Elvin caught the first wave. On the next one came Vince. On the third monster swell came Big Willie—and they all met on the beach.

Reunion. The Slade boys

161

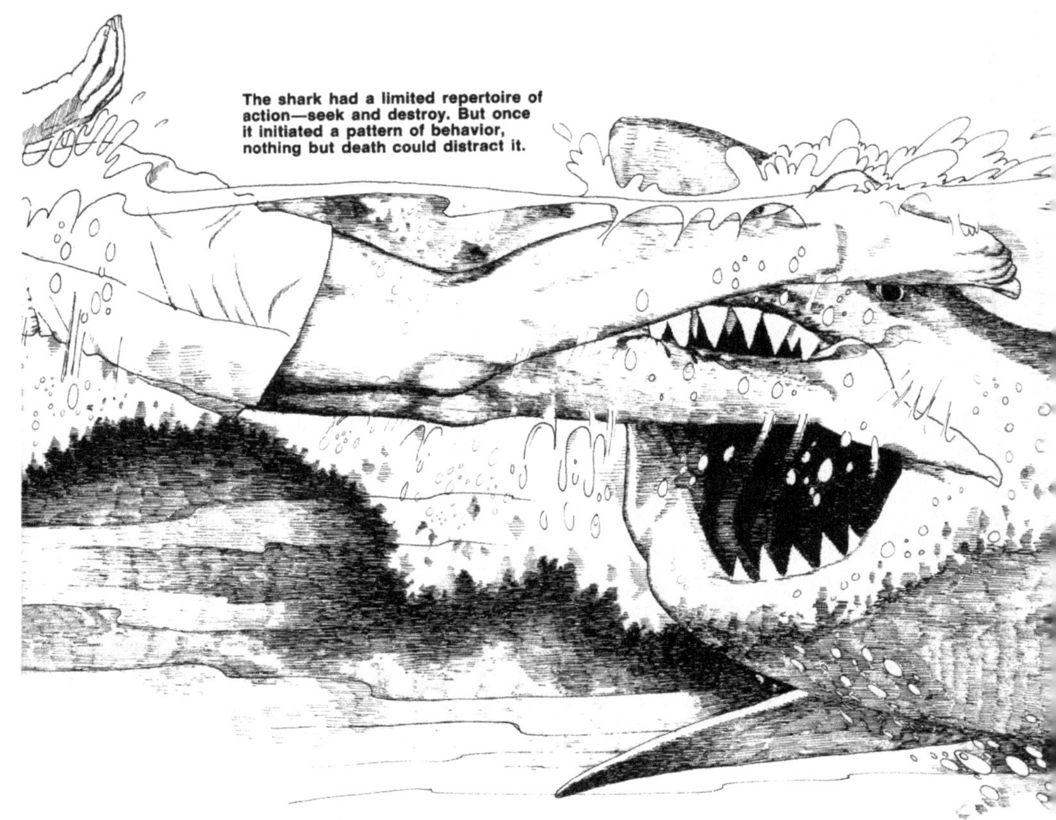

hadn't gathered since a Texas twister broke up the family for good four years earlier. Business on the Panhandle had been about as good as can be expected for a region with a bum rap for a name—Will Slade Sr. would have had some grubbing to do, had he lived to see what that twister did to his ranch.

A falling beam got him as he tried to clear the animals out of the barn. His youngest son Elvin had gone to the hospital with a broken leg. Vince and Big Willie stuck around to see their little brother walking straight, then divided their money (mostly Willie's) three ways and headed for points elsewhere.

Elvin had been hooked on surfing magazines and went straight to California. Vince got drafted and went. Willie'd been too damn big for a uniform, and joined the rodeo to rassle steers.

ROUND about the fifth blink Elvin realized that today would probably be the day Vince got back from Vietnam, and that this was five o'clock in the morning he'd set aside for some surfing. Low tide in half an hour. He splashed some water on his face and held his wet hand out the window. The breeze was offshore, so the waves, if there was a swell, would be hollow, breaking smoothly over the reef in Surf Harbor, Macondo, California.

Macondo was a reborn timber town on a rock peninsula on the Pacific being restored by a lot of carpenters, and increasingly popu-

lated by dropouts from the big cities several hundred miles to the south. Elvin had arrived 4 years earlier, apprenticed himself to one of those carpenters, and stuck around.

Now every aspect of the geography had a label. The tip of the peninsula was now Lookout Point. And the beach area on the south side of the town was now Surf Harbor.

Surf's up!" One guy'd beaten him to the beach—Ed Plimpster, a recent new landowner in town. Only he had no board, and no wetsuit.

"Hope you're not planning to swim too long like that. Gets cold." Elvin said.

"Just a quick dip to wake up. Live right across the road up there."

"Be ready for swimming in

22

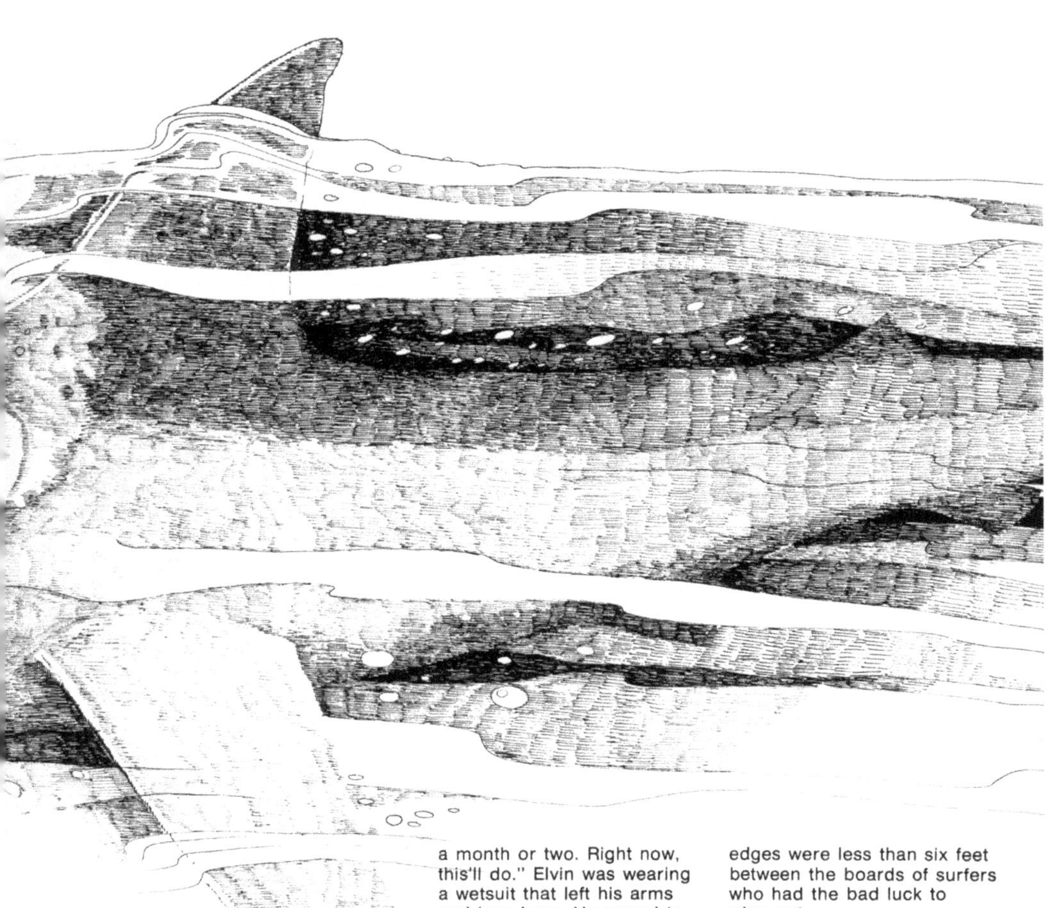

When a shark goes into a feeding frenzy, there's usually nothing left of the victim to identify. But this time, the fish only decapitated one of the Slade brothers, which meant the others would take it on, head to head, one by one

a month or two. Right now, this'll do." Elvin was wearing a wetsuit that left his arms and legs bare. He waved to Plimpster, and ran his board down to the beach. A hunded yards out was the reef, and the waves, which today looked to be topping at about seven feet, breaking sharply and, held up by the offshore, breeze smoothly and evenly.

Elvin barely felt the water chill his skin as he paddled out to the breakers. His adrenalin was running with the surf. He felt the water that slipped between his body and the rubber suit go warm and form a seal.

It took a while to get out there, and he had to fight the waves the last few yards. Surf Harbor had its hazards when you got near the reef. At low tide its jagged coral edges were less than six feet between the boards of surfers who had the bad luck to wipe out.

At first he thought someone had lost their surfboard, and somehow it had remained out beyond the reef. There was a sort of pocket out there that sometimes retained driftwood.

He thought it was an upside-down surfboard because he thought he saw a skeg— what they call a shark-fin rudder.

He was right about the shark fin. And it was moving. Where the hell were the waves?

The waves were upon him before the shark submerged, but unlike the waves in his dream, the first two were losers. By the time the third wave *(Continued on page 90)*

(Continued on page 90)

23

Elvin Slade had to blink five times to be sure he was awake. He was still locked into that dream. Something about riding Waimea with his brothers. Only in this dream there were three good waves for every set of three, instead of just one.

Elvin caught the first wave. On the next one came Vince. On the third monster swell came Big Willie—and they all met on the beach.

Reunion. The Slade boys hadn't gathered since a Texas twister broke up the family for good four years earlier. Business on the Panhandle had been about as good as can be expected for a region with a bum rap for a name—Will Slade, Sr. would have had some grubbing to do, had he lived to see what that twister did to his ranch.

A falling beam got him as he tried to clear the animals out of the barn. His youngest son Elvin had gone to the hospital with a broken leg. Vince and Big Willie stuck around to see their little brother walking straight, then divided their money (mostly Willie's) three ways and headed for points elsewhere.

Elvin had been hooked on surfing magazines and went straight to California. Vince got drafted and went. Willie'd been too damn big for a uniform, and joined the rodeo to rassle steers.

ROUND about the fifth blink Elvin realized that today would probably be the day Vince got back from Vietnam, and that this was five o'clock in the morning he'd set aside for some surfing. Low tide in half an hour. He splashed some water on his face and held his wet hand out the window. The breeze was offshore, so the waves, if there was a swell, would be hollow, breaking smoothly over the reef in Surf Harbor, Macondo, California.

Macondo was a reborn timber town on a rock peninsula on the Pacific being restored by a lot of carpenters, and increasingly populated by dropouts from the big cities several hundred miles to the south. Elvin had arrived 4 years earlier, apprenticed himself to one of those carpenters, and stuck around.

Now every aspect of the geography had a label. The tip of the peninsula was now Lookout Point. And the beach area on the south side of the town was now Surf Harbor.

"Surf's up!" One guy'd beaten him to the beach—Ed Plimpster, a recent new landowner in town. Only he had no board, and no wetsuit.

"Hope you're not planning to swim too long like that. Gets cold." Elvin said.

"Just a quick dip to wake up. Live right across the road up there."

"Be ready for swimming in a month or two. Right now, this'll do." Elvin was wearing a wetsuit that left his arms and legs bare. He waved to Plimpster, and ran his board down to the beach. A hundred yards out was the reef, and the waves, which today looked to be topping at about seven feet, breaking sharply and, held up by the offshore, breeze smoothly and evenly.

Elvin barely felt the water chill his skin as he paddled out to the breakers. His adrenalin was running with the surf. He felt the water that slipped between his body and the rubber suit go warm and form a seal.

It took a while to get out there, and he had to fight the waves the last few yards. Surf Harbor had its hazards when you got near the reef. At low tide its jagged coral edges were less than six feet between the boards of surfers who had the bad luck to wipe out.

At first he thought someone had lost their surfboard, and somehow it had remained out beyond the reef. There was a sort of pocket out there that sometimes retained driftwood.

He thought it was an upside-down surfboard because he thought he saw a skeg—what they call a shark-fin rudder.

He was right about the shark fin. And it was moving. Where the hell were the waves?

The waves were upon him before the shark submerged, but unlike the waves in his dream, the first two were losers. By the time the third wave got to him he was moving and standing, but it was too late.

The shark had been waiting for the third wave. Like a body-surfer gone savage it burst through the white water, smashing the tough fiberglass board like a twig, and sending Elvin Slade backwards head over heels.

He landed on the shark's back in mortal terror, and grasped it around the belly. He was in the middle. Five feet more fore, about seven aft. Five and seven and six—*Eighteen feet*, he thought. He was used to measuring things.

It was his last measurement. The shark sounded, and he held on. The shark veered left, and he fell off. The shark circled and struck. The headless torso of Elvin Slade hung suspended in the water, and the shark sounded again.

The plane nosed down toward the airport. Vince Slade smiled at the stewardess and fastened his seatbelt. There weren't any stewardesses where he'd been flying lately. On the other hand there were a few nurses back in that hospital, one in particular.

But that was old hat. The war was over, and nobody'd want to hear stories this time. His brothers, maybe, but no one else. He hadn't liked killing, and liked remembering even less.

He wondered what the hell he'd do at home. Home? He wondered what he'd do back there. Maybe go into business with one of his brothers, or both. They'd always been fiercely loyal to one another, and word was around their part of the Panhandle that if you messed with one Slade, you messed with three. *"Texas arithmetic,"* the old man had called it, and it had always worked.

The plane landed in L.A. Vince had a bourbon and branch water at the airport bar and went to phone Elvin.

But there was no answer. It was 2 PM. Maybe the kid would be out surfing. Vince decided to rent a car and drive up.

The waves were picture-perfect but no one was out. Vince scanned the beach for a blanket. Zilch. A smashed surfboard lay on the shore. *Phew—maybe the waves ain't so perfect, after all.*

He found a phone booth and dialed his brother's number, No answer. He drove into the center of town and asked after Elvin Slade. Someone said he should try the sheriff's office, down the street.

The news hit him in three places. First in the guts, where he was used to it: someone he knew was dead. Then in the heart, like after Ma and Pa. Later on, in his hotel room, it hit him in the head.

It got him there because of what that obscene enemy had done to his little brother. He'd taken that guy Plimpster's word that it was his brother because he couldn't really be sure. He'd seen headless torsos more than once before. They were lighter to carry than others.

That's the way he was thinking again. First thing back, and some miserable fish defiles his family. Vince Slade had had enough of enemies. And he knew how to use a big knife.

His brother had a boat, and he had recovered the keys from the cops at the station. They figured stay away and the shark would go away. Plimpster had cautioned that there were fish to feed on living inside the reef, and the shark might stick around. Someone else suggested a net outside the reef, and they started talking dollars and dollars. Vince had snapped, "What about my brother's murderer!"

There were condolences but no action, and Vince thought Plimpster might lend him a hand. No telling when Willie would arrive, and no telling when the shark would leave. Vince didn't want the shark to leave.

Ed Plimpster did, but reasoned otherwise. He'd read a little about sharks, enough to know that they'd eat anything that passed through their territory and attracted their attention. Anything from a hunk of metal to a human was edible for this fish.

They were 20 yards from Lookout Point, and circling around from the outside, aiming for a spot not quite in view, around to the left. That spot would be 100 yards out from the beach in Surf Harbor.

"You know, you're mad if you think you can do it alone." Plimpster felt he understood this man's obsession, and would himself be a better man if he did something to lessen the odds. For far be it from Plimpster to try and dissuade a man from blood lust.

"I'm not alone. And you said you could shoot a rifle."

"This fish might weigh more than that car you've rented."

"With this knife, I could kill a Mack truck." Vince wasn't in the same reality as Plimpster, who had things measured up pretty clear. He'd seen the shark hit the surfboard, and heard Elvin scream. When the shark dived out of the wave, there was a long period of curving piscine back. It was a huge shark, probably a blue pointer, maybe twenty feet. That was a good long saber Vince was hefting, and his arms and wrists suggested singular striking power (as did the rifle he was holding in his less workworn hands), but the power of this mega-fish was unfathomable by a man, except in terms of bombs.

"Vince, why don't we go back and find something to bomb it with. One of those grenade-canes."

"You do that if my knife doesn't. Wait and see."

THE FIN was moving in widening circles, spiraling out over its owner's domain. All movement was leisurely and deliberate, never a wasted motion—even when it struck.

Its sensory systems, though mechanically efficient, were geared for a limited repertoire of action. Seek and feed. Once a shark has initiated a pattern of behavior, nothing can distract it but death.

Vince saw it before Ed could turn to tell him. He gripped the knife. It was very sharp. A knife had never let him down, though he remembered the joke about the guy who told the guy with the gun, "I have a knife," and the guy had shot him and he said, "I had a knife." He told the joke to Ed, who didn't laugh.

They were 40 yards from the fin when it disappeared.

"Get ready to shoot."

"It might try to ram us."

It rammed, knocking both men on their butts. Plimpster's rifle flew overboard out of his flailing grasp. Slade's knife sliced his thigh as he fell but he didn't let go. He clawed his way up over the railing and looked down into boiling white water. Through the foam he saw the broad snout and cold eyes.

If he'd had the sense to bring a harpoon, or wait for Big Willie, the shark would have been his meat. But there it was, and here was the knife, and man overboard, hacking into the shark's right flank.

The tail flicked twice and the shark shot backwards, dislodging its snout from the hole in the boat's side, and also dislodging its human attacker. Man and shark hung face to face in the water for what seemed to the man an eternity, then the knife went up in the air and the shark shot forward, mouth open.

The knife fell and glittered to the bottom. The shark glided on. The body hung in the water then drifted toward the surface. Plimpster regained consciousness. No shark, no fin. No Vince. Just something that looked to be part of a body.

"I'm terribly sorry. I did him no good whatever. I didn't even witness his death." Plimpster was drying off, drinking coffee in the small police station. A woman arrived in the room, after parking a small red sportscar outside the open front door. A red TR-7.

She was one of those long, sleek blondes, a sometime companion to Plimpster. She lived in one of the high-priced spreads which dotted the mountains across the Coast Highway. Tom King, the police chief, had phoned her after responding to a panicked radio-signal and dragging a shaken Plimpster from the sinking wreckage of Elvin's skiff.

"Felicia."'

"Hello, Ed. You might have told me what you were up to." She wore a camera around her neck.

"Thank your stars, darling, that you weren't there. Another man has been decapitated. Another man named Slade. I knew him for three hours."

The telephone rang, and Chief King picked it up. A conversation. Yup, two headless brothers and an unapprehended guillotine. Be in tomorrow morning's editions? OK. And one other thing. There's supposed to be a third brother.

BIG WILLIE Slade awoke in a motel room outside Pasadena. He'd been driving three days through from Fort Lauderdale, Florida, wanting to get to the reunion. He'd been in Florida for a year, rassling alligators and working on boats. Someone on the rodeo circuit had seen him bulldogging, and suggested that there might be good off-season money messing with gators.

He fought animals because he was too big to fight a man. And too quick. He tried football in high school, but went straight into rodeo when he got the chance. One-on-one was how he liked it, since the family split up.

People stared at his bulk as he walked into the motel dining room. He picked up a local newspaper, sat in a booth and ordered breakfast, steak and eggs.

"Raw?" The waitress wanted to make sure she heard him right. "Raw eggs?"

"Naw, raw steak. Scramble the eggs."

The waitress looked him over and walked off, smiling to herself. Must be an Oakland Raider.

Big Willie unfolded the newspaper and saw something in the lower right-hand corner about a "headhunter shark." Two brothers. Dateline Macondo. Slade.

Big Willie's smooth brow began to squeeze into a knot. He read through the article twice. His heart started sounding and his shoulders began to quake. He decided to hold it in. The waitress came with the platter.

"Doesn't take long to scramble a few eggs. Want some A.1?"

Willie apologized and paid the bill. The waitress said he didn't have to pay for the steak, since it wasn't cooked. Willie said never mind and left. He floored the Buick till he reached the Coast Highway, and ran some ragged curves up the winding road to Macondo.

He had to duck to get in the doorway. Chief King reckoned that if this guy's shoulders were two inches winder, he'd have had to come in sideways. His eyes were red. This would be the third brother.

He introduced himself, William Slade, Jr., and the Chief started telling him what he knew.

"You tell it like you've been through it all before. What'd you tell Vince?"

"I told him to wait, that you can't take human revenge on an animal, much less a fish."

"And he told you to go to hell."

"Yeah. I'm not going to tell you what to do. You'll be better equipped than Vince was—I had some equipment sent in. You scuba?

"Wrestle alligators, done some scuba fishing. How big's the fish?"

"Be like rassling a Camaro V-8. Maybe 3000 pounds. 'Bout ten times what you weigh, I reckon. Two-and-a-half times as tall."

"And unarmed."

"Except in close."

"Lemme see them. My brothers."

"I don't want to go with you, Willie. Icebox's in the rear. On the right. Toilet's to the left."

But Big Willie didn't go sick when he saw the torsos. He got cold and thought weapons. Something to shoot with, something to smash.

Chief King brought him a harpoon gun and a cane-like device. "Grenade-cane. Bop him on the head with it and swim backwards. Don't miss. And wait till tomorrow. Be dark in half an hour. Fish would have the advantage at night."

"I got some tanks in back of my car. Got oxygen?"

"Pick 'em up in the morning. You et?"

"No food now. Where'd Elvin live? Said he'd built himself a nice cabin. I'd like to sleep there tonight."

THE REFRIGERATOR was full-up with cases of Coors. Two army cots were set up in the bedroom. Elvin should have known I couldn't sleep on a cot. Damn! He looked around the living room. Over the fireplace was a framed photo of three brothers whooping it up at a state fair. Vince on Willie's shoulders, Little Elv on Vince's shoulders. Will would hunch down, they'd both get on, and he'd just stand up.

Big Willie took one beer. He didn't drink much. Went right to his head. He got on the bed, stretched out, and his legs stuck out over the foot of the bed. As his brain faded into sleep, his body became strangely tense. He dreamt he was rassling a gator with a shark's head. He couldn't clamp hold of the mouth.

His body relaxed. After a while a smile came over his face. He dreamt he was with his brothers, drinking beer. One after the other they'd go to the refrigerator and come back. The phone woke him just as he was opening the refrigerator and finding it empty. He picked up the phone. Yeah, in an hour.

The wetsuit was custom-made, and the scuba tanks larger than most men would care to carry, or need. He put on the tanks after parking his car off the road near Surf Harbor. The chief was near the shore, waiting with a pile of gear. A man and woman were with him. The woman wore a wetsuit which exposed long graceful legs. She wore a camera around her neck.

"Willie Slade, this is Ed Plimpster. And Felicia…"

"Felicia Cole. I'm going to take some pictures."

"I tried to talk her out of it," Plimpster offered. "I was with Vince when it happened. I tried to talk him out of it, too.

"Never mind that," said Willie, turning to Chief King. "You just see that the lady stays ashore. I'm gonna try and sneak up on the fish. I don't want anyone else…anyone getting hurt."

He put on his flippers and the Chief gave him the weapons. Harpoon gun and closerange bopper. Felicia, disappointed but not up to arguing, contented herself with a few dry shots of Big Willie as he walked into the water and disappeared beneath the surface without waving, or wavering.

He swam beneath the waves to where the sea floor buckled in a volcanic split. Ahead loomed what seemed a sand bar, but on closer inspection proved to be an encrustation of coral smoothed out by the pounding above. He swum over the top of the embankment and saw the ocean floor bottom out rapidly beyond. Visibility not very good down deep there. He moved slowly along the crest of the reef.

There were no fish nibbling the coral. There was a stillness. Willie pushed off the reef wall, swimming down and out. He stopped swimming and cocked the harpoon gun, holding it out with his left hand. Big Willie was left handed. He held the bopper easily. Big Willie was right handed, too.

And then came *the* fish. Up from the dark water into the sparkle of sun-rays scattering on subterranean white water came a sleek torpedo with lobster eyes, radiating a shimmer of bubbles from its massive flank. The right rocker panel was recently-stabbed. It was ten feet away and Willie was taking aim.

The harpoon lanced between rows of jagged razors down its throat. The tip missed the brain and spinal cord. The fish didn't slow down.

Willie grabbed the harpoon shaft as the fish shot at him and spun around onto its back. The fish broke water and Felicia got her picture.

"I think he's alive!"

Willie was alive and sounding on a fish which was making like a bronc. But Willie was without weapons. The bopper was on the bottom. All he had was this harpoon shaft in his hand which he was trying to grind into the shark's brain.

The shark scraped him off on the coral. Lucky thing it was slowing down, or Willie'd been tartare. As it was, he ripped off some bad chunks of back, and the water was going pink as he spun back to full consciousness.

Miracle. The bopper was by his feet. And the shark was ramming. Willie ducked and the shark smashed into the coral head. Willie grabbed the bopper. Willie sprung and bopped. The shark's head exploded and Willie was knocked over backwards. He hit bottom and saw the shark begin to float up, a bloody hole where the snout was. One eye left.

Willie saw a gleam. He paddled over. A bowie knife. Elvin's knife. He stuck it in his belt, and removed a grappling hook, attached to some nylon twine from his belt.

He dug the hook into the shark's gill and began swimming toward shore. A good set of waves loomed on the near horizon.

Willie waited and caught the third wave in to the beach. The shark, headless, followed. Willie dragged it onto dry beach for the people to see. Felicia didn't take a picture when Willie whipped out the Bowie and gutted ten feet of shark-belly. Two heads rolled out with the gut ooze.

The sheriff became queasy. "Why you want to go do that?"

Willie showed his teeth to the sheriff. "Just want to make sure I got the right fish." ▼

TYLER BOWLING, MARINE ECOLOGIST: This story takes place in California, and the majority of the bites we see there are from white sharks. (California is full of very young white sharks.) And something that we see across species is that normally, bites are from juveniles. We think this is because they're more prone to mistakes while they're still learning their hunting techniques.

"Anything from a hunk of metal to a human was edible for this fish." We don't see most sharks eating metal, but tiger sharks will. They're very, very curious, they like shiny objects. and they'll eat just about anything just to figure out what it is, from license plates to tin cans. Other sharks don't really do this. But tigers do eat metal, and they will vomit it up eventually.

The shark in the story was identified as a blue pointer, which is a common nickname for two species: the shortfin mako, and the blue shark. I assumed the author meant mako, and he claimed it grows to be a 20-foot monster. But in reality, a shortfin mako, a big one, is around 13 feet. And regardless of whether the shark in the story is a mako shark or a blue shark, they're pelagic animals—you're going to find them way offshore, on the open ocean. They wouldn't be inshore in the waves anyway.

"Once a shark has initiated a pattern of behavior, nothing can distract it but death." That's total nonsense. Sharks are always paying attention, and they're very easily spooked. They'll be on task, then something doesn't fit right and next thing you know, they're gone. They're very intelligent predators.

Later, the shark rams the boat snout-first, like in *Jaws*, and it actually gets stuck. Assuming this was a mako, or even a white shark, their snouts are too sensitive to ram anything, really. They've got all those electro-receptive pores at their snout, so they can sense the electric fields of organisms up close; they can zero in on prey without really looking at it. They are sensitive in the snout—they're not going to be ramming any boats. It also says that the animal actually swam in reverse, and for those particular types of sharks, that's real hard to do. I don't think that would happen.

Historically, after there was a fatality or recurring bites, there would be a culling of sharks, by either local government or private citizens, to catch the shark that was responsible. But they usually ended up killing many species with little evidence that they ever got the real culprit.

It's very common that people generalize sharks. In reality, a white shark and a bull shark are about as genetically related as a dog and a kangaroo. So we really can't lump all sharks into stereotypical behaviors.

We need these predators to bring balance to our ecosystems. But people are often less concerned about sharks because they still think sharks are scary. And until we can really get a handle on that, many of these species could be in continued danger of extinction.

ADVENTURE February 1971 Art by Ron Lesser

"The Madman Who Ruled a Killer-Shark Pack"

STORY BY BRET HARPER

THE MADMAN WHO RULED A KILLER-SHARK PACK
An eye-witness account by the Yank skipper who fought him
30

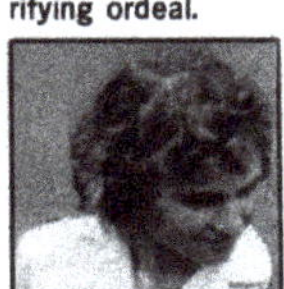

Boat captain Bill Jardine (above) and Claudia Payton (below) after their horrifying ordeal.

At first Jardine was amused by Payton's obsession with sharks, but the amusement quickly turned to terror when Payton used him as live bait for the sea's most bloodthirsty man-eaters

As Told To BRET HARPER　　ART BY BRIAN DAVID

Bill Jardine wished Claudia Payton would stop screaming. Here they were tied back to back—being mercilessly dragged through shark-infested waters by the boat's tow line— and all she could do was scream . . . and struggle. Her sudden movements only drew tighter the ropes that pinned them together.

They were shark bait. Living shark bait.

Water spewed up by the moving boat stung Jardine's cheeks and forehead. Jardine had a dull ache in his side thanks to a hard blow from the butt of an M-1 *(Continued on page 50)*

(Continued on page 50)

As a shark devoured Hurley, on the boat Walter Payton watched with delight—eagerly awaiting the same doom for the bound-up Claudia and Jardine.

31

ART BY GIL COHEN AS BRIAN DAVID

Bill Jardine wished Claudia Payton would stop screaming. Here they were tied back to back—being mercilessly dragged through shark-infested waters by the boat's tow line—and all she could do was scream…and struggle. Her sudden movements only drew tighter the ropes that pinned them together.

They were shark bait. Living shark bait.

Water spewed up by the moving boat stung Jardine's cheeks and forehead. Jardine had a dull ache in his side thanks to a hard blow from the butt of an M-1 carbine, but he wasn't worried about aches and pains. He was worried about being swallowed up by a 30-foot-long white shark he probably wouldn't even know was around until the big predator hit him like an electric meat cleaver.

That was what Claudia Payton's husband wanted.

Jesus Christ, Payton was crazy, thought Jardine. The man had gone completely off his rocker.

It wasn't like he'd encouraged Claudia. From the beginning she had let it be known that she was eager to get laid. And Bill Jardine knew he wasn't the first she'd made a pitch at. Hell, he wasn't even the 15th. She looked like a woman who had been playing the seduction game since she was old enough to experience an orgasm.

But Walter Payton, the crazy bastard, had attacked Jardine and tied the two of them together and dumped them overboard attached to a tow line like a dead porpoise set out to bait a shark. Walter Payton wanted them to attract the giant whites, the meanest predators in the sea. He wanted to see his wife and Jardine ripped into bloody hunks of flesh.

Then he'd go back to port and report they'd fallen overboard while they were wrestling with a big white. A shocking tragedy, he'd tell authorities.

Teeth gritted, Jardine tried again to wrest his arm free of the rope that imprisoned him as tightly as a straightjacket. He had no real hope that he would succeed, but he knew how little time he and the woman had left to live.

Sharks were in the area. Earlier in the day the men on Jardine's charter boat had seen fins slicing the surface of the Gulf of Mexico as smooth and gracefully as skaters cruising on ice. The big fishes' sonar, some of the best nature had handed out to creatures of the sea, would pick up the woman's frantic movements and the whites would speed to the scene.

Jardine couldn't even be sure he'd see them before they struck. If they came fast enough and deep enough, they could circle below and surge up and take away half his body, sever large bits of both his and the woman's limbs, with one lightning-fast run. And if one of the monsters, the big ones that measured 30 feet long and weighed as much as a trailer truck, came up hard enough, he could lift both Jardine and Claudia right out of the water and grind them between his teeth like a fox grinding a chicken bone.

Claudia screamed again and Jardine cursed at her, trying desperately to get her to listen to him. As the wife of a marine biologist who had been on numerous sharkhunting expeditions, she should have known she was doing exactly what she should avoid.

Her long blond hair was damp, her shirt torn and one lovely breast exposed. Jardine didn't like to think of a shark clamping his teeth down on that tender flesh. Once he'd caught a tiger shark arid when they opened the fish up they'd found a third of a young girl's torso in his belly. Claudia could wind up that way…and so could he.

If he had believed the woman's screams would attract help, he'd have urged her to shout *louder*. But they had no chance of obtaining assistance. No chance at all.

They were so far from the Florida shoreline that Jardine had not spotted another boat all day. Only two people were within earshot of Claudia's screams and they were the two men on the boat. One of them, Hurley, was afraid to defy the crazy man who had taken command of the boat. The other was Payton, who had every intention of watching the monster sharks destroy his cheating wife and the charter boat captain he'd hired a week ago…

BILL JARDINE was no expert on sharks. Most of what he knew about them came from oldtimers' stories. He'd encountered a few blues in his time, but he'd never come close enough to a giant white to brag about it. Once he had hooked a big tiger shark and fought the bastard for half a day before winning. Later he and a friend had tangled with a rogue hammerhead while skin diving and the hammerhead took off his friend's right leg and scrotum with one swift, grinding bite. Those two experiences had given Jardine all the personal acquaintance he wanted with any variety of shark.

So when Walter Payton and his party showed up and asked to charter his boat, the *Pretty Lady*, to check on reports that a group of great whites had mysteriously appeared in the Gulf, Jardine felt no burst of enthusiasm.

"I wouldn't count on those reports being true. This is a big year for spotting great whites. Everybody's doing it. And most of the time the sightings prove to be false."

Payton looked amused. He was an Australian who said he'd spent ten years studying the migratory and behavior patterns of great whites, traveling all over the globe. "I've found them in California, New Jersey, Canada, and South Africa. I've even found one species in a lake in Nicaragua and another in the Thyrrenian Sea off the coast of Italy. They love to baffle so-called experts by doing that which we have been told they never do. At one time or another, almost everything man thinks he knows about sharks has been disproved. As recently as World War II, service manuals claimed sharks did not attack man and more recently some scientists believed they had invented an effective shark repellent. In fact, there is no effective chemical defense against sharks and there are at least 27 types that are dangerous to humans. I say at least 27, because we don't even know how many species actually exist. The great white is the most dangerous of all, the one most accurately described as a maneater. From what I've observed, he regards man as his natural enemy."

PAYTON puffed on a pipe as he talked. His tone of voice was slightly condescending and Jardine caught Mrs. Payton smiling at him as if to warn that he'd be better off accepting her husband's boastful lecture.

Then the woman moved in her chair and Jardine felt her knee touch his underneath the table. He glanced at her again and her smile grew, letting him know the contact was no accident.

"Sharks are not intelligent in the common sense of the word. Yet they may be the most cunning creature in the sea. Cunning, that is, at their work, which is, quite frankly, the pursuit of prey. They are more silent than a whisper and yet their movement never ceases. They are always stalking, always moving, because nature has made. it necessary. They have no gas bladder, no natural floating mechanism. If they stopped swimming, they would sink to the bottom of the ocean. Nature intended them to be in constant search of prey."

"Which makes them more dangerous, not necessarily more interesting."

Claudia Payton laughed. "My feelings exactly. Sometimes I accuse Walter of being obsessed with sharks. They're the most important thing in his life."

"They are remarkable," Payton insisted, "especially the great white. He's equipped with an array of instincts that make him a perfect killing machine. The great white can detect a scent a fourth of a mile away. He can sense vibrations of other fishes' finbeats 300 yards away, can detect one part of human blood in from 10 million to 100 million parts of water. The great white has even been known to attack a woman swimmer who has recently had her period."

"I've heard that. I don't know a lot about your great white, but I've watched blues go crazy over blood, attack their own kind in a frenzy. Fishermen tell me they'll even gobble up parts of their own bodies, eat their own insides when they've been gutted. I can't say that arouses my admiration."

"You're one of those who believe they're garbage collectors, are you?"

"They've been found with everything in their bellies from garbage dumped overboard by ships they trailed to bait kegs and barrels. Anything that hits the water, they're liable to gulp down. They don't have sense enough to know the difference when they start eating."

The Australian made an impatient gesture. "I won't argue with you. The point of the discussion is to find out if your boat is for hire. I've heard fascinating reports that great whites are in this area. I want to investigate them."

"Of course I've heard the gossip and saw that newspaper story that probably brought your party here. Some fishermen think there's an entire tribe of whites that moved into the Gulf early this season. They claim some are monsters up to 30 feet long. And one is supposed to be bigger than all the rest. You know what he'd have to weigh? Three tons."

Payton's eyes gleamed with excitement. "More than that, perhaps." He was a tall man with thin cheeks and hair that had started to slip back from his high forehead.

"We want to photograph and observe them for a few days. Later we might try to catch one so that I can examine him. Do you think you could handle that, Jardine?" he asked with a challenge in his voice.

"I'm for hire, but let me tell you the truth. I think that tale about the whites was invented by an old drunken boat captain named Mike Carey. He was the first to report seeing the whites and maybe he encouraged the other stories. Mike's all right when he's sober, but when he's drunk he sees things like flying saucers and mermaids."

"I'll hire out to you, Mr. Payton. But I just want to be sure we understand each other. This may be a waste of your money."

"The money doesn't matter," said Payton.

Claudia held a cigarette for Jardine to light. "Walter's wealthy enough to indulge in this passion of his. Most people couldn't afford to chase sharks all over the world, but his father left him a diamond mine in Kenya."

That didn't explain Payton, but it explained a lot about his marriage, thought Jardine.

They loaded Jardine's boat with the biologists gear the following day. They set out with a chart Payton had marked according to old Mike Carey's instructions. The first two days proved fruitless and the biologist became edgy and short-tempered. He seemed to think he had to find the whites in order to show Jardine and the others that he hadn't been taken in by an "Old drunk's imagination.

During those first two days, Jardine got to know Claudia better and sized up Payton's two male assistants. Hurley, the older of the pair, had been with the biologist for five years and took his work seriously. Rutherford, who liked to boast about his skills as a diver and photographer, was too cocky and abrasive to suit Jardine. He also had his eye on Claudia Payton and spent much of his time hanging around her.

THEY sighted a fin on the third day, but they didn't get close enough to determine if the shark was a white. They put out bait and waited, Payton heated up with excitement.

Claudia approached Jardine, who was at the wheel, and said, "I've been through this so many times I'm bored with it. I'm going below. If you want to come down…" She left the invitation dangling and moved away.

Jardine didn't follow her. The boat was no place for playing around. Besides, he'd caught just a little of the biologist's shark fever. He wanted to know if old Carey had told the truth.

He joined Hurley, who was dumping buckets of bloody gook overboard, forming a slick on the water that raised a stench. "That'll draw them," Hurley said. "Blood drives them crazy. I wouldn't want to fall overboard among them when they're feeding."

"You think they may be whites?"

"Who knows? They're the most mysterious of all. They're supposed to be in all the temperate and tropical waters, but they're seldom seen, so we know only a few facts about their habits. If these are as big as your drinking friend claimed; they have teeth maybe five inches long, four to six rows of them, and they leave bites that are crescent shaped and take off 20 pounds of flesh. A leg, an arm. There was a murder case in Australia. No body was found, but they prosecuted when they caught a shark and found the victim's arm preserved in his belly. They don't chew up their food like you and me. They store huge reserves in their livers. Their livers weigh as much as one-fourth of their entire body. We've had some specimens we captured alive that didn't eat for six or eight weeks because they had so much food stored." Hurley made a sound that expressed disgust. "There was a 13-year-old boy, the whole torso, in the belly of a nine-foot white we found beached off the south coast of Wales. Just imagine what a 30-footer might have inside him. The whole damned chorus line of a nightclub."

"You don't like them as much as your boss."

"No one does." Without looking around, Hurley added, "You were wise not to follow the lady below. He watches her closer than you might think and he's the jealous type. If Rutherford keeps playing around, he's going to lose his job. The old man fired another young diver for getting the wrong ideas. Worked him over first, too. Hit him with a gaff and split his skull."

THEY drew four or five of the creatures before it got dark. One of them broke out of the water as they fed and fought each other in the bloody slick and Jardine saw his dirty white belly.

"They're the ones Carey talked about," Hurley exclaimed.

Payton shook his head. He was smiling now, excited. "There must be more. The biggest of these can't be more than 20 feet. We'll return tomorrow. We'll find the bigger ones and we'll go down in the cage and get some photographs."

"You pleased, Mr. Payton?" Jardine asked.

"Look at them! They appeared as if from nowhere. They can overtake a craft traveling as fast as 40 knots. As I told you, they're marvelous machinery, Jardine. Living, but like machinery. Living fossils, in fact. They're the same as they were three million years ago."

"If they weren't killers, you wouldn't be as fascinated, would you?"

"No," the biologist admitted. "In Kenya years ago, I saw a crazed elephant run into the sea. Great whites consumed him while we watched. It was a bloodcurdling sight, but I'm glad I was there. I'll never forget it."

"They don't know what they're doing. They just hit anything that's in the water."

"Like many people who talk about sharks, Jardine, you have but faint knowledge of the real thing. They are not nearsighted, as many experts claim. They have a limited visibility but within that frame they can quickly detect any movement. Some sharks even have color vision, which is the reason swimmers in brightly-colored suits have been attacked. I've examined them. They have a light-reflecting device behind the retina of the eye."

"I've heard fishermen say sharks are afraid of killer whales."

"They're not afraid of anything in the sea," said Payton as though Jardine had insulted him personally.

The biologist was right about their finding the big fish the next day. They found them. They even spotted the monster Carey claimed to have seen. They also suffered a tragedy…

THEY spent the night in port and pulled out early, Payton nervously prowling the deck. Claudia was sleepy-eyed and surly and had nothing to say to Jardine, who realized his failure to accept her invitation had annoyed her so much she was pouting with him.

The sun began to glow above them. Rutherford sensed Claudia's mood and hung close to her. She responded by deliberately brushing her breasts against the man. While her husband scanned the surface of the water for the glimpse of a fin, Rutherford slid his hand behind the woman and cupped her buttocks with his palm and squeezed.

Jardine already felt the shadow of trouble hanging over them. He wished he'd never seen the biologist and his party.

Suddenly fins surrounded them like ants around sugar. They saw the monster shark, the king of the tribe. He broke out of the water to snap up a baby dolphin they had attached to a tow line and swallowed the bait in one gulp. For a moment he seemed poised in the air like the nose cone of a rocket, his great jaws agape and his dirty white belly glistening in the sunlight.

Payton picked up his camera and ground away. Later he insisted on going down in the shark cage alone to take more photographs.

"If that big fellow hits the cage, he might bend the bars," Hurley protested.

Payton cursed him for a fool and they gave him his way. They lowered him into the water.

The big shark seemed to understand what was going on. He passed under the boat and jarred it. He rattled the cage and jerked it on the pulley, but then he pulled away.

When they pulled Payton up, he was laughing. He shed his gear. "He was right there at the cage, staring at me with his eyes like agates. I could reach through the bars and touch him."

"He'd have taken your arm off," Hurley grouched.

"Jardine, we aren't going in tonight. We'll stay out here. I don't want to take the chance of losing that big monster. In the morning Rutherford and I'll go down in the cage again. Then we'll land one of them. I'd like to catch the giant. I'd love to take him in."

"We didn't come prepared to catch a 30-foot shark, Payton. I've got the gear for a small one and there's a carbine below. But I'm not going to risk my boat trying to catch a monster. You'll have to get another boy for that."

"Afraid, are you?" The biologist thrust his face close to Jardine's.

"Just sensible. If you want to go back and get Carey to help us, we'll come back tomorrow and try for the big fellow. But not without adequate gear and planning and some help I'm familiar with. I didn't agree to risk my life or the lives of these other people."

"If we go back tonight, the big fellow might not be here tomorrow. I won't take that chance. We stay."

He was so agitated that Jardine took the easy way out. He agreed to spend the night on the water.

Payton glanced around. "Where's Rutherford now?"

The others hadn't even missed Rutherford. They had been too busy hauling up the cage.

Payton's eyes gleamed. He stared toward the cabin, but Rutherford appeared first, buttoning his shirt. The idiot, thought Jardine.

"What are you doing?" demanded Payton, grabbing the younger man's arm. "More important, what were you doing five minutes ago?"

"I went to check on Mrs. Payton. She was feeling a little under the weather."

"Like hell," spat the biologist.

Claudia appeared In the door, the top two buttons on her blouse still loose. "Don't be a fool, Walter. Nothing happened between us."

The biologist drew a deep breath. "I won't press the issue now. We've found the big shark and I've seen him face to face."

"Then you're happy, aren't you, darling?" she said sarcastically.

"I said I won't press It now. But we'll talk some more when we get back to shore tomorrow."

Jardine slept uneasily. He heard noises above him during the night and he lay listening and tense. Then Payton yelled. "Man overboard!"

When Jardine reached the deck, Payton was standing at the side of the boat, throwing the beam of a flashlight on the water. "Rutherford fell."

Jardine cursed and swung around the spotlight, put it in the direction the biologist was pointing. They saw Rutherford bob up out of the water, waving his arms.

They saw him for only an instant. Then he burst up as though he'd been blown from the water by a bomb. The big shark, the king, came after him. The men on the boat saw Rutherford's struggling body caught in the shark's jaws like a stick being clamped in the mouth of a playful puppy.

"God," gasped Hurley, who had joined them on deck.

Jardine turned off the spotlight. "Tell me how he fell overboard, Payton."

"I was up here alone. He approached me and started arguing about the incident this afternoon. I told him I was going to fire him when we returned to port. He struck me. We wrestled. In the scuffle, he fell overboard."

"Did he really fall, Walter?" said Claudia in an accusing voice. "Or did you give him some help?"

"It was an accident," insisted the biologist.

"We're turning back," Jardine told them. "We won't be staying out here any longer. We're going in and you can tell your story to the authorities, Payton."

"No!" Payton said. He picked up something off the deck. "Let me make this clear to you, Jardine. We're going to stay. Going back won't help save Rutherford. He's gone. So we'll do as I previously planned and report his death tomorrow when we get in."

"All right," said Jardine quietly. He had other lives besides Rutherford's to worry about now. The thing Payton had picked up was the M-1 carbine.

Claudia clung to Jardine's arm. "He got your rifle while you were asleep."

"Yeah. Can you explain that, Payton?"

"I was afraid Rutherford might attack me."

Payton was now in charge of the boat, enforcing his authority with the weapon. Jardine, who had come up in such a hurry that he was half-dressed, went below to get his shirt and shoes. He sat on the edge of his bunk and wondered if Payton would permit any of them to get back to port alive. Right now the biologist needed Hurley and Jardine to operate the boat, but they were also witnesses who could testify that Payton had reason to push Rutherford overboard...

The same thoughts occurred to Claudia, She joined Jardine, pressing her body against him in the shadows. "He's at the wheel. It's safe to talk. You've got to get the gun away from him. If you don't, someone else may have an accident before we get back."

"I'll look for a chance."

"Jardine, I'm afraid he'll throw me overboard like he did Rutherford."

"This isn't necessary," said Jardine. "I'm as scared of the bastard as you are. He may try to make us catch that big shark tomorrow and kill us all."

A flashlight beam struck the two of them. Claudia pulled away from Jardine and the yellow light fell across her breasts. Jardine heard a weird chuckle from the man in the doorway. "I knew she'd slip below to see you. She's had her eye on you from the first. Rutherford was just a stop in between."

"She's frightened, Payton. She was trying to persuade me to jump you, that's all."

Payton crossed to them quickly and silently and struck Jardine with the rifle. He kicked the captain as he fell to the floor. "The cheating slut will tell the police I knocked her lover off the boat for the sharks to feed on. I know that, so she has reason to be frightened. I'm going to provide some better entertainment than she could give you in bed, Jardine."

When daylight came, he ordered Hurley to tie them together and then he checked the ropes and threw them overboard, dragging them behind the boat on the tow line.

The sharks had come, thought Jardine. One sped past him in the water and he felt a light brush that would cause severe lacerations on his leg. The creatures would circle and look them over and then strike.

He looked toward the boat. Hurley and Payton were arguing. Suddenly Hurley hit his employer and sprang into the water. He swam toward Jardine and the woman with a knife in his mouth. Panting, he began to saw at the ropes that bound Jardine's arms.

Payton put the carbine to his shoulder and shot Hurley. Jardine felt the man's body jerk and then he fell away. With a desperate lunge, Jardine caught the knife and pulled it from the wounded man's hand.

The giant shark, the king of the monsters, surged up and caught Hurley, attracted by the blood from the bullet wound. He rose from the water with the force of his leap and shook the man's limp body as though it were a trophy of victory. Hurley was screaming in terror.

Jardine cut himself loose and pulled the woman behind him as he swam for the boat. Poor Hurley was gone, but the blood streaming from his mangled body was drawing the other sharks away from Jardine and his burden.

Jardine glanced back and saw one of the sharks with the dead man's head in his mouth. Then the creature's mouth closed and the bloody object disappeared.

Some of the sharks were eating on each other in a ravenous frenzy, but Jardine realized that others were now pursuing him. He swam harder, aware of how much dead weight he was carrying, slowing him down.

A shark came at him and Jardine turned the woman loose and bit into the rope to keep her from drifting away. He slammed his fist into the startled shark's nose and saw the creature fall back for a moment to check the situation. Payton leaned over the side of the boat. His eyes bulged. He seemed hypnotized by the drama unfolding before him and had completely forgotten the carbine in his hands.

The motor had been cut off. The boat was drifting. Jardine got a hand on the side and pulled himself up, drawing the woman behind him. She had fainted and was motionless.

A shark leaped for her and opened a cut in her leg. He had bitten down to the bone. As Jardine pushed Claudia over the side, he saw he blood well out and stain the deck.

Payton galvanized into movement. He swung the carbine at Jardine's head. Jardine ducked and grabbed the biologist's arm and spun him around. Payton pitched off the boat into the water.

A shark took him. Jardine could have sworn it was the big monster, the one that had fascinated Payton. It was as though the fish had been waiting for him.

Jardine picked up the fallen carbine. He fired bullet after bullet into the swarming creatures, half-mad with fury and frustration. He saw a bloody hand floating on the water for a moment and then a shark tugged it out of sight.

He started the motor and swung the boat away from the scene. He put a tourniquet on the woman's leg. She would live, but she'd need surgery to sew her together. She was a wealthy widow now, but she'd never forget the terror of this day. Neither would Jardine.

For five minutes he could see fins in his wake as though the sharks were following. Then they were gone.

BITING BACK commentary

CAROLINE COLLATOS, MARINE BIOLOGIST: As a shark and big fish biologist and avid fisher myself, I was entertained by this story's mix of fishing tales, love triangles, and of course, shark behavior! Most interesting, this story is jam-packed with slightly accurate facts about shark biology. But what builds from shark facts turns into exaggerated storytelling, and some facts are embellished to a point where they are no longer accurate.

Sharks and humans cannot chew their food in the same way, as it is physically impossible to do so based on the differences in our jaw morphologies. Sharks do not have a gas bladder like bony fish do. Their body shape and large liver help them remain neutrally buoyant. When sharks stop swimming or are not riding water currents, they do sink to the bottom, as the story accurately describes. Additionally, sharks can go days or weeks without eating, and they do have sensory capabilities to detect vibrations from fish swimming or thrashing.

Shark vision is dependent on species, with some heavily reliant on their eyesight to hunt, and others virtually blind. White sharks do have crescent-shaped bites, but so do some other sharks. Sharks are not fearless in the sea. Many sharks species are prey to larger individuals or species, and have to be alert and wary as any other prey species would be.

Besides these discrepancies, there's the all-too-common portrayal of sharks as mindless killing machines. I have done my fair share of offshore swimming and diving with sharks, fishing and tagging them—even with some of the species mentioned in this story. While many consider sharks to be mindless eating machines, sharks can actually be quite picky eaters. They will not just indiscriminately eat anything, which can be wildly frustrating when trying to tag them! Sometimes they can be just as picky as a toddler you have to convince to eat their vegetables. Like the story accurately describes, a shark bite can cause a human to require a tourniquet, lose a limb, or even lose their life. This is not because sharks are mindless maneaters that will attack anything, but rather because their bites can be very traumatic to humans. In most shark attack cases, the victim is not actually "eaten" by the shark, but rather the shark realizes the victim is not what it thought it was preying upon, and does not continue to eat the human. While there are rare, true accounts of shark attacks on shipwreck survivors, most are cases of mistaken identity.

This story weaves shark fact and fiction together to create an entertaining, dramatic read, but not a completely accurate one. Sharks are not mindless killing machines, nor maneaters. But knowing *human* behavior, I will say I think it is entirely possible someone might tow their wife and her suspected lover through shark infested waters in revenge….

Argosy July 1952 Art by Fred Freeman

American Manhood June 1953   Art by Peter Poulton

Afterword

When I wrote and directed *Mega Shark vs. Giant Octopus* back in '09 (under the pseudonym, "Ace Hannah") I was desperate for cash and feeling the junkie-like need to make another film. I drew upon a childhood love of monster movies, and the sub-genre of rampaging squalus, originating with *Jaws*, but continuing with sillier, exploitative fare like *Tintorera: Tiger Shark*, *Tentacles*, *Up From the Depths*, and Joe Dante's superior *Piranha*. I now realize I must have been channeling the spirit of many MAM writers and artists who also worked pseudonymously and from hunger, both literal and artistic. The result is the same: extreme, insane entertainment.

Perhaps it's the freedom that comes with making pulp. It's cheap and fast and likely inconsequential, so why not creatively "take the gloves off"? This resulted in the most memorably-mad MAM moments in *Mega Shark*, as the 500-foot titular beast takes a bite out of the Golden Gate Bridge, or leaps like a rocket from the ocean and snags a jetliner out of the sky. On the newsstand it'd easily been titled, "SHOT DOWN BY A GIANT FLYING SHARK!"

I was still in the spirit when Warner Bros. hired me to write the sequel to *Deep Blue Sea*. I was the "shark guy" now (at least for the minute), and penned an even more outrageous yarn about weaponized sharks outfitted with rockets and machine guns battling it out with Navy Seals. The studio ultimately balked and did a tamer, more "normal" version. Maybe I had gone too far?

Regardless, the finned pulp of the past is forever linked to that of today. Compare the glorious cover art of the stories discussed herein with the posters of savage shark cinema. Hell, the one-sheet for the most profitable and respectable of 'em all—*Jaws*—could have easily graced a 1950s MAM cover!

Ironically, an important ingredient in all this toothy mayhem, shared across mediums, is that the craziness be played straight. The characters doing battle with ridiculous monster sharks must never acknowledge the absurdity. Or it simply doesn't work. Because the second anyone winks, it simply isn't as much fun anymore. And isn't that the ultimate appeal of this narrative madness—that blood-crazed leviathans tearing people limb from limb is a helluva LOT of fun?

Who knew so much delight could be derived from such operatic carnage! I do know that it's much easier to realize extreme ocean mayhem on the page than to do so convincingly in a low-budget movie. Perhaps in the end, the reader's imagination is the better receptor for these over the top sea-screams; nothing on the screen can ever live up to the promise of the poster anyway. So dive in, keep reading, and watch your back!

JACK PEREZ (aka ACE HANNAH)
Hollywood, CA

About the Contributors

BRUCE AVERA HUNTER ("I Fought the Suez Sea Beast") "When I saw Jacques Cousteau swim with sharks and whales on television in the 1970s, I knew that someday I would, too. Years later, I earned my SCUBA certification and was fortunate to study oceanography at the University of Maryland with ichthyologist Dr. Eugenie Clark, who I joined on a series of research trips to photograph and videotape new species and the behavior of various sea life."

JESSICA MYERS ("The Killer Sharks Caught Us…") completed her bachelor's degree in Marine Science at Coastal Carolina University where she spent over 100 hours volunteering with shark research. She is currently working on her MSc in Coastal and Marine Systems Science at Texas A&M University - CC. While her research focuses on plastic pollution, she aims to educate the public on misunderstood ocean topics using science communication and art through her Instagram (**@goingdotty**). The Minorities In Shark Science (MISS) Foundation is one of her favorite organizations. **Misselasmo.org**

MARK ROYER ("Shark Bait") received his Ph.D. in Zoology from the University of Hawai'i at Mānoa, Hawai'i Institute of Marine Biology Shark Lab where he studied shark behavior, physiology, and ecology. During his studies he worked with the Shark Tagger Hawai'i program (**SharkTagger.org**) to assist in research on pelagic shark conservation. During his free time he enjoys open water swimming and photographing marine life (especially sharks): **SharkMarkPhotography.com**

BRYAN KELLER ("The Sharks Got My Legs") earned his PhD studying the spatial ecology of sharks. His team found that sharks use the earth's magnetic field as a navigational aid, a theory that had been circulating since the early 1970s. Bryan is also interested in the social behavior of elasmobranchs, with some of his group's research demonstrating that sharks prefer associating with familiar individuals vs. strangers.

TYLER BOWLING ("The Shark Who Hated Women," "The Headhunting Shark That Destroyed a Texas Family") Program manager for the International Shark Attack File at the Florida Museum of Natural History, he earned his master's degree from East Carolina University. Currently Tyler studies shark movement and environmental patterns in relation to bites on people. **FloridaMuseum.ufl.edu/shark-attacks**

Sᴀʀᴀʜ Fᴀᴇ Tᴏʀʀᴇ ("My God, the Sharks Got the Women!") Marine Fisheries Biologist for the state of Florida. I have worked with various marine organisms from phytoplankton to great white sharks and specialize in the tracking of marine fish via acoustic telemetry. An organization I am passionate about is OCEARCH and their mission to study large apex predators as well as reduce plastic waste with their "kick plastic" campaign. **Ocearch.org**

Cʜᴜᴄᴋ Bᴀɴɢʟᴇʏ ("Top Oceanographer's Alarming Report: US Shark Epidemic Coming This Summer!") earned his bachelor's degree at the University of Rhode Island and his MSc and PhD at East Carolina University. He is currently a research associate at the Smithsonian Environmental Research Center and a postdoctoral fellow at Dalhousie University. His research focuses on the movement, habitat use, and feeding ecology of highly migratory sharks.

Gᴀᴠɪɴ Nᴀʏʟᴏʀ ("My God—We're Being Attacked by Tiger Sharks!") British evolutionary biologist. Director of the Florida Program for Shark Research. Born in Tanzania. Early childhood in various African countries. Educated in England. Moved to US for grad school. Research centers around using DNA to both estimate relatedness among different species of sharks and to understand their population movements. Field work in Madagascar, Borneo, Sulawesi, Northern Australia, and India. Scared of salt-water crocodiles. **Sharksrays.org**

Dᴀᴠɪᴅ Sʜɪғғᴍᴀɴ ("Shark-Battling Dolphins Saved My Life") Interdisciplinary marine conservation biologist who studies sharks and how to protect them. He is an award-winning science educator and public science engagement specialist. Follow him on Twitter **@whysharksmatter** where he's always happy to answer any questions anyone has about sharks.

Yᴀɴɴɪs Pᴀᴘᴀsᴛᴀᴍᴀᴛɪᴏᴜ ("A Man-Eating Shark Pack Against Scuba Divers") is an Assistant Professor at Florida International University, where he runs the Predator Ecology and Conservation lab. He and his students study the behavioral and physiological ecology of sharks and other predators and use this information for conservation. He has studied sharks all over the world including the Bahamas, Mexico, Galapagos, Alaska, Pacific Islands, and Japan.

Cᴀʀᴏʟɪɴᴇ Cᴏʟʟᴀᴛᴏs ("The Madman Who Ruled a Killer Shark Pack"), a PhD student at the New England Aquarium and UMass Boston, has dedicated the past 10 years of her life to researching sharks and big fish. Her research mainly focuses on shark species habitat use, migration movements, ecological importance, and conversation, and spans areas within the US from Massachusetts to South Carolina to Florida, and areas abroad in Panama and the Bahamas. **AndersonCabotCenterForOceanLife.org**

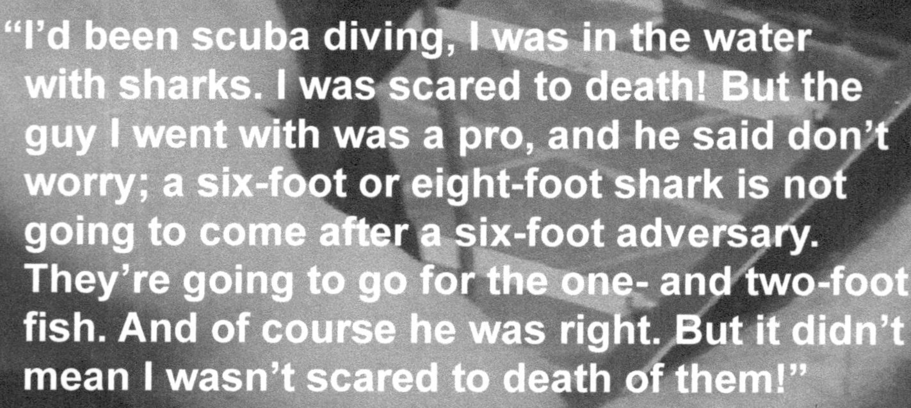

Mort Künstler models for his own reference photo; captured by George Gross.
Courtesy Mort Künstler, all rights reserved

BLACK CRACKER
Josh Alan Friedman

"TELL THE TRUTH
JOSH ALAN FRIEDMAN
UNTIL THEY BLEED"

STOP REQUESTED
WYATT DOYLE
ILLUSTRATIONS BY
STANLEY J. ZAPPA

ERIC REYMOND
NIMRODIA

Eric Reymond
Sub-Sub Librarian,
Extracts on a

I need real
tuxedo and a
top Hat!
words and pictures by wyatt doyle

DUTY - WAVE
IS NOW CLOSED
FOREVER
PHOTOS BY WYATT DOYLE

PHOTOS BY WYATT DOYLE

WYATT DOYLE
DOLLAR HALLOWEEN

Richard Adelman
TEACHER
TALES

a day
at the
beach
Richard Adelman

nu luna
Andrew Bisontini

The Victorious
Triumph of
Superior
Excellence
STANLEY J. ZAPPA

new texture

Pop's
Cookie Duster
story by Don & Lee Doyle
Illustrations by Annette Debevec

THE LAST
COLORING
BOOK
JIMMY ANGELINA and WYATT DOYLE

TO AVOID
FAINTING
KEEP REPEATING,
IT'S ONLY A COLORING BOOK
THE LAST COLORING BOOK ON THE LEFT
JIMMY ANGELINA and WYATT DOYLE

MANZAP REBORN

JIMMY
ANGELINA

GOD
DAMMIT
JoshAlan

free/refuse

CROSSING GUARDS

THE STANLEY J ZAPPA QUARTET PLAYS
FOR THE SOCIETY OF WOMEN ENGINEERS

ZAPPA
singing songs

BALLOONS
Daniel Carter
Nick Skrowaczewski
Stanley J. Zappa

＃ new texture